·MADDIE·

CANDACE ROBINSON
AMBER R. DUELL

Copyright ©2022 by Candace Robinson & Amber R. Duell
Edited by Brandy Woods Snow and Jess Moore
Cover Design by MoorBooks Design

This is a work of fiction. Names, characters, places, and incidents either are the product of the author's imagination or are used fictitiously, and any resemblance to any actual persons, living or dead, events, or locales is entirely coincidental. This book may not be used or reproduced in any manner without written permission from the author.

For Amber Hodges

CHAPTER ONE

MADDIE

Creating a hat was like creating a heart.

For Maddie, it had always been that way. The threads were the hat's veins and arteries. The fabric, its muscle. The pulse seemed to come to life as soon as the hat was placed atop one's head.

Or, at least, her head.

Maddie's fists tightened as she fought to keep her wandering thoughts on hats—wide brims, curving crowns, silk lining, velvet bands, feathered decorations—but all she could focus on was her latest creation, the headpiece she'd just handed over to the Queen of Hearts. *Imogen.*

That *bitch*.

Gritting her teeth, Maddie shook out her hands and exhaled a harsh breath as she stomped away from the Ruby Heart Palace. Her fingers twitched for the collection of hatpins back at her cottage. Plunging a particularly sharp hat pin straight through Imogen's heart and then using it to stitch together a hat made of her flesh sounded enticing. She would love to parade it through Wonderland, giving the queen exactly what she deserved for taking Maddie's sister and holding her as a prisoner in her palace.

Mouse.

Mouse.

Mouse.

Maddie had given Margo the nickname as soon as her baby sister had been born. Margo had been so quiet—always quiet. The mad one and the quiet one. If only Maddie hadn't come back to London after becoming immortal—if only she'd let Mouse believe she had vanished. Mouse had been a child of only ten when Maddie left. She'd returned ten years later to catch a glimpse of her sister each night in her sitting room window after the sun sunk deep into hibernation. Even her hats had ceased to fill the void in Maddie's heart from missing Mouse.

Maddie crouched in front of her old home and gazed through the glass, finding Mouse alone and quilting in front of the fireplace. Several lit candles lined the grime-covered windowsill.

No longer was Mouse a child, but a grown woman. Still small, still frail, her unique pixie-like face seemed straight from a faerie world. Chestnut curls spiraled from her head, the exact color Maddie's had been before they'd shifted to violet once immortality flowed through her veins. Sometimes it was one's eye color that would change, for others it was hair color. Sometimes both, and sometimes nothing at all.

After several long moments, Maddie pushed away from the glass window and the flickering candlelight, then headed back toward the portal to Wonderland. She hadn't made it far from her old home when a hand snatched her arm, making her gasp.

"Please don't go, Madelyn!" Mouse shouted, studying her face.

With Mouse's quiet, stealthy movements, Maddie should have known she would be caught. A mixture of relief and fear flooded her as she faced her sister, who held a lantern, casting yellow light around them. Her white nightgown dwarfed her tiny frame.

"You look different," Mouse continued. "But you're my sister. Don't deny it. You've been coming by the house every night." Not a single sign of terror darkened her sister's eyes.

Maddie's fingers fluttered by her sides, her voice trapped in her throat. The scent of blood wafted through the air, hidden within her sister's veins. Even though she yearned to taste it, she controlled her fangs from lowering. "I'm not the same person anymore."

"It doesn't matter." A tear slid down Mouse's cheek, and she brushed it away. But that didn't stop more from following. "Anything is better than here."

"What happened?" Maddie whispered, her chest tightening. Their home had always been a happy one when she was a mortal.

"While you were away, Mr. Taylor... He took everything from me. Without my consent," she said, her eyes peering down at her feet, her lower lip trembling. "If I stay here another day, I won't survive. I'd rather die."

Fury ignited within Maddie. Their bastard neighbor dared touch her sister? "I won't leave you again," she promised. Maddie wrapped her arms around Mouse, holding her tight as her sister sobbed, and vowed to make Mr. Taylor pay.

And pay he had.

Maddie ensured he'd received no pleasure from her bite, murdering him slowly with her hatpins and knives. Piece by piece.

Mr. Taylor was the only human she'd ever killed. Vampires were another story.

A cloud of bats zoomed over Maddie's head, interrupting her thoughts. Through the trees, howls echoed in the distance,

3

the gray of Wonderland darkening to black. Buildings of obsidian and crimson quickly blocked out the horizon while she ventured farther into the city. She shivered as she passed a dressmaker's shop and cast a glance over her shoulder.

"Bloody hell," Maddie squeaked. "Tonight just isn't my night." She quickened her pace as the howls increased, drawing nearer. The rogue werewolves didn't frequent this side of Wonderland often—unless they were hungry. Most of the queen's guards kept them out, but they sometimes managed to slip into the kingdom of Scarlet. While throats could easily be torn apart with her teeth, she would need much more than that to kill a werewolf. She would need a silver bullet, but she hadn't brought any of her guns to the palace since Imogen didn't allow guests to have weapons.

Maddie's boots pounded the cobblestone path, the ruby lanterns guiding her way. "Hats, Maddie. Focus on hats. Sewing and stitching," she sang to herself, while barreling through the night, passing row after row of red and black homes until she entered the fringes of Scarlet.

Trees replaced buildings and the glow from the ruby lanterns ceased. She darted over wilted plants and hurdled fallen logs until her lone cottage slipped into view—the crooked roof, the black and purple painted exterior, the circular door, the garden filled with red roses. Imogen only allowed red roses in her kingdom.

Tearing open the door, Maddie sprinted inside and slammed it shut, her breathing ragged. Her gaze flicked to the walls lined with hats of all shapes and sizes. Bright pinks, deep crimsons, blacks, grays, velvet, wool, cashmere, lace. There wasn't a single empty spot. Without them—her *safety*—she would slip into madness.

Maddie's thoughts again turned to Mouse as she peered at her sister's favorite blue hat resting on the desk. Imogen and her king, Rav, imprisoned her sister because they believed Maddie knew where the White Queen, Ever, resided. She didn't know, but even if she did, Ever was her friend. Imogen and Rav would murder the White Queen for wanting to put an end to their taking of unwilling humans. It didn't matter that Ever was Rav's sister.

Regardless of the White Queen's location, Maddie remained loyal to Ever and her mission. Feeding or ending a life was one thing, but forcing someone to become immortal was *wrong*. And Rav—

Maddie screeched as she thought about that snake and how her sister was locked up in the palace where *he* resided. She ripped a partially-finished hat off the desk and plopped down on her chair. She shoved the needle into the material as images of Rav spun through her mind. If only it were his eyes she was sewing shut.

Back in London, a couple of centuries ago, Maddie had worked at her mother's millinery shop, dreaming of one day making hats for the queen. While other women yearned for a husband, that had never been her wish. She'd never considered herself pretty enough to receive a second glance from a gentleman. Her sister, yes—but not her. She had neither the looks, the grace, nor the wealth to be considered suitable for marriage. In adolescence, the boys had always found her odd, and it wasn't until she was twenty-two years old that someone gave her any attention, sweeping her off her feet when he'd encountered her mother's shop.

"The queen needs a hat maker, and I hear you're quite good at it," the stranger said. His hair was tucked under a curled white wig, and his brown eyes sparkled as they caught hers. "I'm Rav. And dare I say, you're beautiful."

Maddie quickened her movements, stabbing and yanking the thread through the hat. She hadn't known then, when she'd agreed to accompany him, that it would be for a queen in another world—a world known as Wonderland which had existed just as long as the mortal realm. How could she have known he was the queen's lover? A liar, he was. Deceitful, he was.

Angry. Destroyed. Weak.

Within a few hours of knowing him, he'd made her feel all those things. She'd been green then. Naïve.

The entire town would've called her a fool for being so infatuated with someone after such a short time. All because he'd been the only man to ever pay her any attention. She'd given all of herself to him in the forest that day. There, he not only took her innocence but her mortality, too.

"I hate this hat!" Maddie chucked it at the wall, wishing it would've hit with a loud bang instead of a teeny thud. A melancholy feeling washed over her at the dent she'd just put into the fabric. She didn't really hate the hat. Scooping it from the floor, she dusted it off and brought it up to her face. "I'm sorry. I didn't mean it." She set it down and snatched up a new hat to work on.

Maddie couldn't let Rav and Imogen get to her. She wouldn't allow herself to once again spiral into that dark, mad place. The one where she would either fuck or find a victim to drink the night away. Until her sister helped her to get past those gloomy memories.

The earlier visit to the palace, where she hoped to get a glimpse of Mouse, didn't go as planned. No, not at all.

"You will give me one more hat in a month's time and then we'll come up with a new arrangement." Imogen lifted Maddie's chin, and she studied the queen's yellow irises. *"Understand?"*

"Yes, Your Majesty." Maddie moved out from the queen's touch and rose from the settee. *"Can I see Mouse before I leave?"*

"No."

In that moment, Maddie was pleased with herself for rubbing saliva all over the queen's hat before delivering it.

Maddie adjusted her bright purple arm sleeves, the fabric covering her flesh from elbow to a few inches of her palms, her thumbs peeking out through holes made specifically for them. She plucked up a spool of tulle, twisting the material around the center of a silver hat, creating a golden fishnet veil. Her stomach ached with hunger—she would need to find a human to feed on soon. But even blood cravings failed to pull her focus from her sister and how she continued to let Mouse down.

Maddie's sewing picked up, faster, faster, as she concentrated on her work. For hours and hours, unable to sleep, she added more ribbon and stitching to the same hat, then took it apart before doing the repetitive movements again and again until it was perfect. For all her clients in Wonderland, she wouldn't allow anything less.

A loud rapping at the door startled Maddie, and she lurched forward, the hat falling to the floor. She jumped from her seat, her stiff muscles aching from sitting in the same position for so long, and hurried to the door. Standing on her tiptoes, she opened the small square peephole and peered out. Her breath caught, her lungs halting as her gaze settled on a familiar figure standing outside, shrouded by the gray fog.

What is he doing here? A wave of excitement crashed over her. *He did it!*

Throwing open the door, she grabbed Ferris's arm and yanked him inside, studying his short black hair, dark irises, and flushed cheeks. He'd been working as the Queen of Hearts' Knave. Maddie and Mouse had met Ferris at a club four years earlier. He'd agreed to let them feed on him when their hunger rose, mostly for his own reasons—past demons. Their feeding was his own escape, his high.

"Where is she? You have her, right?" Maddie asked, gazing out the door, hoping to catch a glimpse of her sister. Her heart pounded, trying to free itself from her rib cage when she couldn't spot her.

"I couldn't get her out." His lips tugged down into a frown. "We need to find another way to save Mouse."

"Why so suddenly? You've been there for *two years*." It wasn't his fault, though. His dangerous tenure there hadn't gotten them any closer to saving Mouse.

"I'll get to that in a moment. I just need to catch my breath."

Maddie sighed and gripped his shoulders, though he was much taller than her. "You didn't have to stay so long. Risk yourself. But thank you for doing this, not only for me, but for her. How is she?"

"Quiet." He ran a hand through his hair. "But strong enough not to be broken."

Two years earlier, Maddie hatched a plan—one Ferris agreed to—for him to show up at a club where Imogen frequented to retrieve her male servants. The queen would pluck them from there, fuck them, then make the males immortal. But no one would ever replace her Rabbit, no matter how many lovers she or he took on the side.

After Rav stole Mouse, Maddie needed someone to infiltrate the palace, find out things, and attempt to retrieve her sister. Ferris consented, even though his mortality would be stripped away.

"Now, to answer your question about giving up so suddenly… There's something else you should know." He bit his lip and gripped the back of his neck. "I have a new problem. A big one."

Maddie released his shoulders and stepped back. "What is it?"

"Rav brought a human girl to become a new servant. I was supposed to bring her to the dungeon so she could go through her transition, but I stopped to see Mouse on the way. She asked me to save the girl—Alice."

"You didn't!" Maddie's eyes widened. Why had he listened to her? "Bloody hell. What did you do?"

"Imogen had me dusting rooms with my fucking tongue, and this girl would've suffered the same atrocities. I couldn't deny Mouse's request. I could only stay long enough after rescuing Alice to grab Ever's keys that you gave me from my room or they would've found them." Ferris clenched his jaw. "Alice is back in London."

"As a vampire?"

"A new one..."

"No..." Maddie clasped her hands over her mouth. Not all new vampires made a mess of things, but this was a fifty-fifty stab in the dark.

"She seemed stable enough." He shrugged. "Not wild like some of the others I've seen transition. I promised to help her and will bring her back before anyone gets hurt."

"Not you." Maddie shook her head, her hat sliding against her hair. "We."

Ferris's nostrils flared.

"You know Imogen and Rav will still go after her." If they found her then tortured her, they could discover that Mouse was part of the reason why Ferris helped the girl escape. What would they do to Mouse then? *Horrid things.* "Where are you supposed to meet her? I'll help you."

"Her brother's place. She wanted to tell him goodbye."

CHAPTER TWO

NOAH

The scent of freshly brewed coffee clung to Noah's clothes. He hung his apron near the back door of Bean & Brew and stretched his arms with a satisfied groan. He'd worked a double shift making overpriced cappuccinos and lattes to keep his mind busy. Better to work himself into the ground than to have a weak moment and text his fucking ex.

"Heading out, Noah?" Ava, his co-worker, asked.

He wanted to, but it was getting late. Though London was generally safe at night, one never knew who was lurking about. Ava was a petite girl with a doll-like face and long blonde hair, so he felt better if she didn't lock up alone. "I'll wait and walk you to the Tube."

"Okay." Ava blushed. "Let me grab my purse."

She returned a second later, bag slung over her shoulder, and flicked off the lights. Noah opened the back door and let her step out first. The minute he was out of the shop, he dragged in as much fresh air as he could. Coffee was great, but too much of a good thing ... or whatever.

Ava locked the door and turned to him. "Ready?"

"Hell yes." He couldn't wait to take a long shower and crawl into bed until noon. It had been entirely too long since he'd gotten more than the bare minimum of sleep.

"What are your plans this weekend?" she inquired as they walked side-by-side toward the Tube entrance.

"I'm not sure yet. I haven't had one free in a while, so I'll probably hit up some friends." One of them would undoubtedly be throwing a party and he wasn't about to pass up a chance to drown his break-up woes. Even though Noah had been the one to end things, walking in on her fucking someone else in *his* bed was a bit of a blow to his ego. "What about you?"

"I'm going dancing with some friends." She paused and bit her bottom lip. "Do you maybe want to come along?"

Noah hadn't missed how Ava blushed whenever they spoke or how her gaze landed on him more often than necessary. It had always made him feel good, but he never expected her to shoot her shot, even now that he was single.

"Noah!" Harper's voice carried down the street with a shrill edge. He winced and kept walking as if he hadn't heard his ex call out. "I know you heard me!"

Fuck. "Hang on, Ava. Sorry."

"It's okay," she said, backing away. Ava had been a witness to Harper's meltdown at the company New Year's party last year when Noah had tipped the barista more than Harper thought was acceptable. Months later, he still didn't know if it had been jealousy or because she wanted the money herself. He couldn't blame Ava for wanting to escape. "I'll be fine from here—I can see the Tube. Let me know about this weekend?"

"I will," he assured her. "G'night."

With a fortifying breath, Noah turned to face Harper.

She'd already closed the distance between them, so he held his hands out to keep her at an arm's length. Mascara trailed down her freckled cheeks and her dark hair was in a messy knot atop her head.

"You're dating *her* now? I should've known! She was always staring at you," Harper spat.

"I'm not dating anyone," Noah said in a calm voice. Rising to meet her anger only made things worse and they were in the middle of a public street. "After dealing with your shit, I doubt I ever will again."

Her eyes narrowed. "I said I was sorry. You make me lose my mind, is all."

Noah still hadn't told his parents that, after the breakup, she had splashed paint all over their hand-crafted wall mosaic or purposely snapped the wings off the cherubs sculpted on the living room fireplace. The walls were fixable—a little elbow grease, the right chemicals, and a lot of time would take the paint right off. But the wings were another story.

"Don't make this my fault, Harper. Your issues are your issues and I have too much going on to put up with them, okay? We had a good run." *Good sex, at least.* The rest of the relationship was rather brutal on his psyche, if he were being honest. All two years of it. "But it's over now."

She grabbed his arm as he turned to leave. "Please, just give me another chance."

"You cheated on *me*." With his best friend, no less. "Go leech off someone else, yeah? I'm done with you."

"Noah, *please*," she begged.

But he wasn't having it and hailed a taxi, price be damned. It was worth it to get away from Harper. She'd gotten more chances than anyone should have, and now he was going to relax and enjoy his last year of university. No more drama, no more gold-diggers. Just studying during the week and letting loose on the weekends. When he didn't have to work, that was. His parents were letting him stay in their London flat rent free with two conditions: keep a job and make sure his sister, Alice, stayed out of trouble.

One of those was easier than the other. His little sister had taken full advantage of the freedom university bought her. She'd always been well-behaved and had gotten straight-As, but there hadn't been any other option. Their parents would've skinned them alive for any less. But now that Alice was out from under their thumb, she'd made some ... interesting choices. Not that it mattered to Noah. He was actually proud of his sister for trying to find herself.

"Girl trouble?" the driver asked.

"You have no idea." Noah rested his head on the back of the seat and gave his address. Harper wasn't worth all this trouble.

By the time they reached the front of Noah's house, his eyes had drooped, his head bobbing with sleep. He shook himself out of it and swiped his credit card. "Thanks, man."

"You bet," the older driver said and pulled carefully back into traffic.

Noah walked around the corner to the back entrance in case Alice was napping. Her room was adjacent to the front door, and she was a notoriously light sleeper. If she had any plans to go out again tonight, she would need the rest. She and her friends partied harder than he ever had—he wasn't even sure if she came home last night. *More power to you, sis.*

The gate clicked shut behind him as he entered the small garden. Tall bushes lined both sides of the stone pathway and every inch of dirt between them bloomed in bright flowers. Above them, creeping vines snaked over the brick exterior of the house.

Noah's phone buzzed in his pocket, and he pulled it out to see a text from Harper. He rolled his eyes and unlocked the screen to block her number without reading it. Before he could manage it, he tripped over something large in the middle of the pathway and landed on the ground with an *oomph* next to his sister's prone body. He recognized her black hair and blonde roots immediately as well as the new piercings through the bridge of her nose and in her cheeks.

"Alice?" He pushed himself up with a grunt. "What the hell are you doing out here?"

When she rolled away from him and curled into a fetal position instead of answering, he got to his feet. "You're pissed again, aren't you? I told you not to drink so much."

"Help me, Noah," she moaned.

Such a lightweight. He grabbed her arm and tugged her into a sitting position. "Come on. You're just knackered. Let's get you to bed."

Alice shook her head. "I have to leave."

With another tug, she was on her feet, clinging to his upper arms. Her hair was a snarled mess, the straps and buckles of her white dress were covered in dirt and grass stains, the tulle skirt ripped in places, and her skin appeared paler than usual. His brows rose at the sight. "What happened to you?"

"Vampires," she breathed, her expression wild. Alice's irises were a light blue which was a change from the red contacts she'd been wearing most of the time lately.

Noah rolled his eyes. He knew about her obsession with the mythical beings, knew about the clubs she went to with her new, like-minded friends. She must've meant one of them. Each one he'd met dressed in all black, bodies laden with tattoos and piercings, and a few even sported fake fangs. Still, they'd all seemed decent, harmless. Either he wasn't as good at reading people as he thought, or he hadn't met the person responsible for her condition.

"Who hurt you?" he asked softly.

"There was a man with white, red-tipped hair and fangs…" She released Noah to prod at her own teeth.

"Yes, a vampire. They have fangs." He spoke carefully, running through his memory of her friends for one who fit that description. Demanding their name when Alice was in this state wouldn't do any good. Demanding *anything* from her in any state never ended well, actually. It was just who she was. He had to go easy to keep from spooking her into utter silence.

"What did he do?"

"He took me to a hole in the park."

Noah drew a steadying breath. *Sure, he did...* "Come inside, and I'll put on some tea."

"You're not listening!" she shouted, ripping herself from his grip. "I don't have time to make you believe me. I only came back to tell you that I love you. And ... and goodbye."

His mouth fell open and he blinked, not understanding. "What are you talking about?"

"A ... friend will be coming soon to help me." She paced back and forth, her vinyl Mary Janes clicking on the pavement as she mumbled incoherently to herself.

Noah searched the garden path for Alice's purse. If he could get his hands on her phone, he could call one of the friends she went out with tonight. Ask if they'd seen anything. Maybe someone slipped something into her drink, but he didn't want to get the police involved without knowing more. When she'd started acting out in little ways to find herself, Noah was proud of her, but he was also worried how far she would take her new freedoms. The piercings and vampire clubs were one thing, but he'd made her swear to never touch drugs. If she broke that promise tonight, they would fucking talk about it in the morning.

"Let's wait for your friend *inside*," he urged. A murmured voice sounded behind the gate and Noah spun to face it, putting himself between his sister and whatever *friend* was coming.

"This should be it," a man whispered.

"We need to hurry," a woman urged. "Maybe we should knock on the door, or I can shimmy through a window?"

"She said she would wait in the back garden, so no one saw us."

Noah glanced at his sister over his shoulder. "Are these your friends?"

"I don't know." She sucked her bottom lip between her teeth. "It was just supposed to be the Knave."

"The *what*?" *Knave*? Noah shook his head at the ridiculous nickname. "Never mind. I'll get rid of them. Go inside."

"Wait!" Alice called after him as he approached the gate and swung it open.

A man wearing black trousers and a matching long-sleeve shirt with rope-like rips stood on the other side. A young woman, a head shorter than him, flanked his side. The street lamp behind the duo cast the woman's face in shadow, but she wore an odd hat pinned to the side of her purple hair.

She stepped forward, her hands toying with the skirt of her dress. "Is Alice here?" Her honey-colored gaze shifted past him, her fingers tapping anxiously at her thighs.

Something about the pair made the hair on Noah's arms rise. He couldn't put his finger on *why*, but he knew instinctually they were up to no good. "Sorry, she's not seeing anyone tonight."

"Unfortunately, that's not an option," the man said, and promptly pushed Noah aside before entering the garden.

CHAPTER THREE

MADDIE

This wouldn't go well. A simple task was what Maddie needed. Simple would not be today.

"Noah!" Alice screamed, her dark hair and blonde roots bouncing. Maddie prayed that every door in the building would remain shut. Influencing all the neighbors to go away would waste precious moments.

She assumed the ridiculous blond man, who Ferris shoved out of the way, was Alice's brother. Ferris wasn't one to get aggressive, but they didn't have time to deal with this mortal slowing things to a snail's pace.

Noah pushed off the wall and Maddie adjusted her hat, knowing what he was going to do next as he zeroed in on Ferris. She supposed she should intervene before Ferris, who was too focused on Alice, received a hit to his pretty face.

Leaping forward with the grace of a predator, she clutched Noah's shirt and hauled him back, just as he was about to slam his fist into Ferris.

"What the hell?" Noah growled, attempting to whirl around to face Maddie.

Alice watched with wide eyes as Ferris spoke quickly to her, calming her while Maddie finished dealing with her brother.

Despite her thinner frame, she used her immortal strength to yank him down so he was eye level with her, his back in an awkward position. Her nose skimmed his throat as she drifted closer to his ear, but she couldn't stop herself from inhaling his cedarwood scent and the crimson buried below his skin, all with the bitter scent of coffee mixed in. She'd had a snack in her teacup back in Wonderland before she left with Ferris, but it had been cold. The warm blood flowing through Noah's throbbing vein tempted her. To keep her heart beating, she, and every other vampire, needed blood. It had always been that way in Wonderland. At least, since she'd been there. She yearned for a taste of his blood. *No time.*

"Listen to me," Maddie sang while he cursed and jerked in her grasp, "and listen well. We are not the threat to your sister. She's in danger, and you need to stop fighting us. If I release you, will you do as I say?"

He nodded. Yet by the way his full lips pursed, she knew this wouldn't be the end of it. But she would let him lose his first chance.

Maddie let go of him, and he spun to face her just as she foresaw. *Dear humans, always making bold, yet terrible mistakes.*

With what he most likely believed were quick motions, Noah had her backed into the wall. His hands gripped her arms, his chest pressed against hers. She glanced at Ferris who watched her, his gaze rolling to the sky. He had to know Maddie was having a little fun with the mortal by allowing him some sense of control.

"Just leave him alone," Alice pleaded while Ferris held

onto her. "He doesn't understand."

"Listen," Noah said, his voice low. "I don't know what drugs you're on, but you need to get the fuck out of here before I call the police."

Maddie chuckled then, and he looked at her as if she were mad. But that was nothing new. She quirked a brow and slowly raked her gaze down his lean and muscular form. Now that she was looking, his body wasn't a bad one at all, but it wouldn't tempt her today ... or tomorrow. "You wouldn't have time to pull it out of your pocket and make a call." Noah was a fool for even threatening a vampire. If Rav and Imogen had shown up first, he would've already been dead.

"Now you—"

"Tut, tut." Maddie interrupted his pathetic threats and stared into his green eyes, luring him in with her influence. "Now, step back."

When he obeyed with glazed eyes, Alice gasped, her hands balled into fists against her tulle skirt. "You did to him what Rav did to me."

"It's fine. It had to be done." She turned to Ferris and, with a flick of a hand, said, "Time to go."

"He's going to have to come with us." Ferris sighed as he glanced at Noah. "Rav has her purse, so he'll know where they live. He'll kill him."

Maddie peered up at the mortal, who blinked at her, waiting for her next command. "No. He stays here, Ferris."

"Please," Alice begged, tears sliding down her cheeks, over her silver piercings. "This is all my fault. I—I can't leave him."

Maddie narrowed her eyes. She couldn't let this man or Alice ruin her plans to save her sister, but damn it all, Ferris was right. "I suppose. We'll bring him back for a few days, then he can return home. However, the influence remains on for now. No argument."

Alice nodded, yet her body trembled, still fearing Maddie.

But Maddie was nothing like Rav—he used his influence to torment humans in a variety of ways before killing or turning them. Sometimes even experimenting on the ones he turned.

Footsteps sounded and a couple rounded the corner. Maddie stilled as her gaze latched onto long red hair falling down a woman's back. The breath in her lungs pumped again when the woman's face looked nothing like Imogen's, and the darker-haired female she held hands with wasn't Rav.

The couple didn't spare them a second glance.

"*Maddie*," Ferris warned, his voice serious, "we need to leave now."

Maddie focused once more on Noah's green gaze. "Continue to stay quiet and stick close to me."

Ferris moved down the path first, checking both ways before motioning them on. She wasn't certain Imogen and Rav would appear tonight, but something in her bones told her they would.

Maddie glanced at Alice's still-trembling form. Rav had been the one to take her, and she knew the tricks he liked to pull with his victims.

"Did Rav fuck you before the change?" Maddie asked, her nostrils flaring.

"No," Alice gasped, a look of horror crossing her face. "Nothing like that."

Lucky duck, then.

Alice groaned, clutching her stomach and hunching over.

Perhaps she hadn't turned as easily as Ferris had thought.

"Have you fed?" Ferris asked and pointed at his throat.

"No." A look of disgust crossed Alice's face. "I was hiding in a bin all day until the sun set."

Alice hadn't fed, and if she didn't soon, she might not complete the change and die, or she would grow mad and try to drink from the entire city of London.

"You need to feed," Maddie said as she walked beside Alice. "When we get to the safe house, you can drink from the pouches stored there."

"No!"

"That's your only option for a bit." They didn't have time to scavenge a human in Wonderland to please Alice, and Maddie was certain she wouldn't want to feed from her brother.

"I'll help you through it," Ferris said. "Compared to Maddie, I haven't been a vampire for long."

"I love the lore, the style, but I never wanted to be *this*." A few tears streamed down Alice's cheeks.

Maddie hadn't either, but she'd grown used to it.

"We need to pick up our pace," Maddie whispered. She then turned to Noah, his eyes still glazed. "Follow us and keep up."

No one said another word as they hurried to the park portal near Noah's home. A few stars shone brightly in the night sky, and every now and again the group passed a civilian or a car roared down the street. There were a number of portals throughout London, but the one Rav frequented was in a different city park near the nightclubs. That particular portal led straight to the Ruby Heart Palace. Somehow, Ferris had snuck Alice out through it.

Adjusting her arm sleeves, she looked again at Alice who continued to quiver. Maddie would attempt to lighten the mood while they kept their pace. "By the way, I'm Maddie."

"I'm Alice." She turned to her brother, tears glinting in her eyes, her shoulders sagging. "I only wanted to tell Noah goodbye."

"That's what we all think, but it's never that easy." Maddie peered at Noah in his calmer state, wondering what he was like when not encountering vampires. No human would be able to tell he was under an influence, but any vampire could. If Noah was as close to Alice as Maddie was to Mouse, then Alice would never have just been able to say goodbye. She would've continued to come back, the same way Maddie had returned to see Mouse.

"Which hideout should we take them to?" Ferris asked.

Ever had given Maddie half her set of keys so they would both have protection in case they needed to escape Imogen and Rav. The keys unlocked secret places across Wonderland. Maddie had later split them with Ferris so he could use them once he'd gotten Mouse, which he hadn't. But he'd been able to use one to escape through the palace's hidden back door.

"Rock, paper, scissors to decide?" she finally said.

Ferris rolled his eyes. "Let's just go to the one at the edge of Scarlet."

Ah, Maddie had missed Ferris's eye rolls. "Perfect, my dear." She'd first found him at a club where he'd played drums with his band, or in truth, Mouse had discovered him. He'd been passed out in the hall outside the club's back room, drunk and high. Maddie had said to leave him be, but Mouse chose to save him from overdosing. He'd thought Mouse was an angel when she first drank from him, taking the poison from his blood. After that, he'd wanted that high instead, and it worked out for Maddie and Mouse when they needed their appetites satiated.

The group approached a nearly-empty street and headed across it into the secluded park. Not many humans ventured there. Graffiti covered the playground, and a long crack ran up the yellow plastic slide. A lone swing creaked from the wind, the rest missing from their rusted chains, and a large rat scampered into a tunnel across from a leaning merry-go-round. The picnic tables, long disappeared, had never been replaced.

"I'll let things settle for about a week, then find a way to get Mouse out," Ferris whispered.

The best plan would be for Rav and Imogen to die by the sun's hand. Maddie was about to say just that when the strong scent of sulfur hit her nose. *The portal.* Someone was using it.

Maddie's heart pounded, her gaze settling on the spot

beneath a cluster of bushes beside a row of hazel trees. Vampires from all sides of Wonderland frequented any of the portals they wished, besides Rav's, but she hoped no one was on the other side of this one who could identify Alice or Ferris. Imogen wouldn't give up her search until they found them, alive or dead.

"Hide," Maddie whisper-shouted, shoving Ferris and Alice toward a covered footpath, leading to the playground tunnel that could easily fit two.

She was about to haul Noah with her to take shelter behind—she pivoted her head, searching their surroundings—apparently nowhere. The tree trunks close to them were too narrow, and climbing them wouldn't do with their thin and wiry limbs.

Next option. Act natural. Maddie would look like anyone else coming or going from the portal with an influenced mortal, and no one would recognize Noah.

"You'll thank me later for this." Maddie looped her arm around Noah's waist. She pulled him close to her, like a lover, and walked toward the portal as though they were waiting their turn to enter. "Act like we're *together*."

Out from the bushes, a masculine, yet elegant, hand appeared, then a body. *Bloody hell.* Not what she wanted. Not *who* she wanted.

Scarlet's prince. Chess.

That bastard. Right before Ever went into hiding, she'd told Maddie that Chess had tried to murder her. It had been on his mother's—Imogen's—orders. The White Queen had stabbed him in the chest before fleeing her masquerade ball once she discovered her guards had also betrayed her. But like a cat with nine lives, he lived. Ever should've aimed straight for his heart then twisted the blade like he was a wind-up toy.

It took everything in Maddie not to clench her teeth, but her fingers still dug into Noah's waist, his arm draped over her shoulder. She hadn't asked him to do that, but she didn't shove it off.

Chess wore a tight, dark vest, his full chest on display, his lean muscles flexing as he lazily pushed himself up to stand. He scented the air and his yellow gaze latched straight on them. Layers of brown hair fell to his chin and neck and he tucked them behind his ear.

Damn it.

"What are you doing out here?" Maddie cooed, pretending as if it were any normal night. "Don't you have your own hole to crawl out from?"

"Maddie, Maddie, Maddie, you still haven't learned how to speak to royalty?" Chess purred, licking his lower lip, his gaze flicking to Noah as he stepped closer to them. "Seems you found yourself quite a treat."

"He's mine. Go find your own."

"I'm still full from my earlier dessert." The prince grinned, inching closer to her. "Perhaps when you come to the palace with your next hat, you can stop by my room before you leave." Leaning forward, he whispered, "We can put some of that madness to good use."

Maddie tried not to hurl up her earlier snack. "Tempting, but no."

Chess only leaned in closer, his grin growing wider. "I'm going to find your White Queen soon. Perhaps I'll have a different, *bloodier,* sort of fun with her."

Maddie's heart lodged in her throat, and she held back taking a deep swallow. "Why should I care what you do with her?"

"You may not." He shrugged, then straightened as if he were becoming bored. "But I do know you care about your sister."

"If you touch her—"

"Relax." Chess chuckled. "She isn't my type. She's too quiet. Probably wouldn't even squeak when I fucked an orgasm out of her." He glanced between her and Noah. "Well,

I'm afraid I have more important matters to see to…"

With that, he sauntered away. She clenched her teeth then, so hard she thought she felt one crack.

"I hate that fucking pretentious ass," Ferris said under his breath. Maddie hadn't heard him approach, hadn't known how long she'd been standing there thinking about stabbing several hatpins straight through Chess's villainous heart.

"I feel … I feel," Alice murmured, collapsing onto Ferris. He scooped her up just as her body convulsed, her mouth foaming.

"We have to get her into hiding *now*," Maddie rushed out. "I don't know if feeding will even help her. Something's wrong."

Ferris nodded and lowered Alice to the portal, hurrying them both through.

Maddie turned to Noah and grabbed his hand, tugging him toward the hole next. "Crawl through. Quickly."

After his form slid past the bushes, Maddie pushed the branches back and went in behind him on all fours. A warming sensation tickled her skin as she slipped into the entrance to her home. Deep brown dirt surrounded her while she crawled forward, and a slew of bright scarlet beetles and black and blue caterpillars accompanied her.

Maddie finished venturing the short distance and brought herself to stand back in Wonderland, darkness sweeping around her.

Ferris held Alice, who was now unconscious in his arms, no longer convulsing. To his side, Noah patiently waited, eyes still glazed.

With a grin, Maddie grasped Noah's face between her hands, tilting it down so their gazes met, and she released him from her influence.

He blinked, his breathing hitched, yet his eyes stayed trained on hers as she held him in place.

She parted her lips and her fangs lowered. "I'm giving you

this one opportunity to help us with your sister. She's no longer human. As you can see, I'm not either."

CHAPTER FOUR

NOAH

*N*ot *human.*

Noah heard what the young woman—Maddie—had said. He saw her teeth. *Fangs.* But somehow, it wasn't processing. There was no such thing as vampires. If it wasn't for the fact that Maddie had somehow controlled his mind to get him to— where the bloody hell were they?—then he would've thought the fangs were prosthetic.

But the conversations he'd overheard, a man crawling out of the *ground*, his sister seizing… It was all real, right? And then Maddie had crawled through the very same *hole* in the ground, pulling him along with her, and entered another place entirely. *What in the ever-loving fuck?*

"We have to *move*," Ferris whispered through gritted teeth.

Noah scanned the city behind Maddie. Buildings stood two and three stories high, made from glossy red and black stone and aged wood. Red lights hung in lanterns, casting the entire street in an ominous glow. He stopped breathing when his gaze landed on a man—*vampire*—through one of the open windows facing them. A vampire and a woman. Moving her hair aside, he struck hard and fast, biting her neck. And she arched into him as if she *enjoyed* it. Noah backpedaled from Maddie and Ferris as he looked desperately for somewhere safe to get away from this crazy shit.

No. He couldn't leave without Alice. But she was still in the arms of a damn monster. His gaze snapped to where Ferris held Alice, and his breath left him in a whoosh. The stranger scanned the area like a predator, shifting nervously as he waited for prey. She was one of *them* now. A vampire. *An actual vampire.* Did that mean she was dead? Did she need blood to live? How would he keep her safe when they returned home? Why, *precisely,* couldn't they return home? And how was he going to keep her ... "condition" a secret from their parents? From the world? *For fuck's sake.*

"I need answers to a *lot* of questions before I agree to anything." Noah crossed his arms and dug his heels into the ground. "I won't go anywhere until I have them."

A snarl sounded and Noah whipped his head to the side. Two males seemingly appeared out of nowhere—though likely from behind one of the nearby buildings—and rolled on the ground together a few meters away, their movements a blur. Paired with how dark it was, Noah had trouble making out what was happening. He could hear just fine though—every tear of fabric, each growl. *What the...?* He squinted at the fighting duo and a spray of blood sailed through the air.

"Ignore them," Maddie said, grabbing Noah's arm just as he was about to make a run for it. "We don't have time for questions, but you may ask *one.*"

One. How was he supposed to choose? They all seemed important. What were they running from? Where were they running to? Vampires? Mind control? What were they planning to do with him and Alice? Kill them? Why the fuck were they ignoring the fact that two vampires were tearing each other apart? "What's with the underground tunnel?" he asked before he could stop himself.

"This is where the portal to Wonderland is, and you're in the city of Scarlet. All of the portals are underground. Now"—she put her hands on her hips and looked up at him—"are you coming?"

Noah stared at her as if she'd spoken gibberish. It was a little late to ask him that now, considering she'd already dragged him into this hellscape. What else was he going to do but follow her? Run? With his luck, he'd only get himself drained dry within the hour. Besides, they had his sister. He grunted in anger which Maddie must've taken as a *yes*.

"Welcome to Wonderland," she sang. "I really don't prefer to influence humans but most of the time it's necessary." With a flick of the wrist, she whirled away from him, then glanced back over her shoulder. "Shall we go?"

"Give her to me." Noah stepped up to Ferris and slid his arms under Alice, pulling her away from the vampire. It didn't matter how far they had to travel—he'd be damned if he let anyone else touch her, no matter their motives.

"You sure you can carry her all the way to the safe house?" the vampire asked, relinquishing Alice.

"Don't worry about me." Noah hoisted Alice higher, adjusting his grip. "What's going to happen to her? Will she be okay?"

Maddie ushered him forward and gave a surprised gasp. "I almost forgot! Drink this."

"Drink wha—"

She pressed a smooth glass bottle to his lips. Cool, tasteless liquid flowed over his tongue and down his throat. He sputtered, half of it spraying Maddie in her face.

She wrinkled her nose in distaste and wiped it off with her arm sleeve. "It will allow you to see better since Wonderland has no sun. The muted grays in the morning will be fine for you, but tonight we're going into a lowly-lit part of the city." Maddie poked at his back to make him walk faster. "Now, chop-chop. We don't want to get separated from Ferris."

Get separated? Ferris was right—*gone*. Noah searched the lit street and watched him turn left at a crossroad. How had he moved so fast? It wasn't— Noah winced. *It wasn't natural*, he thought. But it was ... *for them.*

"Go on then, slowcoach," Maddie insisted. "Ferris has the keys to the safe house."

A sharp scream sounded in the distance, quickly turning to a moan. Noah's heart pounded and his breath came quicker. How did a nightmarish place like this exist and no one know about it? If anyone found out, he was sure the world leaders would find a way to bury these portals. They could block the tunnels with cement or throw a bomb down the holes.

"Bloody hell," he whispered to himself. "Where are we?"

"Have you been listening to anything I said, mortal? Your sister has enemies searching for her." Maddie placed her hands on his back and pushed him, holding Alice, farther into the city. "There are many vampires who travel here for the portal. We have to get to the safe house before we draw too much attention."

Noah heard the truth in her tone and hurried his steps to where he'd seen Ferris disappear. It must've been the right direction since Maddie finally stopped shoving him and moved to walk at his side.

Noah kept her in his sights while canvassing their surroundings. No shops stood nearby, but some of the homes featured balconies. Instead of the planters and patio furniture people decorated them with in his world, these were empty. At least for the most part. Two or three contained strange, abstract sculptures that filled the entire space. Spirals and jagged edges, pieces that appeared unfinished. The red lanterns only made them more ominous.

"What are you thinking?" Maddie peered up at him.

Noah swallowed hard, fighting the urge to put some distance between himself and this vampire. He needed her though. Someone had to help him save Alice, and it wasn't like he knew anyone else willing, or even capable, of it.

"Not sure what to think," he mumbled. It wasn't a lie.

"Your sister will be... Well, she'll be fine for now." Maddie gave him a look of sympathy. "Let's have hope that a little blood will fix her right up and one day she'll be able to control her bloodlust."

Bile rose in the back of Noah's throat. His sister, drinking blood... What the fuck was actually going on here? If only he could wake up from this damn nightmare.

"Here we are." She stepped through an already-opened door into a pitch-black room.

Not quite pitch black. Noah blinked a few times until vague shapes formed. Inside the black stone building, Maddie, Ferris, and a few blurred pieces of furniture stood, waiting. He blinked again and an ornate grandfather clock came into focus.

"Get in here, dumbass," Ferris snapped, suddenly in the doorway. He grabbed Noah's arm and yanked him inside before shutting the door.

Noah stumbled over the threshold and nearly dropped Alice. Maddie clasped Noah's shoulders, steadying him, as his gaze fastened on her honey-colored eyes. "Thanks" he said, shuffling away from her touch.

"Set your sister on the settee," she told him, then scurried into an adjoining room with rows of cupboards. She opened one at a time, rifling through whatever was stored there. "Ferris, can you bring me some water?"

Noah's arms ached with the weight of carrying his sister, even though it had only been a few streets, so he took Maddie's advice. After laying Alice on the black velvet settee, he grabbed one of the round decorative pillows and lifted her head. She groaned as he adjusted it beneath her.

"It's okay, sis," he lied, and felt her forehead as if seeking a temperature. Ridiculous, maybe, but what did he know about becoming a vampire? She looked like herself, as she always had, and it was hard to reconcile that she was something different now. "We'll get you sorted."

Alice's eyes snapped open, glowing a bright blue. There was something wild in her expression, a desperation he'd never seen, like the gleam of an animal on the verge of starvation. A growl rose from her throat, low at first, then louder, monstrous. Her fingertips scraped across the velvet cushions. Noah tensed. She dug them in harder, ripping lines through the fabric.

And then she lunged at him. Noah reared back, tripping over his own feet, and landed hard on the wooden floor. Alice was on top of him before he could make sense of what had happened. Something sharp grazed his throat.

Alice disappeared almost as quickly as she'd attacked. Ferris held her to him, her back against his chest, as she snarled at Noah. Blood—*his* blood—dripped off two elongated fangs.

The world slowed as Noah raised his hand to cover the scratch she'd given him. His sister almost *bit* him. What the fuck?

She tried to bite me.
Bite. Me.

"Up you go," Maddie said and lifted him to his feet with far too much ease. "No use crying over a little spilled blood, right?"

He whipped his head to Maddie and stared, mouth open, at her. Was she serious?

"I have to leave now." Maddie shouldered a small bag. "It seems you're coming along with me instead of staying here. Unless you're interested in feeding your sister?"

Noah felt the blood drain from his face. "I'm not feeding *anyone.*"

Maddie shrugged and gave a lighthearted *hmm.* "There's powdered blood in the cabinets for you to mix with the water," she told Ferris. "Use however much it takes."

"It tastes like shit," he grumbled.

"Yes, but it will do." Maddie laughed. "Besides, we can't risk bringing a human here for her."

Ferris fished out a large ring of keys and plucked one off, handing the others to Maddie. "Fine, but don't take too long."

"Wait," Noah rasped. "Where are we going now?"

"You used your one question already." Maddie bopped him on the nose with the tip of her finger. "Let's go, mortal."

CHAPTER FIVE

MADDIE

"Seriously, where are we going?" Noah asked, jogging up beside Maddie in the city street.

The night grew darker, making the red lanterns in Scarlet seem to glow brighter. Maddie hadn't wanted to take the little mortal—or rather, big mortal—with her, but anyway, his height was beside the point. His sister had tried to make a meal out of him, and if Maddie and Ferris hadn't been there, he would've been a dead human.

Noah's warm hand wrapped around her arm and tugged her to a stop. If she wanted, she could easily pull from his grip and toss him to the ground, but she would give the mortal his moment.

"You're a bold one, aren't you?" Maddie grinned. "Any other vampire would've bitten your arm off."

Noah's eyes widened as he dropped her arm.

"I'm only teasing." She paused, laughing silently to

herself. "Or am I?"

"Listen, Maddie. At least tell me where we're going."

Maddie had told him she would give him one question, but to be fair, perhaps she could do another. After all, he did look a bit tense out here. She knew a good way to loosen those tense muscles of his, but with him as frightened as a kitten, a roll in bed would probably not go over so well.

"To my home." She waved a hand in the air and continued her brisk pace.

"Your home?" Noah's voice went up an octave. "For *what*?"

"Quite the little questioner, aren't you?" Maddie cut between two tall buildings lined with diamond-shaped windows. Boisterous growling and screams came from one of the structures. At the other, several of the vampires were feasting and fucking at the windows while some had their curtains drawn tight. Maddie preferred to take a lover behind closed doors, but there was always time to be venturous.

"Well?" Noah asked, arching his impeccable brow at her.

Maddie had only spent a little while with Alice, but already she wished the female's role were reversed with Noah's. Alice wouldn't have been as much of a nuisance.

"We're going to my house to make a hat." She pulled her index finger and thumb across her lips. "Now put a sock in it."

"What the fuck? *Why*? Actually, no. Spare me the illogic," Noah said, rubbing his temples. "We're going to make a hat, then what? Have a tea party?"

Maddie stopped and turned to him with a big smile on her face. "Precisely, my friend. Less talkie and more walkie."

Noah glared but followed beside her, this time keeping his lips sealed. It was a good thing, too, because she didn't want to have to threaten him with needle and thread. He wouldn't find her teasing funny, but a part of her wanted to see the mortal's reaction.

The red lanterns leading to her home grew distant, giving

way to the darkness. If she hadn't given Noah one of her elixirs, the trek home would've been unbearable. No beastly things stirred in the city this night—the werewolves must've gotten their fill, their appetites satiated. However, she did have her gun loaded and ready in the side of her boot.

Maddie and Noah slowed to a stop in front of her door. "How do you like my home?" Maddie sang. It had been a bit since she'd brought a human guest there. She'd been going to the mortal world or the donor compounds in Wonderland for her feasts. Since Ever had been gone, and while Maddie had been plotting to get Mouse out from the Ruby Heart Palace, she hadn't wanted anyone to get too close in case Imogen and Rav tortured them to try and obtain any information about the White Queen.

"It's lovely," he answered sarcastically.

"Such a party pooper, you are." Grinning, she unlocked the door, pushed it open, and waved him in as if he were attending a circus.

"Cut the theatrics." He rolled his eyes, but she could've sworn his lips twitched. As his gaze roamed around the sitting room, a confused expression crossed his face. "What. The fuck. Is this?" He whirled to face her. "You have hats *everywhere*."

"Are you going to be surprised by *everything*?" She stepped over a clump of fabric on the floor and picked up a bonnet from her chair to take a seat. "Yes, dear mortal. They are *mine*. You should try one. It would suit that inquisitive head of yours."

The lack of torture devices was likely a *surprise* to him too, but she kept a respectable distance, making sure he didn't feel threatened. Noah furrowed his brow, his pulse slowing as he examined her home. She'd done her duty—he wasn't frightened anymore. For now.

"So, this is your job? You make weird hats?" he asked.

"Hey now," she whispered and pressed a finger to her lips.

"They can hear you. You don't want to hurt their feelings."

"Whatever." He shook his head and settled on the settee near the wall. "Is Alice going to be all right?"

Maddie truly didn't know. She could be dead when they returned if her heart didn't take well to the blood. The change from mortal to immortal wasn't as easy as one might think. The human body was a very fickle, fickle thing.

"Let's hope. Ferris will make sure she feeds regularly, which will help." Maddie opened her cooler, the contents always cold courtesy of the special ice chests made in Wonderland. She fished out a blood bag and her teacup, then poured the red liquid in. Cold wasn't the best, but it would do to avert her from the lovely smell flowing from Noah's veins. This mortal's unpleasant attitude clashed with his pleasant scent. His cedarwood smell enveloped her once more, sweet as a summer night.

"You weren't kidding about a tea party, were you?" Noah's nose wrinkled in disgust, but his eyes danced with curiosity.

"Nope." She gestured behind her at a pail on the wooden table. "There's water if you're thirsty. I haven't had a human guest here in a while, but I usually refill it just in case. Wouldn't want you to dehydrate and create another problem for us."

Not bouncing back with one of his ridiculous questions, he went and poured water into a teacup.

She lifted her own snack and drank the cold liquid down. A low moan escaped her mouth—it had lost some of its richness due to the chill, but the metallic notes hit her tastebuds just right. When she glanced up, Noah was studying her with an unreadable expression.

She took out a roll of tulle along with a spool of thread.

"You can sleep on the settee if you wish," Maddie said. "I need to finish this fascinator for one of my clients before the morning." She should've had it completed before leaving to retrieve Alice, but her thoughts had been a horse race circling her brain. Or more like a slow drawn-out song that would never end while waiting for night to fall.

Noah relaxed on the settee and took a sip of his water. "Not sure I'll ever be able to sleep, to be honest."

Maddie shrugged and picked up a pair of scissors and a sheet of polka dot felt. She then cut out a large circle and concentrated as she folded, stitched, tore, and looped.

After a while of getting lost in her creation, she glanced up to find Noah asleep, light snores drifting out from between his plump parted lips. Smiling to herself, she grabbed a bowler hat off the wall and placed it onto his head. *There. Now he looks like a gentleman, even if he doesn't act like a proper one.* She then took the folded blanket beside him and draped it across his body, her eyes unintentionally sliding down his muscular form.

He was an unpleasant guest, but it didn't mean she wouldn't have manners. Maddie picked up her project once more and worked and worked until her fingers were tired and her lids shut.

A knock pounded at the door and Maddie jerked out of her seat, snatching a hatpin. Noah studied her hand where it gripped the metal, but he didn't say a word.

"Stay quiet and act natural," she whispered.

He bit his lower lip and nodded, his hands clenched into fists. Those human fists would do nothing to save him here.

The bowler she'd placed on his head was now tossed to the side on the floor. *Poor hat.*

She peered out the speakeasy, expecting to see one of her

clients there. Her entire body stiffened. This was bad. Bad. Bad. Bad. What were *they* doing here?

Imogen and Rav.

Not waiting a moment longer, since that would only make them suspicious, Maddie tossed the hatpin aside and flung open the door with a grin. "How may I serve you, Your Majesties?" She bowed, keeping her gaze trained on Imogen because Rav was more of a piece of shit than the Queen of Hearts.

Without an invitation, Rav bounded into her home, Imogen at his heels. His white, red-tipped hair was pristine as ever, and his brown eyes settled on Noah. Imogen's scarlet curls fell down her back and instead of her usual gown, she wore crimson breeches and a red and black coat with tails.

"It appears we're meeting again, sooner than I expected," Imogen purred, her yellow irises, matching Chess's, met hers. She then sniffed the air. "The treat you brought home smells rather tasty."

Noah's fists tightened even more, and Maddie fought a grin.

"I can share if you want," she sang. "I was just about to have two kinds of breakfasts with him."

"I'll find my own, Hatter." Imogen's lip curled as she retrieved her blasted deck of cards out from the pocket of her trousers. "Now, have you seen my Knave?"

Maddie's heart thumped an extra beat. If Ferris had still been there... But he wasn't. He was safe with Alice at the moment.

She furrowed her brow, putting on false confusion. "The tall one?"

"You know who I'm talking about," Imogen snapped.

"Can't say that I have, but if I do, I will cut out his heart and bring it to you." Maddie knew that answer should please Imogen enough since the queen relished removing the bloody organ of her enemies.

"Hmm," Rav said, pressing close to Maddie and fishing out a photograph from his pocket. "Hopefully you please this human more than you did me." He lifted her chin, his finger caressing her jawline, and she couldn't stop herself from shuddering. "Now, listen close, have you seen this girl?"

Maddie studied the photograph that he held up a few centimeters from her eyes. She focused on keeping her breaths steady because it wasn't just a young Alice in the photograph—a boy, who was maybe sixteen at the time, stood beside her. Even though Alice looked the same except for her locks being completely blonde in the picture, Noah appeared nothing like himself. In the image, he was heavier, sporting a choppy haircut, and he wore glasses and braces. If she hadn't known he was Alice's brother, she would never have guessed this was the same mortal.

"I'm afraid I haven't." Maddie shrugged.

"If you do find the girl or Knave," Rav said, "bring them straight to the Ruby Heart Palace and we will reward you."

Fuck their rewards.

"Come on, Rabbit," Imogen said, shuffling her deck of cards. "I knew coming here would give us no results." She then turned to Maddie. "For wasting my time, bring me a new fascinator in two weeks instead of a month. It had better please me, or Mouse will answer to me again."

Maddie took a deep swallow. "I will." If one thing could make her nervous about anything, it was her sister.

Without another word, Imogen and Rav left her cottage, but not before the bastard gave her a wink while running his hand over his cock. She closed the door behind her and took breath after breath.

"Who's Mouse?" Noah asked, his voice softer than she'd heard thus far.

"My sister. She was the one who told Ferris to save Alice from the palace." Maddie sank down on the settee beside him, his lovely scent surrounding her. "That was the Queen of

Hearts and her king, Rav. They are the ones who changed your sister."

"*Them?*" Noah whisper-shouted. "They were in my home, took my picture? And they also have your sister?"

"It's a long story." Too long to discuss with him now—she didn't have the energy to tell him everything in its entirety at the moment. Not after Rav had put his fingers on her flesh again, caressing, taunting.

"Why is she called the Queen of Hearts?"

"Because she's obsessed with the organ and will easily rip out anyone's heart who she sees as her enemy, then decorate the palace grounds with them. I'm lucky she still hasn't taken Mouse's. My sister has been in her palace for two years, and I just want her home."

"I'm sorry." He blew out a breath. "Once a vampire is changed, can they ever become human again?"

It had been a long time since she had asked herself the same question. There was a time when she'd wanted to return to humanity, but she preferred the cards here. Mouse did as well.

"It would take moving heaven and hell to change back." She paused and then added, "No more questions. Come on, we need to get this hat to my client. It's a good friend of Imogen's which is why it can't be late."

CHAPTER SIX

NOAH

The vampires who'd turned Alice were worse than Noah imagined. Imogen and Rav carried an air of superiority like he'd never experienced. As if they ruled the world and would damn anyone who stood in their way, which, he supposed was true. Except *he* was blocking them from Alice. So were Maddie and Ferris. He would never give his sister up to those two arseholes, yet what motive did Maddie and Ferris have to protect her? Like Alice, Ferris was wanted by the royals, but what about Maddie? He narrowed a suspicious gaze at the purple-haired vampire walking briskly beside him, looking her up and down. His gaze lingered on her legs for a moment—they were rather shapely ... not that he should've noticed...

If Maddie's customer was anything like Imogen, he didn't want to meet the slag. It was likely though, given that the two females were friends. Still, he carried the bright yellow hat box with its oversized, ridiculous blue ribbon through Scarlet while avoiding stepping in the tacky-looking blood stains on the streets. "Are you certain I can't wait at your house while you deliver this?"

Maddie gave an exaggerated sigh. "I've told you already. No, mortal."

"Right." He scowled at the back of her head, a black tulle hat perched on her purple hair. "But *why*?"

"Curiouser and curiouser, aren't you?" She hooked a sharp right down another street.

This one contained only homes made of deep red glass. The walls were too thick to see clearly inside, but he could make out general shapes. Tall furniture, moving bodies. Maddie took another turn and he almost missed it—his gaze riveted to the craftsmanship around him.

"When can we check on my sister?" he asked, almost plowing into Maddie's back as she slowed to match his pace.

"When it's safe."

It would never be safe here, and Alice could be dead for all Noah knew. *No.* He refused to entertain the idea. Ferris was looking after her, and although a vampire and a stranger, he didn't seem to want to harm her. He believed she would be fine until he found a way to reverse what happened.

It would take moving heaven and hell to change back. Maddie's words played over and over in his head. That meant there was a cure, even if she'd refused to elaborate. But whatever the hell it was, getting it was instrumental. "Don't fret about your sister—we'll go soon enough. I cannot drag a mortal around Wonderland with me and hope to succeed," she continued.

"Succeed in saving your sister?" he asked.

Maddie whirled around and placed a finger on his lips. "You talk too much about things that shouldn't be spoken of."

Noah arched a brow and inched his head back, away from her warm touch. While it was clean now, he could only imagine how many throats she'd ripped out with the same digit. "But you *are* dragging me around Wonderland."

Maddie rolled her eyes and continued down the street, this time at his side, her arm brushing his. "I won't be going directly home after making this delivery, and I can't very well leave you alone. What if Imogen and Rav return, hmm? So I need to take you somewhere else—somewhere safe—to wait."

He certainly didn't want to run into those two, but more importantly... "What am I waiting for?"

Maddie patted his shoulder as if comforting a simpleton. "To go home, of course."

"I can't go home." Noah clutched the box tightly. "I need you to tell me more about the cure for Alice so I can find it."

Maddie released a high-pitch laugh. "Impossible."

"You said one exists," he insisted.

"And it does. Deep in the swamp, in the heart of werewolf territory. The beasts would eat you long before you came close to the cure. A simple mortal man against an entire pack of wolves? No, no. It's best to accept your sister's new life and move on."

A sudden burst of rage seared Noah's veins. Accept that Alice would be reduced to a blood-thirsty creature? That she would live in this alternate world under the rule of arseholes as fearsome as Imogen and Rav? Fuck no. What would he tell their parents? Not the truth, obviously, but to let them think she ran away would be torture.

"Then I suppose *you* should accept *your* sister's imprisonment," he snapped.

Maddie inhaled sharply, immediately stopped walking, and dug her fingers into his upper arm. "Watch what you say, mortal."

"Don't threaten me," he said, pulling from her grip. It was stupid to taunt the one vampire who was helping him. She could easily turn on him, kill him, and lie to Alice about it. If Alice was told he returned home, she would believe it—she was too trusting. There would be no reason for her to question it when Wonderland was a deathtrap for humans. But if she ever returned to visit, only to find their flat empty, what would she think? That he was murdered or he'd moved on with his life? Still, he had to do whatever he could to help his sister now, while he could. "Tell me where this swamp is and how to get there, and I'll be out of your hair."

Maddie reached up and twirled one of her curls. "I don't have time for this now. We'll be late."

"Tell me where it is." Noah lifted the hatbox into the air, high above his head. "Or you won't have anything to deliver."

Maddie blinked at him in surprise, then brought the outer edge of her hand down in the crook of his elbow. His arm bent under the hard blow, and she easily snatched the box away from him, cradling it to her chest. "If you behave yourself, we'll discuss her situation *after* I complete my sale."

Noah rubbed his arm and grinned. Damn, she was strong as fuck. He could wait the few minutes it would take to drop off the hat. "Deal."

With a nod, Maddie strode down the empty streets, her skirt riding up her toned legs. The faint hint of death lingered in the air, pulling him back to the present. Noah had attended an autopsy for one of his university classes and he would never mistake the distinct scent of human decay. He pushed the knowledge away before it was able to take root. Losing his mind wouldn't help Alice get out of this shithole. He held his breath, hoping by the time he needed another, they would be far enough away from whatever corpse was nearby. A bat swooped down from a hidden perch, streaking straight at his head. He cursed, ducking, and tasted the scent on his tongue. A cough shook his chest as he fought not to vomit, especially when his gaze connected with half a skeleton resting beside a rose bush.

"There, there," Maddie said without a hint of sympathy. "Pull yourself together."

Noah slapped a hand over his mouth and tried to drag in a

breath without smelling anything.

"We're here," she added.

Noah took in the large stone house she stared at. *Of course, their destination was likely a murder scene.* The building was three stories high with a slate roof, a small stone gargoyle fixed to each corner, and massive, arching windows draped in red curtains. Maddie didn't wait to see if Noah followed as she climbed the six steps to the door and lifted the knocker. A snarling wolf's face peered back at him with a chain wrapped around its snout and something about its carved expression made Noah uncomfortable.

A few moments later, the front door swung inward to reveal a woman with sunken eyes. She wore a long black dress, a large white bow tied neatly in the front, and her dark blonde hair was pulled into a tight bun at the base of her neck. Noah couldn't tell if she was human or vampire, which, he supposed was going to be an ongoing problem now that he knew the sun-fearing creatures were no fucking myth.

"May I help you?" the woman asked.

"Hello, Robin. I've come with Osanna's new hat." Maddie held the box up in the woman's face as if she would've missed it otherwise. "She's expecting me."

Robin wordlessly stepped aside, and Maddie waltzed in. "Come along, mortal," she sang when Noah didn't immediately follow.

He cleared his throat and slipped in after her. Robin clanged the door shut behind them and Noah swallowed hard. This was nothing like Maddie's home, but empty, a shell of a house, devoid of all life. The stone walls were bare, the marble floor gleaming. No furniture decorated the entrance hall, but a large crystal chandelier hung from the ceiling. Two sets of stairs curved up either side of the room.

"In here," Maddie said, and entered through a door to the left without waiting for an answer. When Noah caught up, she leaned in. "I *always* meet her in here."

Noah studied the room with the red curtains he'd seen from outside. Pleated silver fabric covered the walls, and a large black settee faced the door. Two iron lamps hung from the ceiling, candles burning behind the metal bars. On the matching black ottoman, sat a tray with two glass goblets full of thick red liquid.

Blood, Noah realized. His skin crawled, not only because of what it was. *Where—or who—had it come from?*

"We always have a drink," Maddie said, following his gaze. "Sit there."

Noah slipped around the ottoman to take the corner of the settee. The metallic tang of blood floated in the air, and he pulled in a shallow breath. A drink with an enemy in exchange for a hat? He rubbed his forehead against the first hint of a headache.

"Hatter," a female cooed, bursting into the open doorway a moment later. "I'm dying to see what you've brought me this time."

Noah's lips parted as he took in the vampire. A gold silk robe hugged her body, the color bringing out the bronze tones in her flawless skin. She looked as if she had just stepped out of a magazine spread with her high cheekbones and winged eyeliner.

"Hello, Osanna. It's just what you ordered," Maddie told her as she handed over the box.

The vampire lifted the lid and pulled out a cobalt hat with stiff, curled ribbons and a giant sapphire. She placed the hat on her sleek emerald hair and turned her head this way and that to see if it fit. Then, her gaze finally landed on Noah.

"Who's this?" she asked, swiping her tongue along her lower lip.

"My mortal," Maddie answered, her voice sounding protective. "He's staying with me for a little while."

Osanna removed the hat and returned it to the box with a curious expression. "I thought for a moment, perhaps, you brought refreshments this time."

Maddie laughed, the pitch higher than what he'd heard prior to this moment. "Unfortunately not. He's already given what he could for today."

Noah's eyes drifted between the two vampires, his pulse quickening. Osanna didn't mean she wanted to feed from him, did she? *She did.* He was no vampire expert, but the drop of her fangs seemed like a damn good indicator. At least Maddie was lying to try and keep his blood where it damn well belonged.

"He does seem tired," Osanna admitted. "Perhaps you would allow me to entertain him briefly? Just to see if he would be interested in extending his stay once you've finished with him. He's *very* attractive."

Maddie hesitated. Her gaze met his and she gave him a look that told him to play along. Why did this feel like part of her plan *before* they'd struck their deal in the street? Noah narrowed his eyes at her, letting her sense his suspicion. He had promised to behave, but that didn't mean Maddie was allowed to throw him to the wolves.

"That would be fine," Maddie agreed, wringing her hands in front of her.

"Splendid." Osanna licked the corner of her lips. "Go see Robin about payment."

Maddie cast him one final, almost guilty, look, before slipping from the room faster than it took Noah to realize what the hell was happening. Then Osanna sat beside him, and he caught a whiff of her perfume—a horrible cross between baby powder and coffee beans. He hadn't even seen her move. "Hi," he murmured. Every alarm bell in his head alerted him to her proximity.

"Hello." Osanna trailed one of her gold-painted nails gently down the side of his neck. "You have no marks here. I didn't expect the Hatter to prefer more private feeding locations."

"Wh—"

Osanna's hand landed on his knee and slid up his inner thigh. Noah attempted to shift away but she tugged him closer. "Don't be coy, human," she whispered in his ear. Her hand skimmed down the opposite thigh and back up. "You seem not to have any sensitive bite marks hiding here. Did she bring you here to feed a different sort of appetite?"

Noah opened his mouth to tell her he had no idea what she meant when Osanna cupped his balls over his trousers. He attempted to wiggle out of her touch, but she simply began stroking him, effectively holding him in place. "Excuse me," he shouted.

"Unlike her, I like to mix business with pleasure." This time the words took on an edge of anger—anger directed at Maddie. "If the Hatter wants to hide Ever from my queen, I will see no reason not to break her toy."

"I'm not a toy." His heart pounded in his chest, his muscles begging him to *run!* But he was trapped. Paralyzed by fear and cornered by a predator.

"Silly boy." Osanna laughed. "Of course you are."

Osana lunged forward, her teeth slicing through the flesh of his throat. Blinding pain radiated from Noah's neck. He sucked in a breath to shout when she covered his mouth. Pressure built beneath her bite, the agony coming in waves as she sucked and released with each mouthful of his blood. He kicked out, sending the goblets of blood on the table shattering to the ground. Then the pain dissolved into a wave of pure ecstasy. Noah moaned, feeling the suction at his neck all the way down to his swelling cock. Osanna's hand stroked him over his trousers as she continued to drink from him. His eyes fluttered and his back arched into her touch.

Noah's limbs fell limp at his sides, useless and weak. But he didn't care. Not when he was experiencing the most intense pleasure of his life.

Osanna ripped herself free from his throat. Noah slumped

backward and slid down, his head bent at an unnatural angle into the crease of the cushions. He didn't mind the discomfort as euphoria washed over him.

"Delicious," she rasped. "You would've been wonderful to bottle. Too late now."

Noah moaned as the room faded in and out of focus. "Maddie," he called as pain began to leak through the bliss. Or … he tried to call for her. His voice didn't seem to be working anymore. *No,* he cried out, the word never making it to his mouth. *I can't die here. Not like this! I still have to save Alice.*

Osanna stood, wiped at the corners of her mouth, and lifted her new headpiece again. "I shall let the Hatter know I'm finished," she purred as Noah continued to bleed out.

CHAPTER SEVEN

MADDIE

Maddie wandered the bare halls to the library to meet Osanna's housekeeper, Robin, for her payment. Osanna was a flashy female, golden and silver gowns, sapphire and emerald headpieces. But she wasn't much for decoration around her home. Maddie could easily spiff up the place if Osanna asked her to. Walls lined with ruby cloches and bronze bowlers would be positively delightful.

And then she remembered Noah... She hadn't wanted to leave the mortal with Osanna, yet it wasn't as if she hadn't left humans with her unattended before. If anything, she may take a small bite from him, have a quick drink, but no permanent damage would be done.

Maddie rounded the corner to find the library door wide open. Inside were two high-back green velvet chairs, an elegant ivory table, a fireplace accompanied by walls and walls of books, mostly erotic. She didn't think Osanna even knew how to read—it would be too much work for her. The tomes were just there to look pretty or to supply her with pictures for browsing in her boredom.

Where was that blasted Robin? She was usually in here. While waiting for the housekeeper to show up, Maddie pored over each pristine book, not a single crack or bend in their spines. "Oh," she said, coming to a stop on a bright white one with golden letters. She drew out the *Kama Sutra* book and flipped through its crisp pages.

She arched a brow as she took in each position—delicate, rough, unusual. "I've done that one. Definitely that one. Wouldn't do that one. Ah, that one I certainly like. Bloody hell, how do you even get in that position?"

Footsteps echoed in the hallway, pulling Maddie out of her rehashing of past partners. She pushed the book back into its place and peered up as Robin's blonde head entered the room. "There you are," Maddie sang, gliding toward the housekeeper across the floor and holding out her hand. "Payment?"

Robin bowed with a strange smirk and took out a silver key from her pocket. The housekeeper had been here for years, unlike the Queen of Hearts who constantly replaced the majority of her servants after she grew bored. Osanna kept hers, or the one. As long as Robin didn't speak too much, anyway. But Robin would help Osanna with her vicious deeds when necessary. A follower, like Igor was to Dr. Frankenstein.

Robin went to the wall beside one of the bookshelves, wiped away a few specks of dust, and placed a key into the small rectangular jeweled door. It squeaked open and she withdrew a velvet sack that clinked with coins.

Maddie wiggled her fingers as Robin dropped three scarlet coins in her hand, which the Hatter quickly tucked into the skirt of her dress.

"Good day, Robin." Maddie waved a hand in the air and spun on her heel. Now that she was finished with Osanna for a few months and wouldn't have to see Imogen for another two weeks, Maddie had the freedom she needed to focus on saving Mouse.

It was time for her to take the mortal and head back to Ferris to figure out what their next step would be. When Maddie delivered Imogen's hat to the Ruby Heart Palace, she would have to try and make a move—Mouse had been there too long. And she also needed to figure out what the bloody hell to do with Alice, who couldn't stay in hiding for the rest of her life. But wasn't that what Ever was doing? When, if ever, would the White Queen finally make her appearance? Maddie had thought she would've already returned by now. Unless something was wrong...

As Maddie turned the corner of the hallway, Osanna's green hair flowed around her when she stepped out from the sitting room, her golden robe dragging on the floor. The sapphire hat Maddie had made was atop Osanna's head, and the immortal brought a hand to her own face. To wipe away a streak of blood from her chin... Maddie halted. She must've decided to have a small snack from Noah. Maddie would apologize to him, then they would be on their merry way.

"Your human tasted lovely, Hatter." Osanna grinned, bringing a hand to her fascinator. "But I may have *purposely* gotten carried away. Now, clean his body up and leave. Robin will walk you out and I'll see you in two months." She paused, her grin growing wider. "You know better than to cross my queen—she'll find Ever soon enough."

Maddie couldn't show her concern. Not for the mortal and not for Ever. Even though her heart thrummed faster in her chest. "As I told our queen, if I stumbled upon Ever, I would escort her myself to the Ruby Heart Palace with a brand-new white hat atop her head. I have the perfect one ready with lace and—"

"Next time, bring each of us a dessert, along with the hat that *I'll* use on Ever." With that, Osanna turned on her heel, swaying her hips as she headed down the hallway.

Gritting her teeth, Maddie rushed into the room. The metallic scent of Noah's blood permeated the air, strong, so strong. She yearned for just one taste, for her tongue to gather his flavor. But she shook the allure away and found Noah slumped on the settee, deep crimson blooming at the spots where Osanna drank from him. "Oh dear." What did the curious mortal do? Ask too many questions?

Maddie grabbed Noah by the shoulders. "Mortal!" she hissed. "Wake up."

He groaned, his breath ragged. At least he wasn't dead ... yet. His tan skin grew paler by the second. She had to get him home because he was running out of time. Once she got him there, she could ... what? She wasn't a human doctor. She didn't have a way to give him a blood transfusion, and he sure wouldn't last long enough for her to get him out of Wonderland and to a hospital.

There was one way to save him, though...

The cool steel of a knife was at her throat, interrupting her thoughts. "Osanna said to clean his body up," Robin growled in a low voice. "Not turn him."

"Deepest apologies," Maddie said. "I shall carry him out the door then."

As soon as the blade was lifted, Maddie whirled around and ripped the knife from Robin's hand. "After I kill you, that is," Maddie sang. Then she shoved the blade into the female's heart. The housekeeper's body collapsed to the floor, her eyes closed. She knew she should leave things how they were, but the need for revenge pulsed through her. Maddie searched around for something to decapitate Robin with, but the walls were bare of anything useful and the knife, too small. So she would just get messy. She gripped Robin's head between her hands and twisted it hard to the right, tearing it from her body. Thick blood spilled from Robin's neck, and Maddie tossed the head on the floor beside the vampire's still body with a sickening *thump*.

Shrugging, she spun to face Noah. Enough time had been wasted. Maddie didn't think—she brought her wrist to her mouth and sank her fangs into her flesh. A slight sting came as she bit down, hot crimson blossoming to the surface. She shoved her wrist to Noah's mouth, and it took a moment for his lips to move. But she knew as soon as a drop touched his tongue, he would crave it. She knew because she remembered that first taste when Rav had held his wrist to her mouth, when ecstasy rolled over her in waves, how she wanted more and more of his blood, him inside her. The *bastard*...

And then Noah's lips brushed her flesh in an almost caress, drawing her away from thinking about Rav. Noah flicked the tip of his tongue across her skin, his lids closed, as he began to suck. His eyes fluttered while he groaned. It felt just as good to her as she knew it did for him, maybe even better than making a hat.

But a mortal who hadn't changed yet didn't have the control to stop on their own, so she forced herself to rip her arm away when she'd given him enough. "You don't want to bleed me dry because then how would we help you-know-who?" Maddie whispered.

Noah's eyes cracked open, dazed, but his skin wasn't as pale as before.

"Now, off we go."

He mumbled something when she pulled him to stand. His body sagged as he leaned his weight on her. Maddie helped him wrap an arm across her shoulder and she looped hers around his waist.

Osanna was a bitch and Imogen's friend, but Maddie truly didn't think she would've drunk him almost dry. And why should Maddie care anyway? Noah was just a mortal who was getting in the way of her trying to help her sister. Besides, Mouse had asked Ferris to save Alice, not Noah.

And then... Maddie had done the one thing Ever was fighting against: turning mortals into vampires without their consent. But if she hadn't, he would've died, which was a practice generally accepted by both her and Ever. Dying was a natural part of life, but being turned wasn't, so it should always be the human's choice. However, she didn't *want* him to die, even when he made her life harder than it already was. He might still die though, if his body wasn't made for the transition...

As Maddie and Noah left Osanna's and hobbled down street after street, the sky became a lighter shade of gray. A storm of bats beat their wings as they flew above, their squeaks echoing across the city. When Maddie had first brought her sister to Wonderland, Mouse had wanted to keep one for a pet. Maddie would've gotten her one too, but those bastards were impossible to catch.

Noah groaned, his pace slow, his weight becoming heavier.

"Keep going," she said, lifting and tugging him along. "You're lucky I returned when I did." If she'd left him at her cottage, he wouldn't be in this position. But all things happened for a reason, good or bad. If he'd had enough strength to hold onto her, she would've attempted to carry him on her back.

It didn't take much longer for her cottage to slip into view. A light fog covered the rose garden surrounding her home. They walked through the light mist with baby steps until she finally thrust open the door.

She stumbled into her home with Noah in tow. As his body started to slump, she thought about just dropping him there on the floor for now. She used more of her strength instead and picked him up, cradling him in her arms. She should've probably just done this earlier—it would've been easier. Vampire strength and speed were highly advanced, but a pity it only lasted short increments before a rest was necessary. She could've handled the distance to her cottage, however.

With a sharp turn, she sat him on the settee, his body

collapsing into the cushion. She wiped a hand across her cheek with a sigh. "How about we *not* play that game again, all right?"

Beads of perspiration dotted Noah's upper lip and forehead. Bloody hell, what a nuisance he was. She still needed to meet with Ferris, but now she must tend to this mortal to make sure his arse didn't die. It was all for Mouse because this was what her sister would've wanted her to do.

She stared at his features—the light stubble on his face, his square jaw, his plump lips. Then her gaze dipped to his tight black shirt, his broad chest, his muscular arms—she couldn't help noticing how attractive he was. So different than that picture Imogen and Rav had showed her of when he was younger. What had happened to him? Damn. Now she had questions for him about his magical transformation.

Maddie stepped over rolls of tulle and a pile of cut squares of different furs and leathers. She picked up a piece of cloth and poured cool water from the pitcher onto it. She then walked back to Noah and placed it on his forehead. There would be blood bags in her ice chest for when he woke, and she still had boxes of bottled powdered blood for emergencies if he needed them. Once he was well enough, she would need to find a live donor and teach him how to feed properly. Alice would eventually need that too.

She propped her fists on her hips and stared down at him. "There, all better." She was about to call it good and begin working on a new fascinator until he needed her, when his hand gripped her wrist.

Already?

Noah released another groan and drew her toward him. His groans were starting to sound like those zombie films mortals tended to watch.

With a strong tug, he pulled her into his lap, and she squeaked when her legs straddled his thighs. She arched a brow as his strong hands gripped her waist, his fingers digging into her hips. His eyes were still shut.

And then she felt his cock against her, hard and ready. Maddie's breath hitched when he rolled her hips forward. Her heart pounded, all her heat rushing straight to her core. And she wasn't even sure if she liked this man. But she knew how mortals were during their transition, some more lustful than others.

"Tut, tut, mortal." She grinned, lifting both his lids so he could see her. "I don't think this is what you want after such a dreadful day of suffering."

Maddie released his lids and he blinked. His bright green eyes focused on her and widened, his hands stilling on her hips, his fingers digging in harder.

"No, not mortal anymore, is it?" She shrugged and gave him a sympathetic look. "Immortal."

CHAPTER EIGHT

NOAH

Noah used every ounce of strength he had to lift Maddie from his lap. *Damn.* He'd been dry humping her like a fucking teenager ... and he'd *liked* it. *And* she'd *let* him. Maddie cocked her head and stared at him, then shrugged.

"Sorry," he muttered, leaning back into the settee.

"Don't be." She padded through the living room, carefully moving hat materials from her path. Noah found himself staring at her long legs as she bent over to chase a rolling bobbin. Her skirt was just long enough to prevent him from seeing more. The view of her legs was tantalizing enough but he still cursed the extra inch of tulle.

Get it together, man.

Maddie finally made her way to the cupboards and grabbed a teacup, quickly filling it with bagged blood. "You need to drink."

His veins were parched, his mouth a desert. There was no

pain in his neck like he expected and, when he lifted his hand to Osanna's bite, it was already healed. But the ache in his chest intensified with every slowed beat of his heart. *My heart is still beating.* Vampires were dead, weren't they? He was still very much alive, though he was quickly coming to regret that fact as pain rattled through his bones. His body spasmed, joints locking, jaw clenched, as he fell over onto the cushion. Maddie rushed to the settee and rolled him to his side. The fit lasted only a handful of seconds but left him sweating through his shirt.

"Here," Maddie said softly, holding the teacup right under his nose. "It will make the pain go away."

Drink blood? Never.

But his body disagreed. It begged for the thick red liquid. *Craved* it. His eyes had tracked Maddie's movements as she poured it, but the idea sent chills through him.

Soon though, he would need to. He knew it, even if he didn't want to admit it. There would be a point where he couldn't deny the mounting hunger. His gums tingled at the mere thought of a sip, and he squeezed his eyes shut to erase the image of Maddie's fangs dropping down.

"I have to check on Alice," he croaked. If she'd experienced even a sliver of this agony, he needed to see her.

Everything made sense now: why she'd been sprawled on the ground behind their flat, the reason Ferris had carried her, why she'd attacked him at the safe house.

"Drink and live. Don't and die. It's all the same to me," Maddie said with a flippant wave of her hand. "But you can't see your sister if you don't survive the transition."

He scowled. "You turned me. You *should* care if I survive it."

Maddie cast her gaze to the floor and chewed her bottom lip. "If you don't pull through, it will be the same as if I didn't turn you. This was the only way to give you a chance."

"Vampires are dead either way," he said, focusing on the

painful *thump thump* in his chest.

"No." Her laugh came out high-pitched as she sat beside him. "Mortals all think that, but it isn't true. We are alive and we will remain that way forever."

Alive? He'd think more on what that meant later, but it gave him hope. It would be much harder to cure death, yet, if what she said was true, this seemed like more of a disease. The cure existed—Maddie had confirmed it. All he needed to do was find the location of this werewolf swamp. *Because werewolves were a fucking thing now too...* "Unless someone drives a stake through your heart," he said.

"More nonsense. We die by sunlight, fire, or if someone cuts off our heads." Maddie shrugged. "Imogen removes hearts, which is also effective."

At the mention of the queen who'd turned his sister, Noah pushed up into a sitting position. "We have to go—"

"Hush." Maddie slipped from the edge of the settee where she'd perched and spun to face him. "You need to drink and finish the transition before we do anything. I'd prefer you do it quickly as I have my own sister to save."

Noah swallowed hard. He'd forgotten Maddie's sister was imprisoned, and that she was the reason Ferris saved Alice. "Fine," he said through clenched teeth. "Hand me the cup."

Maddie scooped it off the end table and placed the cup into his hands. "I promise you'll like it," she said as if that made drinking blood any better.

She's completely mad. Noah raised his brows and gave her a final look before bringing the cold liquid to his lips. The metallic scent filled his nose and a groan slipped from him, unbidden. *Bottoms up*, he told himself and took his first sip.

A bright memory exploded behind his eyes. One of a sunny day at the beach with his parents and Alice—years before impossible rules controlled every moment. He was three, Alice two. His father spun Noah and threw him up into the air, only to catch him a moment later. That was what drinking blood felt like. A rush of soaring, the fear of falling, and the relief of being caught all at once.

And Maddie was right—he *did* like it.

Noah tilted his head back, downing the cup's entire contents in two gulps. Then he licked the inside of the porcelain clean, followed by his lips. Whatever reservations he'd had about his new diet were officially gone and he couldn't bring himself to feel ashamed. He glanced into the cup to find it spotless, and he frowned at Maddie. "More."

"No." She plucked the cup away. "You'll become ill if you drink too much at once. Rest and let this settle, then you may have more."

"But—" A mild cramp twisted his stomach and he clutched at his abdomen. Perhaps she was right.

Maddie tutted. "Told you so. Now, lay back and sleep."

Noah had no choice but to listen as a stronger cramp took hold. Another round of cold sweats broke out along his forehead. Maddie tucked a blanket around him as he drifted away from the pain. While he slipped toward peaceful sleep, he clung to the memory of that day at the beach—the laughter and the warmth of the sun—and he smiled.

Hours blended together as Noah slept. At one point, Maddie had dragged him into her bedroom in case Imogen and Rav made another visit, but he slept better on the bed anyway, so it was worth the struggle to get there. He had woken for another cup of blood before his eyes slipped closed again. Each time was easier. The cramps stopped, the pain in his chest subsided, and the dryness in his mouth quenched.

He owed Maddie for taking care of him so diligently—

though, he supposed, she owed him. After all, she *had* turned him. It was only fair that she wiped the sweat from his forehead and set cool cloths on the back of his neck. Regardless, he was grateful for her attention. For a vampire, she wasn't half-bad.

When Noah roused again, his body hummed with energy. He kept his eyes closed, scanning himself, concentrating on each part to ensure nothing was wrong. Arms, shoulders, neck, hips, legs, ankles. Everything seemed to be in working order, and he felt ... almost normal. Except he could smell *everything*. Scents of wood furniture, to soft linen blankets, to old metal spicing the air in Maddie's room. *Blood*, he instinctually knew, noting the difference between that metallic aroma and the metal tools Maddie kept for hat making. It carried a tangy undercurrent that made his fangs threaten to drop.

"I know you're awake," Maddie sang from another room.

Noah opened his eyes and sat up slowly, waiting for his body to revolt. When it didn't, he released a breath and slipped from Maddie's bed, walking toward the living room. There, he found Maddie pleating pieces of felt. She sat cross-legged on a large, padded chair, the skirt once again teasing him with what was beneath. He pursed his lips. Why were his thoughts so focused on seeing Maddie hike up her skirt? There was no denying she was attractive, and anyone would be drawn to the perfect swells of her breasts, but there wasn't time for fantasizing. Both he and Alice were fucked if he didn't learn how to reverse their conditions.

"I'm surprised you let me sleep in your bed," he said with a small smile.

Maddie shrugged. "You looked uncomfortable."

Undoubtedly, she was correct seeing as he was at least a head taller than the settee. He plopped down on it and watched her work on her hat. "How long was I sleeping?"

"This time, about two hours." She stuck the dull end of a

needle between her lips and brought the felt closer to her face. After a moment of inspection, she lowered it and plucked the needle from her mouth. "If you're asking how long since you started the transition, it's been five days."

"Five *days?*" he blurted. That was impossible. It couldn't have been more than one day and one night at most. Every time he looked outside Maddie's window, it had been dark. But *how* dark? The gray mornings in Wonderland were comparable to London's evenings. He was certain he'd been fired from his job, but who gave a fuck about making coffee at this point? It was all a blur now, but he knew one thing for certain: they needed to get back to the safe house. "We have to go."

"If your sister died, Ferris would've returned by now," she mumbled, narrowing her gaze at her work.

"How do you know?" he demanded. "Maybe he ran off alone."

She smirked. "I have all the other keys."

"Fuck the keys," Noah growled. The last time he'd seen Alice, he'd left thinking she was a monster, but now he understood. What a shit brother he'd been. He had to go back to help her, to *cure* her. And himself. "I need to see my sister."

"Noah." Maddie sighed and set the pleating down on her lap to look him in the eye. "Ferris would never abandon me, and he would never give up on saving Mouse. We're days late in returning, so he would've come searching by now. Since he hasn't, it's because he's stuck watching Alice."

"Or because Imogen found them." The thought stole his breath.

Maddie sucked her bottom lip between her teeth and Noah's cock stiffened slightly. What would it be like if she sucked *him* into her mouth instead? Ran her tongue slowly up the length of him from tip to base? He raked a hand through his hair and looked away.

"Unlikely," she said after a moment.

"Not impossible though," he insisted.

Noah tensed when a soft knock sounded at the door, but Maddie simply stood and placed her supplies in a basket. "That will be your meal."

Meal? Had she ordered more blood bags to be delivered? How was it she even got the blood bags? Stole them or bottled them herself? Never mind, he didn't want to know.

Maddie opened the door and motioned in a man in his mid-thirties. He was dressed in a nice pair of trousers and a neatly pressed dress shirt as if he'd just come from a day at the office. Following him was a rich, warm scent that immediately made Noah's fangs drop.

"Hello," he greeted. "My boss sent me."

"Yes, I've been expecting you." Maddie quietly shut the door behind him and turned to look at Noah. "While you were asleep, I left for a moment to secure a mortal for you."

"You left to *secure a mortal?*" Noah repeated in disbelief. Humans weren't *things* to be acquired.

"There's a company in Scarlet that contracts us," the man said with a big smile. "We get paid handsomely and enjoy the work."

"This is his first feeding," Maddie whispered to the stranger.

"I figured as much." The man's smile was kind as he rolled up his sleeve and approached the settee. "My name's Elijah."

"Noah," he replied through clenched teeth. He did *not* want to bite someone. Let alone some stranger they pulled off the street like some sort of prostitute. People couldn't just go around drinking random blood. *Or any blood*, he reminded himself. But he was a vampire now—that was exactly what he needed to do to survive.

"Nice to meet you." He held his arm out to Noah. A few light-colored scars dotted his skin from prior bites. "Don't worry. As a vampire, you can't catch anything from blood—not that I have anything to catch."

"Are you a mind reader or something?" Noah grumbled.

Elijah laughed. "No, I just recognize that look. I've been doing this for a while."

Maddie hovered beside them, glancing from Noah to Elijah and back as if she was worried that Noah would refuse. He damn well *wanted* to refuse, but the sound of the steady heartbeat mixed with the warm, heady scent wafting off Elijah had his mouth watering.

He sighed in defeat and took Elijah's proffered arm. "Let's get this over with."

"You'll like this even better than the bags." Maddie smiled encouragingly as Noah swiped the tip of his tongue across a fang. "And I'm right here to stop you."

Noah closed his eyes for a moment, mentally preparing himself, and lifted the wrist to his mouth. Saliva flooded his tongue as an intoxicating scent reached his nose. *Ah, fuck it.* Instinct took over and he sank his fangs into Elijah's soft flesh.

Hot blood exploded into his mouth and he moaned as the different flavors mingled together on his readied tongue. Iron and … and he couldn't identify everything he tasted. Whatever it was, it was euphoric. A crackling fire on a cold day, bringing him back from the edge of death. This was so much different than the bagged blood. Those bags quenched his thirst, but this was like drinking life itself.

Noah pulled in a deep mouthful and swallowed, again and again. Energy sparked through his body, blazing through his veins. And still he drank. Until it felt as if he would explode with power. And then he drank some more.

"Noah," Maddie called through his haze.

He ripped his mouth away from Elijah's arm and gasped for breath. His body practically hummed, and his cock was hard as steel. *Shit.* He'd just gotten a hard-on from drinking blood? Was that supposed to happen?

Elijah said something, but Noah was too preoccupied with the new sensations flowing through his body to comprehend.

Maddie leaned down to look Noah in the eyes. "He's fine," she chirped to the human. "I'll see you out."

Noah's gaze landed on Maddie's arse as she led Elijah to the front door and placed a coin in his palm, exchanging a few quiet words. How he wanted to see that arse bent over for him, him unbuttoning his trousers, freeing his cock, then sliding into her with one swift thrust and… *Stop.* He rubbed a hand over his face and his fangs retracted on their own.

"Feeling better?" Maddie asked, returning to him.

Noah let out a long breath and peered down at himself. Other than the raging boner straining against his trousers, there was blood dried into his clothes from where he'd bled out on Osanna's settee. He sniffed himself and blanched. Sweat and blood—not a good combination. If everyone in Wonderland could smell as well as he could, it would definitely draw attention. "Do you have anything else I can wear?" he asked.

"I stashed some clothing for Ferris here, but they might be large on you." Maddie quickly disappeared into her bedroom and Noah winced at how loud the squeak of the dresser drawer was.

"Are sounds always this … grating to the ears?" he called.

Maddie laughed as the sound of her rummaging through fabric filled the air. "It's only because there's nothing but us here to make noise so your ears pick up on more. Outside, for example, there's the sound of animals and bugs and the wind to contend with."

"I know you don't want to waste time, but you should probably clean yourself as well. Everyone will know you're newly-turned if you go around like that, and fresh vampires tend to turn curious heads."

He wanted to argue, but she was right. There wasn't time. Nor was it wise to draw attention to themselves when that could lead Imogen and Rav straight to Alice. "Fine."

Noah hurried toward the door across from Maddie's bedroom. Swinging the door shut with what was meant to be a gentle push, it slammed with a loud *bang*. He glanced at his hand. With the amount of effort that took, he was sure he could've turned the wood to splinters with a single punch. Part of him wanted to test the theory, but he might destroy Maddie's home in the process.

"Sorry," he called.

"You'll get used to it," Maddie replied from the other room.

Noah wasted no time cranking the water on and sealing the plug in the clawfoot tub. Every second he spent wearing the crusty, ruined clothing, nausea churned his stomach more. Once everything was removed, he shoved the fabric into a bin and hoped it was meant for either the rubbish or dirty linen.

The bathtub filled quickly, and he stepped in, purposely ignoring how badly his cock ached with need. As he sank down, a groan escaped him. The warm water felt fucking amazing against his skin, his muscles, and he immediately began scrubbing. Maddie thankfully had a bath sponge and soap in plain sight, even if it did smell like cherries. He scrubbed every inch of his body, thinking about how she would have used this same sponge on her milky skin, her breasts, in between her legs... *Stop, damn it.*

When his body and hair were both clean, he settled back into the curve of the bathtub. *Only for a moment,* he told himself. He still didn't have anything to put on anyway. He thought about borrowing Ferris's clothes. The vampire was larger than him, but not so much bigger that his clothes would fall off.

A sudden suspicion crept into his mind and before he could stop himself, he called out, "Why do you keep clothes for Ferris here?"

"In case he ever got released from serving at Imogen's palace," Maddie replied immediately. "Which he now is. Or more like a fugitive."

He scowled. "So you and him aren't..." *Dating? Fucking?*

The door swung open, and Maddie bustled in with an armful of clothes. "Aren't what? Together?" She laughed as if the idea were ridiculous. "Definitely not. I've just been friends with him a long time and he risked his life to help Mouse."

Noah quickly covered his cock with both hands. "Do you mind?"

"Not at all," Maddie assured him and let herself study him from head to toe.

Noah's skin prickled at the attention, his member hardening behind his hands. A blush filled his cheeks as his gaze locked on her shapely lips. "See something you like?" he said, attempting to embarrass her into looking away, but his voice came out gruff, full of want.

She grinned. "I was only thinking you're pretty." Her eyes drifted toward his body again. "If I may..."

Noah scowled. "What?"

"It's nothing to be embarrassed about." She stared directly at his hands and Noah drew in a sharp breath. "You'll feel the lust for a few days after the change is complete, especially after feeding from the source."

"Great," he said in a higher-than-normal voice. "We can stop talking about my hard-on any time now."

"If you want my help, it will make things easier." Maddie shrugged. "Towels are in the cabinet."

Lust for days? He didn't want to go see his sister with his fucking dick hard as a rock. "Wait," he called as Maddie turned. "What do you mean by *help*?"

She walked back toward him. "If you feel comfortable, lean back and let me take care of it."

Noah hesitated. Was he really going to let her do this? Whatever *this* was? The way his veins throbbed against his cock, he knew his hand wouldn't totally resolve the issue so he consented.

Maddie peeled off her arm warmers and slowly knelt on the tile beside the bathtub. She leaned over the edge, her lips so close to his. A wave of desire pulsed through him like a second heartbeat. He wanted to rip off her ridiculous outfit, drag her into the bathtub with him, and have her lower herself onto his cock. Fuck her and fuck her hard.

Maddie wrapped her nimble fingers around his hard length, and he gasped as her hand tightened. She didn't say a word as she stroked. He leaned his head back and groaned as her pace picked up. One of his hands slid into her hair while his other gripped the edge of the bathtub. She tilted her head and lowered her lips to his neck. The scrape of her fangs against his skin sent a jolt through him. He wanted her teeth to sink into his body as he slipped his hard length into her.

Noah closed his eyes and groaned at her touch, her movements. He was so close, her hand going faster, faster, *faster*. Then one of her fangs lightly pricked his skin and he came in a hard rush, muscles tensing, body spasming, as he shouted, "Fuck!"

"All better?" Maddie lifted her head from his throat, gently releasing his length.

His chest heaved as he peeled open his eyes and he could've sworn he saw lust reflected in her gaze. But then she rose, water sliding down her arm. "Yes," he rasped.

"After you get dressed, we'll go." Then she walked out of the room, leaving him unsure what the hell had just happened.

CHAPTER NINE

MADDIE

Maddie straightened her hat as she left the bathroom with Noah remaining in the tub. Still naked... Still wet... She hadn't meant to kiss his throat, taste him with her tongue. Had only meant to rid him of his lust for a little while. But now, as she closed the bathroom door behind her, she'd created a little problem for herself. Her core thrummed with the same tightening Noah had just felt. She *needed* to purge her own lust and working on a hat would not help with this.

It wouldn't take long—she could finish the task before he even stepped foot into the hallway.

Maddie slipped inside her room and hiked up her skirt as she pressed her back to the wall. She then dipped her hand inside her panties, finding a pool of wetness between her thighs. Noah had done this to her without even a single brush of his fingers. All it had taken was the touch of his cock in her hand, the press of her lips and tongue to his neck. He'd smelled of cedar, tasted like honey. She wondered what he would've tasted like if he'd spilled himself into her mouth instead of in the water.

"Bloody hell," she rasped.

The water's swishing echoed, and she knew Noah was stepping from the bathtub, beads of water sliding down his naked form—she stroked her center. A cabinet creaked as Noah must've grabbed a towel, and she imagined him running it over his abs, his tight arse—she circled her clit. The rustling of him getting dressed reverberated—she came at that movement, imagining every hard muscle of him pressed against her softness. Her body pulsed, spasms rocking through her as she thought about what it would be like to have him inside her, thrusting, growling. Her chest heaved while taking a cleaning rag from her bedside table. She wiped her hand with the rose-scented cloth and straightened the skirt of her dress before stepping back into the hallway, just as he opened the door.

Maddie grinned, hiding the aftereffects of her orgasm that still purred within her. "Ready?"

"Are you going to tell me the exact location of the cure now?" Noah said, raking a hand through his damp hair, the muscles of his arm flexing. Ferris's clothing fit well enough, although she preferred his tighter dark T-shirt. He now wore a black, long-sleeved collared shirt with pleats across the front and arms. A single line of obsidian buttons ran up the length of his trousers from ankle to thigh. Maddie's eyes lingered on the slight bulge of his trousers before flicking them up to meet his gaze. His hair hadn't changed in color since the transition, but his eyes were an even brighter shade of green.

"Past Ivory in the center of werewolf territory, as I said. Now, chop-chop. Let's go. Grab the smaller ice chest and one of the backpacks on our way out." Maddie waved a hand in the air and spun on her heels, then lifted her bag of necessities for them.

Noah slammed the front door a bit too hard behind them and winced. The immortal would get used to his new strength eventually.

As they headed into the night, the sky was already shifting, and it would turn into morning soon. They didn't have any more time to waste, and she needed to get to Ferris. Five days had passed. Five days too long. And Ferris would be getting antsy, especially since she had planned to visit him after delivering the hat to Osanna. But then this messy immortal situation with Noah had come about.

Maddie supposed she could've left Noah and went to the safe house, but she hadn't wanted Noah to die, not after she'd turned him without his consent. She had also needed to stay with him at the cottage in case Imogen and Rav ventured back to have a chat—she'd risked enough by leaving Noah for a short while to request a donor be sent to her home for him to feed. Maddie didn't know how good of a liar Noah could be.

Since days had passed, perhaps the little deviants had grown tired with their search for Ferris and Alice and found new toys to play with. But Maddie knew better—Rav and Imogen would never stop the hunt until their bodies were discovered.

As they stepped onto the trail leading to the outskirts of the city, Noah strode beside her with his hands buried deep in the pockets of his trousers. He hadn't said a single word since they'd left, not even one of his silly questions. "Cat got your tongue?" Maddie asked.

His green gaze met hers then, a hesitant expression on his face. "Thank you," he said softly.

Maddie quirked a brow and drawled, "For…?"

"The bathroom." He scratched the back of his neck, pink staining his cheeks.

"Ah, yes." She grinned, thinking once again about her hand around his velvety length. "That. You should make it through tonight just fine. It's the least I could do after, you know, turning you."

Noah scowled, his lips forming a tight line.

Maddie didn't know what she'd said to damper his expression. "Speak, immortal."

"So, you did it because you felt guilty?"

No. If it had been Ferris in Noah's position, she would've told him to use his own hand and be on with it. "Yes," she lied. He didn't need to discover that she'd been wanting to know what his cock felt like since he'd taken her into his lap. It was a help-help situation. Help him while helping her quench her curiosity. Although, her curiosity now led to wanting to know more. "Anyway, you had asked about a cure for Alice, so I know you don't want this life. But, I did it to save you. I wanted to allow you the opportunity to still live, albeit a different life. However, if you want me to, I can rip your heart out right here."

Noah stopped in his tracks, a look of horror crossing his face as he stared at her.

"I mean," she continued slowly. "I don't want you to die. Just, I'm sorry. I shouldn't have taken you with me to Osanna's. I thought it was safer if you were with me here in Wonderland, but apparently, you were fated to die no matter where we'd left you. But hey"—she clasped both of his upper arms and lightly rattled him—"you're not dead now!"

"Wow." He chuckled, shaking his head as he peered up at the sky before returning his focus to her. "All right... I'm not sure how to respond to *that*. You aren't so bad, though. Maybe a bit of bad luck, but you're sweet."

What? No one had ever called her *sweet* before. Even when she was a human. *Odd. Mad.* His words sent a rush of tingles straight to her chest. It was quite possible bats were flying in her stomach at the same time. With a tilt of the head, she patted his cheek. "Let's go check on you-know-who."

He lifted a brow, then his expression turned serious as they walked. "I hope she's all right."

"As I said, *he*"—she wouldn't risk saying Ferris's name out in the open—"would've let me know if she wasn't." Unless something happened to him... Unless he'd been caught. Even without a key, if Rav and Imogen knew the location, they could always find a way in.

Noah gave a brief nod.

"Now, act casual with me." She wrapped her arm around Noah's waist as they trekked through the city toward the outskirts, the red lanterns becoming dimmer as the sky lightened. They passed a few bloodied corpses sprawled on the ground, as well as several alive immortals and humans. One couple seemed to be having a role-playing sort of day. The mortal wore fake fangs and nibbled at the vampire's neck. Some were bustling about the city, carrying baskets of goods and ice chests, while others yawned, most likely on their way home for their daily rest.

Noah draped his arm around Maddie's shoulders and drew her closer as they entered the outskirts, the lanterns lessening. "So," Noah drawled. "Since you and Ferris aren't dating, when was your last boyfriend?"

Boyfriend? Maddie had never had a boyfriend. Only lovers. "Ah, there's my questioner." She pressed her head to his arm so they appeared like any other couple to lookers. "Never. I've only fucked. There was the one time with Rav... I thought... Before I was turned. But I was foolish then."

"So you—"

"We're here," Maddie interrupted, preferring not to tell him how she'd taken lover after lover to take away the sting of Rav's betrayal. She hadn't even known the bastard for more than a day, yet his effect on her had lasted more than she would've wished. But when someone was one's first, no matter how long they knew them, they always lingered. No matter that her instant attraction to him had turned to instant hate.

Straightening her spine, she rid the memory of that tainted

arse from her mind. Maddie removed her arm from Noah's waist and raised her fist to knock the secret code. Noah took his arm from her shoulders as the click sounded from the lock and the door flung open.

"I'm going to kill you," Ferris said between gritted teeth. He stood there, peering down at her with a hard stare. "Where have you been? I thought you were fucking *dead*."

"Oh, you know, just been roaming Wonderland, creating hats, and making Noah immortal." Maddie shrugged then grabbed Noah's hand and pushed their way inside past Ferris.

Ferris shut the door before whirling around to face them. "What the hell, Maddie?" His eyes widened as he scanned Noah. "I *know* he didn't ask you to make him immortal. He was freaking out days ago."

"I wasn't freaking out." Noah rolled his eyes while resting the ice chest and backpack on the floor.

"Whatever, man." Ferris focused on Maddie. "Well?"

"There could've been a lovelier circumstance," she started. "But alas, it wasn't intentional. I promise. Imogen and Rav came asking questions at the cottage, parading a photograph of Alice and offering a reward for her. Then I had to deliver Osanna her hat and that bitch nearly killed him."

"Wait, Rav and Imogen came to your house?" Ferris's throat bobbed, and for the first time since he'd escaped the palace, he truly looked worried. "Do they know anything? If they know we're connected, they'll hurt Mouse. *Kill* her."

Maddie blocked out the images of her sister bloodied and broken, her head lolled to the side, eyes blank. "I don't think they suspect anything. They only came to see me since I was at the palace the day before. However, they didn't leave without threats."

"Fuck!" Ferris hit his fist against his leg.

"Where's Alice?" Noah asked, searching around the room, his gaze settling on the velvet settee.

Ferris rubbed the back of his neck. "That's what I needed

to talk to you two about. I've been giving her blood, but she's rejecting it."

"What does that mean?" Noah stiffened. "If I'm walking about and feeling stronger than I ever have, then she should've been fine days ago."

"It doesn't work that way," Maddie said softly. "Some don't make it. Some die the night of transition. Others, days or weeks later."

Noah ran a hand down the side of his face. "I need to see her."

Ferris nodded and opened the door to a guest room for Maddie and Noah to go inside. Boxes of powdered blood took up most of the space in a corner, a stack of books in another, and a small mattress holding a frail Alice was against the opposite wall. She lay in bed curled on her side, her skin pale and sweat slicking her brow. The blankets rested in a rumpled heap on the floor beside her.

"Alice." Concern filled Noah's voice as he rushed to his sister's side and knelt beside her.

"Noah," Alice whispered, peeling open her eyes. "I'm so sorry. I didn't mean to attack you."

"You didn't." He smiled warmly. "You only tried to."

"What's wrong with your eyes?" Her gaze widened and she clenched his shirt. "You're not human anymore? What *happened*?"

He blew out a breath. "It's a long story."

This was a moment that Maddie needed to bow out from. A moment between family. "I'll leave you two alone for now." She shut the door behind her before Noah could respond.

Alice was going to die. Maddie had seen this time and time again. There had been numerous instances where she'd changed mortals over the years—some made it, some didn't. There wouldn't be any saving Alice. Not without a cure, and the cure was nearly impossible to get. Yet… A dark thought slipped into her mind. One that wouldn't make her feel guilty.

It could possibly get her sister released. And Rav had mentioned a reward for Alice. Mouse had wanted Alice saved, but if the female was dying, then what would it matter?

"What are you planning?" Ferris asked, narrowing his eyes.

"Oh, nothing." She rocked back and forth on her heels.

"Bullshit."

"It's going to help Mouse, so don't you dare try to stop me." She knelt to draw out a cold blood bag from the ice chest then held it up to him and smiled. "Here, I brought you this. I know the powder is hard to swallow."

Ferris's gaze softened and he reluctantly took the blood bag. "Thanks, Maddie."

"No, thank *you*." Her shoulders hunched forward as she stood. "You're in this position because of me." Because of the foolish mistake she'd made with Rav all those years ago. Mouse, Ferris, Noah—all except Alice led back to that mistake. So Maddie wouldn't let herself feel guilty about what she was going to do.

Ferris sighed and wrapped his arms around her, pulling her to his side. "Mouse saved me when I overdosed. The both of you are what kept me going after that. I would do anything for her—you know that." That included him giving up his humanity for only a small chance of saving Mouse. Which hadn't worked. But if Maddie gave Alice to Rav and Imogen, she could get Mouse back. It would not only help her sister, but would make everything Ferris went through worth it. She didn't know everything he'd done in the palace, what all was done to him, but she did know he had to fuck Imogen before his change and clean palace rooms with his tongue. His sacrifices wouldn't be for nothing. Maddie loved him like a brother, almost as much as she loved her sister. Once Mouse was out, she would need to figure out a way to help him find somewhere safer to stay. He couldn't remain hiding in this safe house forever. But, for now, one step at a time.

The night had already lifted and after everyone was asleep, Maddie would sneak Alice out and take her back to the Ruby Heart Palace.

CHAPTER TEN

NOAH

*W*ater dripped against stone, the only sound in the empty room. Noah walked from corner to corner, seeing perfectly through the darkness, yet unable to find a way in or out. No windows, no doors, no air ducts.

Drip, drip, drip.

He wasn't afraid, but there was a deep sense of foreboding that grew as he continued walking around the room. Hunger prickled through him the longer the captivity lasted. He needed blood. Warm, thick, human blood. If someone were in front of him, he would sink his teeth into their neck and drink and drink and drink...

Dust rained down from the ceiling as a large crack appeared overhead. The drip of water stopped, and maniacal laughter replaced it. A boom. More dust. The crack widened.

"Baby immortal," came a vaguely familiar voice. "Bow to your queen."

Noah inhaled sharply, realizing who was speaking. Imogen. The female who'd turned his sister. "Never!" *he shouted at the ceiling.*

The ceiling crumbled, raining down on him in large chunks.

Noah sat up with a gasp, drenched in sweat, just before the stone crushed him. *A nightmare. It was just a nightmare.* He dragged in a long breath then let it out slowly through his mouth, accidentally pricking himself on his own fangs. Lifting a finger to his mouth, he prodded at them. He'd desired blood in the nightmare, but he was fine now, no thirst coursing through him. How did he get the fangs to go back in without feeding? They'd simply retracted when he drank his fill at Maddie's house.

He let his arms fall back to his sides on the lumpy single mattress and sighed. With Maddie going in and out to check on Alice, he wouldn't have gotten any rest if he stayed with his sister. Not that he was getting a decent sleep anyway, but it would still be difficult now that he wanted blood. Fresh blood, like he'd tasted at Maddie's cottage. The richness of it … the boosted strength. He felt as if he could rule the world now, more so when he fed, and he wanted— No.

His fangs finally retracted into his gums. What he wanted was to go home with his sister. Once he got the cure—with or without help—they would both take it, then never have to worry about blood or fangs or fucking vampire queens again. Despite knowing that his sense of wrongness stemmed from the dream, the thought of his sister made him desperate to see her.

He slipped out of bed and walked softly through the house, not wanting to wake anyone. Maddie had said she would nap on the sofa if she got too tired, so he didn't dare look in that direction in case she sensed his gaze upon her. If she woke, he would end up distracted.

"Alice?" he whispered as he padded into her room. With

the others asleep, they could have an honest conversation without anyone else chiming in. "Are you awake?"

Silence.

And ... *fucking hell.* The sheets were flung back, the pillow dented from his sister's head. Yet there was *no Alice.*

Noah scanned the small room, but she was nowhere to be seen. "Alice?" he called louder as he left the room, not giving a shit if Maddie or Ferris woke up. She was sick. Where could she possibly have gone?

Racing from Alice's room to the living room, it quickly became clear she was no longer there. Noah's heart pounded as he struggled to remain calm. Alice couldn't have gotten far. Not in the state she was in. *Maddie.* She would know where to look. If she wasn't in Alice's room, she would be on the sofa ... but she wasn't there. He stared at the empty black cushions as the truth set in.

Maddie and Alice were both *gone.*

That couldn't have been a fucking coincidence. He didn't overlook them. There'd been nowhere to hide in Alice's small space. The gut punch stole the air from his lungs. His mind immediately conjured the worst-case scenario of Imogen and Rav kidnapping them, but wouldn't he have heard the commotion? Unless they were extremely stealthy as he was certain vampire royalty would be.

"Ferris?" Noah called and hurried to the third bedroom. "Ferris!"

"What?" he grumbled through the door.

Relief whooshed from him, and he barged inside. Ferris was on his stomach on top of his covers, completely naked, with an arm slung over the edge of the mattress. Noah quickly averted his eyes from the vampire's arse. "They're gone."

"What?" Ferris mumbled, clearly still half asleep.

"Alice and Maddie, they're gone." Kidnapped, most likely, but he refused to accept that. Perhaps Alice had just needed some air... He winced at the obvious lie.

Ferris sat up and yawned. "What are you going on about?"

"Alice—you remember my sister, don't you?" Noah spoke slowly, despite the adrenaline pumping through him. Was the vampire a fucking idiot? "And the quirky, purple-hair hat maker?"

"Maddie's watching Alice tonight," he said, waving a hand through the air.

"Watching her *where*?"

Ferris rubbed his eyes. "What's all this about?"

Noah lifted a dusty vase from a table just inside the door and threw it at Ferris. "They're *gone*, ya daft pillock!"

Ferris caught the vase with one hand and gave him a withering look. "The transformation still affecting your brain? Damn. Let me get them for you."

He stood, grabbed a pair of black tracksuit bottoms and, after putting them on, brushed past Noah. Ferris wandered through the entire safe house as if Noah was the fucking moron here. Then his steps became a little less hurried as he doubled back to check the bedrooms a second time. Noah nearly screamed when Ferris sprinted into Alice's bedroom for a third look.

"Are you satisfied yet?" Noah asked.

Ferris came back into the living room, chest heaving, pupils blown wide. "They're missing," he concluded.

"No shit," Noah shouted. "Where could they be?"

Ferris paced the living room, hands clutching the sides of his head. "I don't know. Maddie offered to watch her tonight. I could tell she was upset about Mouse. It felt like she was up to something but—*oh fuck*."

"What?" Noah demanded. "*What?*"

"It's just…" He swallowed hard. "No. Maddie wouldn't…"

Noah's hands balled into fists. He was no expert, but he'd guess there wasn't much Maddie was incapable of doing. Between hiding Alice, dragging him to Wonderland, turning him into a vampire, and jerking him off in the bathtub, *kidnapping Alice* didn't seem too outlandish. "She wouldn't what?"

"Ah, hell," Ferris snapped, and left Noah standing alone in the sitting room.

"Ferris?" he called, his voice rising along with his anger. "What's going on?"

The vampire stormed back into the room fully dressed in a black knit jumper and boots to match his trousers. "Get your trainers on. We have to stop them before they reach the palace."

"The palace?" Noah quickly collected his gym trainers from his room. They were hiding from Imogen and Rav so why the hell would she be going there?

Ferris stared at him. "Maddie had said Imogen offered her a reward to bring Alice back."

And she thinks the reward will be Mouse's release, Noah pieced together as he finished putting his trainers on.

Ferris grabbed the key off the hook on the wall and peered outside before opening the door wide. "Let's go."

Noah followed Ferris outside, trying to even his breaths. Ferris strolled through the street at a leisurely pace, far *too* leisurely for Noah's liking. Then, without warning, he vanished down a side alley. Noah's new vampire reflexes managed to follow the movement and he rushed after him.

The city smelled the same as it had when he'd followed Maddie to Osanna's. Like blood and decay. Only now, it didn't bother him so much. The metallic scent was pleasant while the decay was more of a nuisance than stomach-churning. They avoided the red lanterns as they navigated isolated side streets, but he could see perfectly fine without the lights. The claw marks and blood spattered on the sides of buildings were as clear as day.

A discarded pair of lace gloves beside a large blood stain doubled his concern for Alice's fate. They weren't *her* gloves, but she would've worn them. And the blood smelled stale which, he assumed, meant it was too old to belong to his sister. But that didn't mean she wasn't bleeding somewhere in the palace.

It was obvious what had happened now—Maddie had taken Alice from the safe house with the intent of delivering her to Imogen and Rav. How long ago had they left? Alice could be withering away in the royal dungeons already. Or worse... He felt the blood drain from his face.

"Why would she do this?" Noah whispered. "I mean, I know why, but..."

Ferris held up an arm to stop Noah in the shadows as two vampires appeared on the street ahead, laughing hard. "Alice is dying, yeah? I'm certain Maddie wouldn't have done this otherwise," he said once they passed, leaning forward to scan one side of the street and then the other.

Noah rubbed at his chest, his heart beating out of control. She was going to turn Alice over to those two arseholes? What did it matter if his sister was dying? Noah had been planning to get the cure before that happened and then they would've been fine. "Does she really think they'll trade her sister?"

"Obviously," Ferris muttered.

After nearly fifteen minutes of walking, Noah followed him around another corner, out of the alleyways, and across the main street into a different alley on the other side. In those brief seconds when they weren't between homes or shops with slate roofs and enormous windows, he spotted a castle, aglow in red lights, perched on a cliff. Tall spires rose from the red stone structure and black stone parapets speared the sky. Light shone in the windows and shadows moved along the footbridge.

How had he never noticed it when away from the safe house? Though, he supposed he'd been preoccupied with everything going on—been distracted by Maddie on the way back to the safe house ... after she'd touched him in the bathtub.

Such a beautiful fucking deceiver.

"They won't give Mouse up, will they?" he asked, already knowing the answer.

"Depends." Ferris glared at the palace for a moment. "But my guess is they'll throw Alice in the dungeons to die alone and keep Mouse exactly where she is now."

"And Maddie?" He hated himself for asking—for caring, given the circumstances—but he didn't want to imagine her suffering. Maddie had done a despicable thing, yet no one deserved torture.

Ferris clenched his jaw shut. "It's better not to think about it."

Noah scanned every side street they passed, hoping to catch a glimpse of purple hair, but the closer they got to the looming palace, the more panic squeezed his insides.

"You're being too conspicuous," Ferris warned. "Try to move your head less when you—*damn.* There she is."

Noah's head jerked up. Maddie was talking to Alice outside a small cave at the base of the cliff. He made a quick step forward and Ferris yanked him back. "What now?" he snapped. Alice was right there. Safe, for the moment, and he wanted to keep it that way.

Maddie patted Alice on the shoulder and strode away from her. Alice shifted back until she was barely visible behind a large boulder. Noah shoved at Ferris's arm so he could get his sister before someone else saw her hiding there.

"I'll go first, grab Alice, and take her back to the safe house," Ferris whispered. "Once we're gone, get Maddie's attention and bring her back with you."

"Like hell!" He wasn't about to trust Ferris with Alice's safety now that Maddie proved untrustworthy. For all he knew, Ferris would take the opportunity to trade Alice for his own pardon.

"Shut the fuck up," Ferris hissed as a group of vampires

meandered down the street. "Do what I say."

Noah fell silent, only because he knew other vampires finding them would thwart their rescue efforts. While the group took their time passing, Maddie started up a long, winding staircase carved into the stone.

"Now?" he asked when the strangers disappeared into a nearby red house. Though, once Alice was safely away, he couldn't guarantee he wouldn't shout at Maddie for her betrayal. A scene wouldn't matter much if Alice was safe, so what stopped him? He scowled at Maddie as she climbed higher and higher.

Ferris released him and moved so fast, he was a blur. One second, Alice was hidden with only a small piece of white fabric visible, the next, she was gone.

Noah took a deep breath and stormed forward. None of Imogen and Rav's lackeys knew him, so he didn't feel the need to sneak around like Ferris. He barged forward, hands in fists, and stopped at the bottom of the staircase.

"Maddie!"

"Bloody hell!" she yelled, whirling around. Then her gaze landed on Noah, and she froze. "Noah?"

"What the fuck?" he demanded.

She raced back down the steps, darting around him to peer at where Alice had been. Finding it empty, she turned and grasped Noah's shirt. "Where is she?"

"I'll tell you where she *wasn't*." He grabbed Maddie's wrists and pried her hands away from him. "Tucked safely in bed. Where she belonged."

"She's *dying*," Maddie whispered in a cracking voice. "Your sister wouldn't suffer long locked up, but Mouse will be tormented for eternity."

"You're out of your fucking mind. Are you listening to yourself? I never would've done this to you."

Maddie took three heaving breaths, eyes blazing with desperate fury, before her shoulders curled forward in defeat.

"I'm sorry, but you don't understand."

"You're sorry?" Noah scoffed. He *almost* felt sorry for her, but she'd just kidnapped someone he loved. "I don't think that's quite good enough."

A male vampire passed by in a long trench coat and studied them both with a curious expression. "I'll talk to you about it when we get back," Maddie urged.

Noah didn't know what there was to talk about. She had planned on serving Alice up on a silver platter to her king and queen. *And* she was likely doing so while fully aware it wouldn't work. Noah had met Imogen and Rav once and even he could tell they weren't the sort to negotiate. Especially since they already seemed to loathe Maddie.

"Now, we need to leave," Maddie whispered. "There are guards inside the palace."

"You weren't worried about the guards two minutes ago," he snapped.

"We can't do anything for either of our sisters if we're locked up," Maddie hissed. "Don't be a fool."

Noah pursed his lips. She was right—he couldn't get the cure for Alice if he was locked in a cage. "Fine," he relented. "But this doesn't mean we're square."

CHAPTER ELEVEN

MADDIE

Maddie was caught red-handed as though she'd held a blade to Alice's throat. She just as well could've been. She knew Noah would come after her when he'd discovered Alice missing, but she'd hoped she had enough time to switch out one sister for another. However, she wasn't foolish enough to think Imogen would simply hand over Mouse. No, that wouldn't have been the heart-stealing queen at all. But with a carrot dangling in front of her, Imogen may have given in. Which was why she hadn't brought Alice with her onto the palace grounds. Imogen didn't keep guards outside her palace as they did within the mortal world. The queen only kept her slaves inside.

Maddie had hoped Ferris would've sided with her on the matter, but even then, she had an inkling he wouldn't. Because Mouse had told him to save Alice.

Clusters of large red beetles trailed beside her while she

and Noah trekked back toward the safe house. As they passed through the city, a male vampire's head lay, torn clean off, beside a body, blood pooling out from both wounds. Most likely an altercation between two males over a female.

Noah pressed a fist to his mouth like he may lose the nutrients in his stomach, but he said nothing. In fact, he hadn't asked a single question, only kept those shapely lips of his in a tight line. Her fingers fidgeted with the skirt of her dress, wishing she had a needle and fabric in her hands right then.

"Look, Noah," Maddie said slowly. "Tell me what you would've done in my position. If it was *your* sister in Mouse's place, and my sister was going to die anyway."

His shoulders stiffened and his voice came out even. "I wouldn't have taken your sister."

"I don't believe you." Maddie narrowed her eyes. "Not if you knew what Mouse has been through. Not if you knew how they've been treating her in that palace. For two years, Noah! And that is only two years. This may go on forever. Do you realize *that*?"

He stopped. Turned to her. His piercing green eyes met hers then. "I get it. I do. But Alice is *my* sister, and I was only human a few days ago. Maybe you forgot what humanity is like."

Maddie sucked in a sharp breath. She didn't usually do things like this and didn't *normally* turn mortals without their consent. She knew exactly who she was. "I did save you, didn't I?"

"About that..." Noah bit his lower lip, studying her intensely. "You mentioned the cure and that it's just past Ivory in werewolf territory. I want it. For her and for me."

He was asking about that damn cure again? If Maddie could pull one out from her pocket right now, she would, but she couldn't. "There's no way you'll ever get it. Only a couple have, and they didn't go unscathed. One lost an arm, the other a leg. All the others never came back."

A look of fear crossed Noah's handsome face, and she didn't want to put it there. But he needed to understand that he would most likely die. This wasn't playing with a few bats here—these were true monsters.

"Would you risk it for Mouse?" He turned the tables on her, just as she had done to him a moment ago.

"Yes," Maddie said simply. For her, for Ferris, for Ever, if any of them wanted to go back to being human, she would risk her life for theirs.

"Then help me, Maddie," Noah pleaded, placing his arms on her shoulders. "And I'll help you."

Help her *how*? She thought again about how she'd already tried to infiltrate the palace with Ferris. He was much cleverer than anyone she'd met, and still, he hadn't succeeded.

"My, my, my, look what we have here." Maddie froze at the sound of Rav's voice. What had the bastard heard? He slinked out from the side of a building, wiping blood from his mouth with the back of his hand.

Maddie clenched her jaw. Why did she always have to run into him? It was as though he sought her out on purpose to toy with her.

"I just came from Osanna's and was on my way to give you my condolences, but lucky me, I found you. Although, it looks as though your mortal lived." He raked a hand through his hair, smoothing out his white and red locks as he sauntered toward them. Noah clenched his fists at his sides, and Maddie screamed inside her head for him to quit showing their cards to the bastard. Rav would take notice.

"Perhaps," Rav continued, his finger stroking his lower lip as his gaze fixed on Noah's. "I can help you with whatever you need instead of Maddie. A pity you are no longer mortal, I wouldn't have minded turning you myself. After fucking you of course." His stare slid to Maddie's and he smirked.

"Sorry, I'm taken," Noah said. "I'm Maddie's." Her eyes almost widened at the sentiment, but she kept them relaxed.

"Mm. For now." Rav remained smirking as he turned his attention back to Maddie. "If Ever isn't found soon, he may end up in a cage beside your sister. Cheers then."

Maddie's nostrils flared as Rav walked away with a pep in his step, disappearing through the city. Perhaps she would rip a head off today because she wanted to rip his off right now, then cover his face in hatpins. Before she could decide to chase after him and get herself killed, Maddie stormed off in the direction of the safe house. Noah easily caught up beside her with his enhanced vampire speed. He must've seen by her expression to not ask anything because he stayed silent.

After they left the city, screams echoing in the distance, the safe house slipped into view. The night was already starting to fall as she pounded the secret code for Ferris a little too loudly on the door. He should've already made it back … with Alice.

Ferris threw open the door, a scowl on his face as his mouth opened to say something. Most likely to reprimand her.

"Not now." Maddie waved her hand in the air and skirted past him. Alice sat on the settee, her expression one of sadness. When she'd taken Noah's sister, Alice was too loopy to know what was really going on. It had almost been too easy to lure her through Wonderland. Had it been that easy when Rav had brought Alice here? She was incredibly naïve. Just as Maddie had once been. A part of her hated what she had tried to do while the other still wished she'd succeeded.

Maddie avoided looking at Alice, trudged into the room where Noah had slept, and slammed the door behind her before plopping down on the mattress.

Why couldn't it have been Imogen she'd run into today? Why did it have to be that bastard?

The door didn't remain shut for long, though, its loud creak echoing. "Ferris, I…" Her words trailed off when Noah stepped inside the room and closed the door behind him.

His expression wasn't hard as it had been earlier—it was

softer, kinder. "What the hell just happened back there?"

"Rav," Maddie muttered.

"I don't understand. You mentioned him before, that you two... But there has to be more to it. Tell me." His throat bobbed as he studied her, and she felt she owed him this after taking his sister.

"Fine, I'll tell you my story and you may understand a bit more on why I don't want Mouse there a moment longer." Maddie then explained to Noah how Rav turned her over two centuries ago, pretended he was a gentleman taking her to become a hat maker for the queen who was really Imogen, how she thought she was in love with him after a day. And how, when she got to Wonderland, Imogen didn't choose to have her as a servant in the palace and believed her too pathetic to make any hats. Maddie was tossed out in the city, starving and weak, and she'd kept walking through a world she didn't understand. Then, she'd stumbled into Ivory and met a female whom she believed was a nobody like her. But that female ended up being Ever, the Queen of Ivory. Ever had chosen Maddie to make hats for her, and only then had Imogen taken notice of Maddie.

"That motherfucker." Noah's chest heaved, angrier than he'd been earlier.

"It's fine. Rav didn't take advantage of Alice in that way."

"It's still not *fine*. He did this to you, and he did this to my sister. I want to beat his fucking arse."

"It gets worse," Maddie said. "While we want to save our sisters, he wants to kill his. The White Queen—Ever—is Rav's sister. He already turned the Ivory guards against her, sending her into hiding, so for now, Ivory belongs to Rav. He isn't really the king of Scarlet either. Imogen may say he is but the true heir, if anything were to ever happen to her, is Chess, the male you saw at the portal before we came to Wonderland. Rav isn't his real father. Ever told me how Imogen and Rav murdered Imogen's husband, the last king, his father, the same night she turned Chess into a vampire. Then she brought her immortal son to Wonderland after leaving him in England until he was an adult. The king and Imogen had given up their lives and their son to become vampires."

"Bloody hell." Noah's eyes widened. "He wants to murder his own sister? How were Imogen and Rav not arrested or whatever you do here? Though after all I've seen so far, I shouldn't be surprised. But damn…"

"Yeah…"

A tense silence spread throughout the room and her gaze stayed trained on his. So many thoughts slipped into Maddie's mind. Her sister, what she'd done to Alice, when she'd had her hand around Noah's hard cock. For once, she had nothing to say. Nothing else to give in that moment.

"What if I offer you a trade," Noah finally said, breaking the silence.

Maddie arched a brow. "What kind of trade, immortal?"

Noah knelt in front of her, appearing as though he were her knight. "If you help me retrieve the cure for Alice, I'll help you save your sister."

"How would you help me save Mouse?" Maddie sighed, her stomach sinking.

"We'll retrieve Mouse from the palace ourselves."

Maddie tilted her head to the side and patted his shoulder. "Easier said than done. Imogen has ripped out the heart of everyone who has defied her."

"What about when you deliver her hat?" He perked up. "She'd mentioned two weeks, right? Since you've done this before, she wouldn't be expecting you to just barge in and take Mouse."

Maddie mulled it over. When she'd delivered the hats, Rav was always prowling around the mortal world. He would most likely be gone… Even then, it would be difficult. There was always the chance Chess would be there too. But what did she have to lose? If she failed, then Ferris could continue trying to save Mouse. Her sister had waited long enough.

"Perhaps we can try. I'll help you locate the cure first, but we may not make it back in time to save Alice." Maddie didn't know how much longer Alice would last. It would be a few weeks at the most.

"I want to risk it," Noah said.

"Does this mean you forgive me?" Her mouth curved into a wide grin.

Noah blew out a breath. Then a small smile crossed his face as he lifted her chin. "Would you forgive me if the roles were reversed?"

"Yes," she whispered, liking the feel of his fingers on her chin a bit too much.

"Liar," he whispered back. "Alice is safe for now, so yes, I forgive you." His hands cupped her cheeks. "But I still want to throttle you."

"You're doing mighty fine on that threat, immortal." She waggled a finger at him. Before she ruined the moment by asking if he wanted her to make him come again, she changed the subject. "Go check on Alice. I need to talk to Ferris anyway."

"All right. I'll see you soon." His hands left her cheeks and she missed the light touch, his warmth.

As soon as Noah slipped out from the room, Ferris brushed past him and entered, that scowl still on his face.

Maddie cocked her head and grinned. "Were you hovering at the door, *listening?*"

"Fuck yes, I was."

She laughed, louder than she'd intended.

"It's not funny." Ferris's scowl deepened. "You put your life, Mouse's life, and Alice's life all in jeopardy. Imogen would've killed you all."

"I knew what I was doing," she drawled. "A reward was offered for Alice, remember? Besides, Imogen never found out you were connected to me or Mouse, did she?" Maddie purposefully left out that Ferris was included in that reward. She didn't need him traipsing to the palace and sacrificing himself. He wouldn't be held in a cell like Mouse—he'd be dead. And that would destroy Mouse if she knew he'd done that for her.

Ferris lowered himself on the mattress beside her and wrapped his arm around her shoulders. "Your new plan is shitty."

"It really is."

"You're falling for that wanker, aren't you?" Ferris smirked.

"If by some Wonderland miracle we get the cure, then Noah's taking it and going back home." So there was nothing to fall for anyway, even though the feel of his fingertips on her face still lingered on her skin.

Ferris lightly shook her. "Whatever, Maddie."

She took a deep breath, her tone serious. "Watch over Alice and if something happens to me, then don't give up on Mouse, all right?"

"I'm not giving up on her or *you*."

Maddie circled her arms around him and rested her head against his shoulder. "Werewolves and Imogen, no big deal. Now, let's have some fucking bloody tea before I head out into true monster territory."

CHAPTER TWELVE

NOAH

Noah scooped Alice off the settee and tucked her into bed before mixing her a cup of powdered blood. "You have to hang on. Maddie and I are going to get something that will cure you," he told her as she shivered beneath the covers. At least, he hoped they would succeed. There was a chance the werewolves would kill them both, but he couldn't let Alice doubt. "All you need to do is survive long enough for us to get back."

"What cure?" she asked through clacking teeth.

Ferris grumbled from the other room, and Maddie's cajoling reply was muffled by the door. Noah knew this was dangerous and that Ferris didn't like it, but too fucking bad. Alice was dying and he wasn't going to let her be stuck in Wonderland forever if she did live. He glanced at his sister's frail form. An ache built in his chest and he rubbed at it. Failure wasn't an option. Not when the stakes were this high.

He sat on the edge of the mattress by his sister and tried to hand her the cup. The mixture of powdered blood smelled stale and did nothing to entice him, but it was all he had for her at the moment. "Drink this."

"No," she whispered. "It makes me feel worse."

"You need to keep your strength up," he insisted.

Alice grabbed his free hand and squeezed it, a gleam of true fear in her eyes. "I don't want to die."

"I know." He set the cup down as Maddie and Ferris continued their hushed conversation. "We'll get the cure, I promise."

Alice clung to him and rolled onto her side, burying herself farther under the covers. Noah rubbed small circles on her back and waited for Maddie to fetch him when she was ready to go. He had nothing to pack nor prepare. All he had were the clothes on his back. For everything else, he relied on Maddie.

After a few minutes Alice's breathing evened with sleep, and he stayed a long while by her side. He didn't know how much time had passed when Maddie cracked the door open. "Ready?" she whispered.

"Yes." Noah kissed Alice on her forehead and stood. He spared her a final look, offered up a prayer that she would survive until they returned, and slunk away to join Maddie.

Ferris's eyes tore into him as he followed Maddie across the living room. He couldn't blame him for being annoyed. If it weren't for Noah and his sister, Maddie wouldn't be risking her life to get a cure. She and Ferris would be on their way to saving Mouse instead. It seemed almost too easy to convince Maddie to put Alice above her own sister, but she *had* attempted to trade one for the other. Whether or not it was guilt that got Maddie to agree to finding the cure, he was grateful.

"Stay safe, Ferris." Maddie grabbed a backpack from just inside the front door and handed it to Noah, then slipped one on herself. "We should be back before the end of the week. Don't do anything I wouldn't do."

Ferris pulled her into a hug. "You better come back or your sister will never forgive me."

At least, if they *didn't* succeed, Mouse had someone left to save her. Alice only had him. He envied their sense of security. Ferris wouldn't keep fighting for Alice and, honestly, there was no alternative. The cure was her only chance. It wasn't as if their parents would come to bail them out of trouble, and no one in Wonderland owed him any loyalty. He swallowed hard, forcing down the swelling sense of dread.

"Thank you," Noah told Ferris. "For looking out for Alice."

"Mouse wouldn't absolve me if I abandoned her," he grumbled.

Noah wondered why the opinion of Mouse mattered so much to him. To Maddie, it was obvious—they were siblings and very close. Ferris and Maddie were nothing more than friends. He'd been around enough people to know when they were interested in each other.

Maddie tugged on the hem of Noah's shirt and led him out the door. His gaze fell immediately to the back of Maddie's black boots. The weight of his worry and guilt refused to let his gaze travel higher. Was it the right thing to risk Maddie's life for Alice's? Not that he truly had a choice. He would never let his sister die if he could help it, but perhaps if she gave him directions he could—*no*. There was no way he would survive this without help. He wasn't *that* naïve.

After what felt like ages, long after the cobbled streets turned to dirt paths, Maddie slowed. "He was right."

"What?" Noah jerked his head up and found they were no longer in Scarlet, but in an empty field with tendrils of blue smoke floating overhead. He sucked in a breath as he studied the glimmering wisps.

"Ferris. He said Mouse wouldn't forgive him if he abandoned Alice and he was right. My sister has the kindest heart."

Noah nodded, unable to tear his eyes away from the sky. Was Mouse anything like Maddie? He and Alice were very different, but he loved her all the more for it. Mouse had to be centuries old like Maddie. It seemed strange to think of the age difference between himself and these vampires, but it didn't *feel* like they were born generations apart.

"Alice has a kind heart too," Noah started. "Our parents became really strict as we got older, and she spent most of her time studying to please them. Then she moved in with me for university and rebelled. I was worried she would take things too far and fall in with the wrong crowd, but she never stopped being kind."

Maddie tapped her lips. "She looked very different in the photo Imogen and Rav had."

Noah turned, taking in the endless glow of the scenery. "It was an old picture. She didn't always dye her hair." Then, feeling Maddie's intense stare, he glanced down at her. "What?"

"You looked different too." She arched a brow, making no effort to hide her perusal of his body.

Noah's head fell back with a laugh. He'd hoped Maddie hadn't noticed. *Shit, that's embarrassing.* "I was the biggest nerd."

"Ah, my dear immortal, a nerd no longer. You aged quite well." Maddie smirked.

"No. I finally noticed girls and started caring about how I looked. Hit the gym four times a week, cut down on sweets, and discovered the magic of face wash."

Maddie gave a thoughtful *hmm*. "I bet the girls all fawned over you then."

Noah shrugged. He couldn't lie—it had been the biggest perk of working out. All of the hottest girls in school wanted to date him. It had been a huge ego boost for a previously self-conscious kid, but it had gotten old fast. There was far too much drama that came along with it and too many of them only wanted him for superficial reasons—looks *and* money. "I suppose. There's been my fair share of hookups, but I've only dated one person since then. That ended quite badly though."

"Only one?" She cocked her head. "What happened?"

He sighed. Were they really going to do this? Have the ex talk? "We dated for two years, then she fucked my best friend."

"You want me to stab her with a hatpin?" She patted his shoulder, her expression serious. "Not kill her of course."

"I'm better off." He exhaled sharply. "Or I was. Dying sort of put a dent in that, if I say so myself."

"You didn't die," Maddie said matter-of-factly.

Right, right. He was technically alive, but what good was that if he was stuck in a dark world with a craving for blood? He wanted to go home. Though, if he was being honest, it was fucking amazing seeing in the dark and having super strength. "Where are we going?" he asked to change the subject.

Maddie pointed ahead. "Ivory is that way, but we won't get there for a while yet. Tonight, we'll make it to one of Ever's safe houses, then I'll give you a *lesson*." She waggled her eyebrows at him.

His cock pulsed. It wasn't an innuendo—*was it?*—but he couldn't stop his thoughts from traveling down a lurid path. Her teaching him *exactly* how she liked to be touched, him learning *exactly* what she tasted like in every way. He shut the thoughts down, before he sported a full boner, and cleared his throat. "A lesson?"

"Let's do three lessons." She stopped and whirled toward him with an excited gleam in her eyes. "We need to test your vampire speed. Race me to that tree."

"What tree?" He squinted ahead but only more blue smoke swirled. There, in the distance, he caught sight of a silhouette so far off he barely recognized the shape.

"That one," she blurted and took off.

Noah stood there for a moment, mouth hanging open,

before he raced after her. The wind whistled in his ears as he ran, focusing on the purple blur a few lengths ahead of him—Maddie. He smirked as he pushed himself harder, letting the adrenaline fuel his speed, and soon caught up with her.

"There you are," she said with a bright smile. "But you're too late."

Noah opened his mouth to ask what she meant, when she dug her heels into soft earth and placed her hand on a tree. He slowed too quickly and nearly toppled over his own feet. "Well, damn," he said with a long exhale. The tree came out of nowhere. "You're fast."

Maddie laughed and poked playfully at his chest. "Faster than you."

"Hey now." He captured her wrist and tugged her closer. "It wasn't a fair race."

She cocked her head and pretended to think for a moment. "You have longer legs, so I was at a disadvantage."

Noah chuckled and she leaned into him. A whiff of sweet cherries hit him. The air between them thickened and Maddie's gaze trailed up to his lips. They'd already done other things together, but he wanted to find out what she tasted like. Would she be as sweet as she smelled? Sweeter? How soft were her lips and would she part them for him? He lowered his head the smallest fraction as if drawn by an invisible force, about to find out if she tasted like cherries.

Maddie waved a hand in the air and quickly stepped back. "Time for lesson two."

"Oh?" Noah cleared his throat, straightened, and took in the forest. Anything to keep his thoughts from circling back to what he thought the second lesson could be. Black trunks. Gray leaves, with the occasional red one ruining the monochromatic scheme. The trees grew thicker together farther out, it seemed, but here, they appeared sparse. "What is it this time?"

Maddie slipped her backpack off, set it on the grass, and

dug into it. When she stood again, a pistol rested in each of her hands, pointed directly at him. She looked between them, then up at him. "Do you have a preference?"

The fuck...? He'd never seen a gun in real life, and it instantly had him stepping back. "Where the hell did you get those?"

"There's a seller in Scarlet who brings them back from the mortal world." She held both out toward him. "So?"

"What?"

"Which would you like to use?"

His eyes widened. "Neither, thanks."

Maddie shoved one of the pistols into his hand. "Don't be a silly goose. How do you expect to enter werewolf territory without one? I have plenty of silver bullets, but we'll practice with regular ones now. They're easier to come by."

"I don't know, Maddie..." He gripped the weapon carefully, keeping his finger off the trigger. This would make going up against the werewolves much easier, though, so he'd just have to get over his reservations. "I've never shot a gun before."

"That's why we're *practicing*," she said as if it should've been obvious. "Look, it's easy."

Noah's gaze lifted slowly—or at least it felt slow. He barely had time to see that she had raised her gun. In his direction. The boom reverberated through his skull as the bullet whizzed by his head, the sound extra loud to his immortal hearing. A wave of dizziness swept over him.

What the fuck? What the actual fuck? "Did you just shoot at *me*?"

"No, I shot *past* you." Maddie lowered her arm and grinned. "My aim never fails."

"Like I give a shit about your aim? What if I'd moved?" he shouted.

"Well," she said, dragging the word out. "I suppose you'd heal then. Now it's your turn."

Noah shook the ringing from his ears, cursing his amplified hearing at the moment. "I don't know how to shoot a fucking gun. It's not like they were lying all over the place back home."

"Don't be a coward." She bent down and set her pistol on the ground, then circled around behind him. "It's simple."

"I'm not a coward. A lesson is supposed to come with instructions though." He'd much rather kill than be killed, but he didn't want to accidentally shoot the wrong thing. Like Maddie, for example.

Maddie's hand gently slipped down his arm from where she stood a little to the side behind him. "You don't want to become a meal for the hungry beasties, do you?" Her hand reached his wrist and lifted his arm up. "Turn off the safety here," she said, pointing to a small lever. "Now aim." She steadied his arm, her fingers skimming his wrists, and her breasts brushed against his back. The contact sent an immediate heat straight to his cock, but he had to concentrate. This was important. So when Maddie's warm breath skated along his arm, he squinted ahead at his target. "Put your finger on the trigger and—"

Noah curled his finger around the trigger as she spoke and the gun blasted. His arm jerked back, his body practically humming from the blast. "Oh my God," he whispered, his heart pounding, a smile crossing his face. He hadn't expected such a power rush to come from shooting a weapon.

"Well, you weren't supposed to squeeze it yet," Maddie said patiently.

Noah took a steadying breath and nodded. Shooting was the smartest option. Quicker for everyone involved. He scowled at the gun in his hand—if only he wasn't a shit shot.

"Try again. Hit that tree over there."

Noah lifted the weapon, attempted to line it up with the trunk a few yards away, and shot. The bullet blasted through the air and completely missed its target.

"No worries." Maddie shrugged. "Werewolves will be bigger and closer."

"I'm not sure that's comforting," he grumbled. If he couldn't hit a target standing still, how did she expect him to hit one that *moved*?

"We've made enough noise for now. You can try again tomorrow." Maddie took the gun from him and slid it into his backpack before skipping to retrieve her belongings. Pulling her key ring from a pocket in her skirt, she sang, "Come along, immortal."

Noah rubbed his hands together as he plodded behind her up to the tree they'd raced to. He watched quietly as she slipped one of her keys into a crack in the bark. "What's this?" he asked curiously.

"Our safe house for the night."

With a single push, the side of the tree shifted inward, revealing a spiral staircase leading beneath the ground. Maddie ushered him inside. When he was three steps down, she came in behind him and shoved the door closed, locking them in the pine-scented safe house. He blinked twice to adjust to the darkness, but then everything was completely clear, thanks to his improved vampire vision. And by everything, he meant the smooth brown walls and matching wooden staircase.

"Go on," she said.

Noah descended the steps with Maddie on his heels to a rounded room. An *empty* room. No bed, no sofa, no nothing except for an open crate full of powdered blood.

"It'll do to keep us safe," Maddie assured him, as if she'd read his mind.

Noah slid his pack off and plopped down on the carved-out wood floor, stretching his legs. "Yes, it'll do." He wasn't going to be awake long enough to care about comfort anyway. Now that he was sitting down, exhaustion washed over him in a wave. "Sweet dreams, Maddie."

"Don't let the Wonderland bugs bite," she replied as she rifled through her bag for something. "I'll wake you when it's time to leave."

The scent of cherries invaded his nostrils. Noah wasn't sure if he'd be able to sleep with the images in his head of Maddie slipping her dress off her petite body and straddling him. He pressed his eyes shut and rolled to his side, facing away from her. *Fucking hell. Think of werewolves instead, Noah. Big beastly ones.* But it wasn't working. Not one bit. Fuck, he was in trouble.

CHAPTER THIRTEEN

MADDIE

A smidge of alabaster tulle there. A little ivory lace curved and braided between. Perhaps frosted felt entwined with chiffon near the front. Folded and shaped pearly roses of wool could be sewn into a small arch. Then at its center would rest an anatomical heart, crimson paint appearing to leak from its veins, coating the other white areas in splashes of scarlet, as though the organ were bleeding. That was it! This was the fascinator Maddie would gift to Imogen, as the perfect distraction, before attempting to retrieve Mouse. *If* they came back from this journey.

The image in Maddie's mind of the hat was one of the finest she'd come up with, one that would anger Imogen. Yet, she knew it would distract the queen for a moment, a moment where Maddie and Noah could possibly make their move. She wasn't sure what the plan would be following that, but as long as they could get Imogen's arms behind her back before she tore into their chests, then it would be a good day.

Once—*if*—they got Mouse out, where would they go? To hide in one of these safe houses forever? To see if there was anything left in the dead Red Queen's abandoned territory? To hide somewhere in the mortal world? The mortal world may be their best option, but Maddie didn't want to constantly move every few years when humans realized they didn't age. Then to pretend she was human and hide from the sun? *No*—she liked her freedom. If they were able to retrieve the cure, and there was enough, then perhaps she, Mouse, and Ferris could also take it. *No to that too.* None of them would want that.

As Maddie contemplated the what-ifs, a strong arm folded around her middle and drew her to a firm chest. She gasped at the sudden movement, and the warmth forming in her belly. Noah nuzzled into her neck, and they were like two spoons fitting together perfectly. His hard length pressed into her, her eyelids fluttering at the contact. His breathing came out soft, even ... *sleeping.* She'd been in this position many times but never while the male wasn't awake.

Noah's impish hand then slowly slid up her stomach and she stilled, wondering what was going to happen next. His palm cupped her breast and he growled into her neck, pressing harder against her. Maddie naturally arched into his touch, but she needed to wake Noah before this got too awkward for him. She didn't mind his hands on her one bit.

"Immortal," Maddie whispered, jabbing him in the ribs with her elbow.

"Mm-hmm," he groaned, somehow moving even closer, his fingers kneading her breast.

"Noah," she said louder, jabbing him harder.

His hand loosened from her breast, but remained frozen there, his entire body stiffened.

"Fuck." Noah removed his arm from around her and shifted back. "I'm sorry. I didn't—"

"No worries." With a smile, Maddie rolled to face him and placed her hand to his warm cheek, giving it a light tap. "It's natural. I told you the lust would come again." She paused, remembering her hand around him in the bathtub only a couple days ago, him enjoying it, her liking it just as much. Not only that, but it had helped him. "Do you want me to take care of you again?"

His throat bobbed as his bright green eyes studied her. "Only if you want to," he said softly. "Not out of obligation."

"I don't do anything I don't want to do."

"All right," Noah whispered. "It helped last time."

She scanned him up and down. "Let's remove your clothes, so we don't get them too messy."

Noah seemed to fight a smile as he slowly nodded before lifting his shirt over his head. Not taking her eyes from his bright green irises, Maddie reached between them and unbuttoned his trousers, then pushed them down. He kicked the material off until he was bare before her. She took in each hard muscle, his defined chest, his strong thighs and arms. This male never would've given her a second look in her past human life, and she didn't truly know if he would in this immortal life either. But they were stuck together, and she was starting to rather like having him around.

As she gripped his hard length, Noah released a deep groan and wrapped his arm around her waist. He rested his forehead in the crook of her neck when she gently caressed at first. Maddie inched closer as she circled the head of his cock with her thumb, then stroking up and down, adding firmer pressure, her movements increasing their pace.

Noah's breathing hitched—her heart pounded.

Maddie unintentionally shifted even closer, a heat spreading through her, consuming her, and she yearned desperately to sink her fangs into his throat. Not for a treat like she did with mortals, but for the pleasure that vampires gave to one another. With all the immortal lovers she'd taken to her bed, she'd never once let any of them push their teeth into her flesh though, not after Rav. Only hers penetrating them.

Her lips pressed to Noah's throat, her fangs lowering on their own accord. Maddie grazed his tender skin with her teeth, then flicked the area with her tongue, tasting his salty flesh. He shivered at her touch, and let out a delicious sound just as she pumped and stroked him even harder. She liked the feel of him, the sounds he made.

"Maddie," he rasped while his muscles tightened, his body spasming, his cock throbbing as he spilled himself.

Noah's chest heaved, her body now coiled tight, aching for a release of her own when she let go of him.

Before she could retrieve a cloth from her pack to clean them up, Noah said something unexpected, enticing, his voice curious. "Can I touch you now?"

Maddie stilled. She'd assumed she would've just taken care of herself as she had the last time. And even though anticipation stormed through her at what his fingers would feel like on her, inside her, she answered, "You don't have to."

"But I want to," he murmured, his fingers running up the length of her spine in a delectable caress.

And that matter was settled. "All right, show me what you can do, immortal."

He chuckled, then his gaze grew serious, daring. "To be fair ... and less messy, how about you get undressed?"

Fair indeed. Maddie grinned. "One of my hands is already messy, so you may have to help me."

Noah didn't hesitate as he loosened the buttons at the front of her dress. Her heart beat faster, preparing to break her rib cage in half. He then reached over and peeled down the straps from her shoulders, exposing her breasts, the cool air hitting her nipples. Fangs lowering, he drew the dress down from her body, and as he reached her panties, he took them with the other material until she was naked before him.

He tossed the dress and undergarments aside and his gaze

drank her in while studying her for a long moment.

"Go on," she instructed.

Noah rolled his eyes and licked his lower lip before he brought his shapely lips to her breast. She moaned when he took her peaked nipple between his teeth, sucking and nipping while his hand ventured to her center. As his fingers brushed the sensitive area, her moans grew louder—she knew her wetness was already pooling around his digits. He circled and rubbed while sliding two fingers inside her heat. Her hands balled into fists and her eyelids fluttered at his practiced movements. Noah's mouth trailed kisses up her throat, to where his fangs grazed her this time. The fear she'd experienced in the past didn't come, instead, she wished he would sink them in. And as she imagined it, as she focused on the rhythmic movements of his hand, as she thought about what it would feel like to have his cock inside her doing the same thing his fingers were, a wave of emotions pounced through her. Her body quaking and quaking and *quaking*. This was nothing like what her own fingers would've been able to do. Nothing at all.

Noah lifted his head above her, his mouth so close to touching hers. Chest heaving, Maddie pressed her forehead to his before their lips could brush. Because if she kissed him, she may just be as foolish as she'd been with Rav when she'd given all of herself to him in that forest. A kiss never mattered before, but something about a kiss with Noah seemed different.

"Next time, we'll take care of each other again," Noah said softly, pressing a kiss to her forehead before helping her back into her dress. Like a gentleman.

But all she could focus on was *next time*.

Maddie woke and stretched her arms to the ceiling with a yawn. She turned to Noah to find him still asleep on his back, breathing evenly.

He looked angelic as he slept with his chiseled features and his curled blond hair. She tapped his cheek. "Good morning, sunshine. Are you ready to find the werewolves?"

Noah's eyes cracked open, his gaze meeting hers. Crimson stained his cheeks, and she was certain he was thinking about their night before. After all, it was a memorable night.

"Come on. We'll be in Ivory soon." Maddie stood and shoved on her combat boots. She grabbed her backpack from the ground, placing the straps over her shoulders while Noah mirrored her movements.

"What's Ivory like?" Noah asked as they ascended the stone steps leading out of the tree safe house.

"Beautiful," Maddie said, opening the door to the fresh air, laced with hints of vanilla and honey. "Decorated in mostly whites and silvers."

As they entered the night, the world around them grew boisterous from creatures' activities.

"What is that?" Noah squinted his eyes as he peered around the large trunks.

"Sounds like mostly mating." Maddie paused, tilting her head to get a better listen. "And perhaps some feeding. We're in the very outskirts of Scarlet. Occasionally a werewolf will slip in."

"What the fuck?" Noah's eyes widened. "I thought they had their own territory."

"They do, but the rogue ones still prowl about. That's why most of us keep guns and silver on hand at our homes." She tapped his cheek. "But they aren't like you and me. They would be like a wolf in your world—focused on their predatory natures. Vampires like to feed, but not all of us are heartless."

"Watch out," Noah shouted, grabbing her by the shoulders and pulling her to his firm chest.

Maddie's gaze fell to where Noah stared. A group of five badgers watched them around a crimson log, their teeth razor-sharp, their skin pale and wrinkled. She laughed. "Noah, they're only a different breed of badgers than what your world has. They're harmless ... well, to us anyway. Not mortals. They would drink them dry."

"They have no fur," he stated, not loosening his grip on her.

Maddie batted his arm away and crept closer to the clan of badgers. She knelt beside a smaller one with a shriveled face, then reached down to pet it, stroking its soft head. The badger let out a light purring sound. "See?" She glanced up at Noah with a smile. "Come on."

"Uh..." Noah hesitated, but then slid down beside her, shakily pressing a hand forward. The badgers focused on him yet didn't scamper away as he awkwardly petted each of their heads—if one could call it that. "These don't run like ours do," he said in awe.

"One reason why I love Wonderland." She grinned and stood, straightening the skirt of her dress. The wildlife in Wonderland had their oddities compared to the mortal world which made her feel more at home here, even if most could be deadly. But they were outcasts like she'd been. "Let's go."

They continued walking through the forest, the sounds of mating lessening with each step they took. The trees were of black and red—obsidian trunks and crimson leaves, or scarlet trunks and onyx leaves. Crows cawed above them and Noah stepped toward one near a trunk.

Maddie yanked him to her by his shirt sleeve. "Don't get

near any of the birds in Wonderland—they peck out anyone's eyes who draw too near."

"Bloody hell." Noah sucked in a sharp breath. "You just told me the wildlife here was different than back home."

She shrugged. "Well, do crows try to peck out your eyes in London?"

He rolled his gaze toward the sky, a smile tugging at his lips.

Leaves crunched beneath their feet, and the trunks of the trees appeared as if they'd been braided.

"Thirsty?" Maddie asked, her throat growing drier with each passing moment.

"Very," Noah said.

"Better to eat before we get to Ivory anyway." She fished out a canteen of water, then two pouches of powdered blood and handed him one. "At least Ever's territory is more calming. I miss it."

"Why don't you still live there instead?"

"Because once Ever went into hiding, Imogen forced me and Mouse to live at the cottage in the woods. And then, eventually, Mouse was taken."

"What a bitch." Noah cocked his head. "How long has Ever been in hiding?"

"Almost four years." Maddie shrugged and peeled open her blood pouch. She moistened her fingers and pushed them inside before bringing them to her mouth. The powder was chalky, the flavor weak, but it would do. Sometimes it was hard to swallow, so she took a swig of her water before tipping the pouch's contents onto her tongue to make a thicker, tastier liquid.

As she finished, her throat was no longer dry, her appetite satiated. Up ahead, white and silver trees poked through the slits of Scarlet's foliage.

"What is that?" Noah asked as they inched closer, taking a swig of water.

The white and silver of the tree trunks were splashed in something bright red... *Blood.*

CHAPTER FOURTEEN

NOAH

Blood splattered the silver trees. Long streaks of crimson with speckles all around, and large droplets oozed toward the white grass beneath their feet. The trails followed the lines of the bark, slipping between the cracks and making a strangely beautiful design. But it was *a lot* of blood. More than Noah felt comfortable passing off as some wild beast securing dinner. Unless that dinner was human-sized.

"Is it always like this?" Noah asked before his imagination could run away from him. She'd claimed Ivory was relaxing, but they apparently had different definitions of that word. Under different circumstances, she could've been telling the truth though. Some of the trunks were white with silver leaves, others silver with white leaves, and a light, fresh scent lingered beneath the metallic scent of blood.

"No." Maddie ran her index finger along one of the stained trunks, then inspected her red fingertip. She licked the crimson from her digit and Noah's stomach churned. "It's fresh human blood."

Noah's brows rose. If it was fresh, then whatever did this could still be lurking around, yet she didn't seem overly concerned. Another vampire wouldn't be a threat to them unless they worked for Imogen and Rav, but he'd rather not waste time talking to anyone. "What could've done this?"

"Well…" Maddie's gaze slid from the trees to the ground and back up as she tapped her lips, thinking. "It could've been vampires, of course, or some beasties. Or the Jabberwocky."

"The what now?" The Jabberwocky *sounded* like a beastie, as she put it, but if she was making a distinction, it had to be something else.

"The Jabberwocky." She slid between trees, careful not to rub against the trunks, and steered them straight for the white dirt road ahead. "It's a horrid beastie as big as a dragon with long talons and barbed quills sticking out from its fur. Its face is dragon-like with scales and hundreds of teeth, but don't you fret! The Jabberwocky rarely comes into Ivory and Scarlet. It usually stays just past Red, but once Ever left, the creature became a little more daring. This blood most likely came about from a vampire's doing though."

Rarely was not never, but Noah chose to go with Maddie's theory. Another vampire wasn't a threat to them in the same way as some vicious beast the size of a fucking dragon. They wouldn't be hunted down for food. For other reasons, perhaps, but being a vampire removed him from at least one menu. Crazed murderers roamed all over the mortal world though, so if humans could pick off other humans, arseholes in Wonderland could do the same. The best thing to do was get the fuck out of there.

"How much farther is the swamp?" he asked.

Maddie wrinkled her nose as she thought. "If we walk all day and sleep at the next safe house, we can get there by morning."

"We can get there tonight if we don't rest then?"

"Tut, tut. We need our wits about us."

"Fine," Noah conceded. Time was ticking for Alice, but a few hours to rest could make the difference between success and failure. Facing werewolves with a fresh mind had to be for the best. "While we walk, let's go over the plan for when we get there."

"Get where?" came a tauntingly curious male's voice. Noah's pulse immediately began to race.

"Bloody hell," Maddie grumbled.

A vampire leapt down from a tree directly in front of them. Chestnut hair fell halfway down his neck, shorter pieces framing his face, and he studied them with yellow irises. He wore black trousers with a matching vest, abs on full display. This was the same male he'd seen in the park just before they first arrived in Wonderland, when Noah was under Maddie's trance. *Chess*. Imogen's son. The *prince*. Noah fought the urge to step forward and beat his arse.

Chess smiled at Maddie, fangs fully descended and a smear of blood on his lips. "Did I frighten you, little plum? I was certain you noticed me a moment ago when you looked around, but I guess you were too preoccupied with the mess I made on the trees."

Maddie shuffled slightly in front of Noah. "Weren't you searching for something before in the mortal world?"

"I'm the king of multitasking. Search for a human, search for a queen… But instead, I found a hatter and a new vampire." His yellow gaze landed on Noah, seeming to bore down to his soul. "You were a mortal last time we met, weren't you?"

Noah opened his mouth to reply just as something large fell from the same tree that Chess had leapt from. It hit the ground with a loud *thump*.

"Found a snack too," Chess said with a shrug. "Meant to tie him up there to bleed slowly, but I got carried away."

Noah peered around the flippant male and drew in a sharp

breath. *A body.* The heavyset man was nearly decapitated, his skin waxy, his eyes bulging from their sockets. Noah's stomach churned at the sight. There was drinking from someone like he had at Maddie's and then there was draining people dry.

"A royal servant from Ivory?" Maddie asked, peering down at the man's dead body. "I wasn't aware those traitorous guards had left anyone alive."

Chess shrugged, all humor fading from his expression. "Where are you off to, Maddie? You know you're not allowed to leave Scarlet unless it's for the mortal world."

Maddie shifted into Noah's side and her arm circled his waist. Following her lead, he settled his arm around her shoulders. "I'm just showing my boyfriend around Wonderland. He's new, like you said, and we wanted to take a little trip. I'll be back in time to deliver your mother her next hat."

"Boyfriend..." Chess licked the corner of his lips, spreading the blood smeared there. Noah narrowed his eyes, growing uncomfortable with the scrutiny. "You know, Maddie, I never thought you were the type to sire anyone and keep them."

"It was a happy accident," she said with false cheer. "Now, if you'll excuse us…"

She tapped Noah's side, steering him away without breaking their embrace, and walked across fallen leaves. Noah released a quiet, relieved breath. He wanted to get as far away from Chess as possible, as fast as possible. But running would only make them look suspicious. Maddie hadn't mentioned not being allowed out of Scarlet before they'd left, but would it have made a difference?

Chess sidestepped in front of them and chuckled, a predatory glint in his eyes. Noah scowled, his hand tightening around Maddie's shoulders.

"Oh, Maddie," Chess whispered and tapped the tip of her

nose. "You know I can't let you wander off into Ivory."

Maddie rolled her eyes. "I don't know where Ever is. Besides, you still have Mouse."

"So you keep saying, but I..." Chess prowled a step closer, forcing Maddie to look up to see his face. "Don't..." He gripped her chin. "Believe..." His eyes turned to thin slits. "You."

Noah tensed, ready to knock the prince away from Maddie. The way Chess was touching her lit his protective instincts on fire, but she wasn't even trying to defend herself. For that reason alone, he held back, grinding his teeth together to the point of pain.

Maddie squeezed his side as if in warning, rolling her shoulder slightly, and he loosened his grip on her. "You're welcome to join us then," she offered.

"I don't do threesomes." Chess paused. "With only vampires." A hiss escaped Noah without warning and Chess eyed him. "Don't sass me, child."

Noah froze. He wanted to rip the prince's face off. Tear him apart. Somewhere, deep inside, he recoiled at his own thoughts, but he'd work through *that* later.

"Now," Chess continued. "Come back to Scarlet with me like a good girl. Mother will be interested in your sight-seeing itinerary."

"Okay," Maddie said in a slightly slurred voice. Chess's grip had tightened so much that her lips puckered.

Chess stepped back and wiped his hand on his trousers. "Stay there for one moment, won't you?" He climbed the tree again without waiting for a reply, leaping and swinging on the branches like a damn monkey to reach the top.

Noah spun Maddie to face him. "What the fuck? We can't go back to Scarlet," Noah said in a rushed voice. They needed to keep going without distractions.

"We can't fight Chess either," she whispered. "He's older than I am and much stronger. Trust me and play along."

Maddie looked the same age as Chess. Immortal... Noah supposed that meant he would look like this forever. No pain, no memory loss, no deteriorating. Another perk of being a vampire.

Chess leapt down in front of them again and produced a blood-stained rope. "You don't mind, do you?"

Noah's fangs dropped. "Fuck yes, I mind."

"I was only being polite." Chess lifted one of Maddie's arms and started wrapping the rope around her wrist. "She may be weak and you may be new, but I'm far too lazy to chase you."

A growl slipped through Noah's lips as he bared his fangs, and Maddie tensed beside him. "We aren't going anywhere with you."

"You picked a feisty one," he said to Maddie, his tone somewhere between amused and annoyed.

Before he could stop himself, Noah lunged at Chess. The prince easily sidestepped him, and Noah skidded across the dirt path. He barely caught himself and whirled around, straight into Chess's fist. The force of the punch sent Noah stumbling back two steps before tripping over his own feet and landing hard on his arse.

"It seems you'll be traveling as my prisoners instead of my guests," Chess said with a sigh.

Before Noah could even attempt to stand, Chess had him flipped to his stomach, face pressed to the ground. Blood trickled from his nose where the prince had hit him, and he fought the urge to lick it away. But the urge only lasted a moment as Chess yanked Noah's arms behind his back, straining his joints. The rope cut into his circulation two seconds later.

"Chess," Maddie shouted. "He's newly-turned—don't go overboard. You know how impulsive a new vampire can be."

"Excuses," Chess grumbled. "I'm too old to deal with this shit."

"Bastard," Noah growled, and some of the white dirt found its way into his mouth. He'd been in his fair share of fights, but it had never lasted longer than a few punches. This was far more serious. He meant to tear Chess limb from limb.

Chess stood, one foot on either side of Noah's hips, and gave the rope a sharp tug. Then, to Maddie, he said, "Your turn."

Without a word, she stomped forward, a scowl on her face and her hands held out in front of her. Chess moved away from Noah and used the other end of the rope to secure her wrists together, then patted her head.

"Splendid," she sang.

"Wait here while I gather my other things." Chess stepped over Noah, purposely kicking him in the ribs as he did so. He bent over the corpse and rifled through the dead man's pockets.

"Now look what you've done, immortal." Maddie leaned down and helped Noah roll to his side. "As if escaping wasn't going to be difficult already."

Noah hauled himself into a sitting position, his arms trapped at a painfully awkward angle. "At least we're tied together."

Maddie grabbed one of his elbows and pulled him to his feet. "Insufferable," she muttered. "The both of you."

CHAPTER FIFTEEN

MADDIE

Noah just had to go ahead and muck things up and make the situation worse. Chess had stepped a few paces away, always slinking. He wasn't the brightest bulb in the box which may have been the reason Ever had been able to stab him so easily before escaping. But he was ridiculously strong.

Yet Maddie could be sneaky. She had a plan—one that now would have to come to fruition another way because of Noah's hotheadedness a few moments ago.

Chess stood near the dead man's body, the scent of metal filling the air. A heavenly smell, but she was still satiated from her powdered meal yesterday.

"Ah, here we are," Chess purred, holding up a closed switchblade that he'd fished from the man's pocket. Swiping the tip of his tongue at the corner of his mouth, he popped open the switchblade and sauntered toward Maddie. "Don't worry, little plum, I'm only taking you home." He paused. "Which means you'll owe me. But if you come back here, I'll have to get my hands dirty." The prince drew a gentle line across her throat with the blade, and Maddie held back spitting in his face while Noah glowered.

"Come on then. I've still got other jobs to do." Chess grinned, placing his hand in the middle of the rope, and tugged them forward as if leading two horses.

Maddie didn't need this delay. If he took them back to Scarlet, they wouldn't have enough time to complete their journey to save Alice before she had to deliver the hat to Imogen. She glanced at Noah and found his gaze trained on her, as though he'd been trying to silently catch her attention. Then he flicked his stare to the rope, motioning his head at it.

She frowned, not understanding what he wanted her to see. If Maddie could get closer to Noah, then she could untie him, but Chess's hand hovered between them. Noah cleared his throat and bulged his eyes at the rope, then at Chess.

Oh. She knew precisely what he wanted them to attempt. A distraction would have to do the trick first.

"What if I offer you a trade, Chess?" Maddie sang, a smile spreading across her face.

"I have everything I could ever want," the heartless prince said without looking at them, his shoulders square, his body relaxed.

"Do you?" Maddie asked.

Chess glanced back, smirking, his chestnut-colored brow arched. "Do you plan on giving me sweet Ever?"

"I told you," Maddie drew her words out slowly, "for the last time, I don't know where she is."

"Pity then." He jerked them forward and Maddie stumbled. "I may change my mind and take you to Mother instead."

The blood in Maddie's veins turned to liquid fire as she thought about Ever, what Chess would've done to her if the White Queen hadn't gotten away. Would he have slit her throat then removed her head or ripped out her heart the way his mother did with her enemies? "Yes, a pity you won't tell your mother you saw me here because then she would know you lost us."

"What are you rambling about, Hatter?" His movements stopped.

Maddie cocked her head at Noah, giving him a silent signal to do it now. With one quick jerk, the rope was out of Chess's hands, and they slammed it into his neck, backing him against an alabaster tree.

Chess seethed as Noah and Maddie both pulled on the rope from opposite sides to trap him against the trunk. Even with the rope binding Noah's hands behind his back, he had enough strength so Maddie could truly yank on it. The prince bucked and writhed so hard that Maddie thought her hands may get ripped off.

"You fuckers!" Chess's face turned bright red, spewing every curse word at them. But with each sound, she could hear him growing weaker, see it in his face. His fight lessened until his body stilled, his eyes falling shut.

Maddie released the prick from her angle and Chess slumped to the ground with a *thump* before collapsing on his side.

"Untie me," Noah rushed the words out, already in front of her with his back turned.

It took only a moment for her to unravel the knot. Noah shoved the rope from his wrists and whirled around to untie her. Not once did she remove her gaze from Chess—she didn't know how soon he would wake.

Maddie shimmied out of the rope, lunged for Chess, and grabbed his head before twisting it to the side with a loud snap that echoed through the forest.

"He'll be out for a long while." Her chest heaved as she released the prince and plucked up the rope from the ground. "Still, we should hurry."

"Why don't you just kill him?" Noah asked, Chess's

switchblade now in his hand.

The thought of ripping out the prince's heart sent a thrill through her, but she had to be reasonable. For now. "We can't yet. We don't have Mouse, and if I killed Imogen's son, then she would murder my sister in the worst possible way before we could get her." Maddie lifted a finger. "However, we will revisit the matter after collecting Mouse. Now, hold up his body."

Noah easily lifted Chess and propped him against one of the thin trees. Taking the rope, she wrapped it just below the prince's rib cage. There was only enough to circle his body once—it would have to do, but she tied it tight enough so that he couldn't easily shimmy out of it.

"We'll tear off pieces from the dead man's shirt so we can bind his wrists and gag him," Maddie instructed after confirming the knot was tight enough.

Noah didn't hesitate as they ripped off two long black pieces of fabric from the dead human's T-shirt. Maddie shoved the fabric in between Chess's teeth and wrapped it around to the back of his head while Noah bound the prince's wrists together behind his back.

"If he withers here forever, then too bad." She glanced up with a grin and shrugged. "He should've left us alone."

"He's a fucking arse."

"Well, we made a great team today." Maddie straightened out the skirt of her dress. "Now, let's go since the bastard made us lose time."

Without another word, they hurried through the forest to widen the gap between them and Chess. The night was at its full peak, black and silver owls hooting from the tops of trees around them. They needed to get to the safe house before morning so they could stay on track, giving Maddie enough time to make Imogen's hat. But there was still a while before they would arrive at the hidden house. Ever had told her exactly where each safe house was located on the keyring she'd given to the Hatter. Maddie may not have been to all of them before, but Ever had shown her the ones in Ivory, long ago, when they'd both lived here.

As they pushed farther through the forest, cool gusts of air blew, and a strong scent permeated the air.

"More blood?" Noah said, his nostrils flaring as he drew in the smell.

Maddie slowed at the edge of the forest and inhaled again. Blood always tinged the air in Wonderland but it was normally a sweet odor. Ivory had never smelled like this, colder, staler. Close to four years had passed since Maddie had been here last, but not that much could change during this amount of time.

Could it?

She broke out of the forest, the city of Ivory resting before her. Tall, white structures with silver-tinted windows flooded the area. Some buildings were shaped like chess pieces, and other rectangular structures contained a single game piece in the center of their roof with spheres in the corners for decoration. A heavy quiet blanketed the city, a far cry from the peals of laughter that used to ring out through the streets. That part disturbed her most of all.

"Why's it so quiet?" Noah's eyes opened wide, his hand still clutching the knife.

"I don't know, but there isn't anything we can do about it now," Maddie said softly, wishing she could.

Farther in the distance, the Ivory Palace sat like a gothic castle that could be read about in one of Edgar Allan Poe's works. Only, it was a beautiful pearly white, its towers tall, multiple spires steepling the sky, the moat surrounding the grounds a sparkling silver. Sharp alabaster thorns covered the top along with ornate chess pieces circled with roses.

Nostalgia washed over Maddie, and she missed her home. Missed how she and Mouse would play games of chess with Ever in their spare time. Missed the celebrations the White

Queen would have there, when Maddie would get lost in a lover, where Mouse would happily dance alone, while Ever would think of ways to make Wonderland better as she played her viola. Inside the palace now resided some of the guards who betrayed Ever—the others were turned unwillingly ... just like in Scarlet. The kind that Ever wouldn't want. Due to their nature, Ever always said that draining a mortal dry was one thing, but turning them into something they didn't want was another.

"You all right?" Noah clasped Maddie's hand, his warmth pulling her out of her staring spell.

Maddie shook off the feeling. "I'll be fine. Now, come on. We'll stay on the outskirts of Ivory."

They distanced themselves from the city, stalking the edge of the forest, the buildings vaguely taking shape in the distance.

Her hunger wasn't there, but Maddie forced down the powdered mixture of blood and water. Neither she nor Noah spoke too much so they could hear if someone drew too near, the way Chess had. But nothing besides forest creatures made any noise.

The darkness started to lighten and morning would arrive soon. A glistening lake slid into view and Maddie's shoulders relaxed.

"We're here." She sighed, studying the waterfall, the white flowers and pale grass surrounding it, the clusters of trees creating a canopy feel.

"This is probably the most beautiful thing I've seen here," Noah said, stepping to the edge of the lake.

"Maybe one day you'll get to see the rest of Ivory. There are much prettier lakes. Trust me." But then she remembered he was going home, and that she wasn't allowed to venture freely through Ivory anyway.

Maddie halted next to a waist-high boulder. She pressed her hands against its rough surface and pushed hard until it rolled out of the way.

Retrieving her keys from her backpack, she found the one she was looking for, then ran her fingers across the pale grass. "Aha," she sang.

"An interesting place for a safe house." Noah knelt beside her. "And smart."

"Indeed." Maddie grinned while pushing the key inside the lock and turning it with a small click. "Home sweet home for the night. If you want to take a quick rinse beforehand, now's your chance. Be fast."

Maddie stood and peeled off her arm sleeves, followed by the rest of her clothing while Noah stared up at her. "I said fast, immortal." She arched a brow.

"Oh, right." Noah bit his lip, lifting his shirt over his head, exposing his ripped abdomen. He unfastened his trousers and Maddie reminded herself that she didn't have time to sit and stare either. They needed to hurry before anyone spotted them. But she couldn't stop her mind from drifting to the night before, his fingers in her, her hands on him, the taste of his sweet flesh against her tongue.

A small squeak released from her lips when the freezing water brushed her skin. She quickly washed away the dirt and grime of the past couple days as best she could.

"Anything dangerous in the water?" Noah asked when he slipped in beside her.

"Not in this one." As she took a step, a sharp pain pierced her foot and she grimaced. "Bloody hell, I mean, yes. But not creatures. Just watch where you step."

"What happened?"

When she opened her mouth to answer, a loud noise, *howling*, not too far away, roared through the air. Then another and another, reverberating in the forest, shaking the trees, rumbling the ground.

"Well, that's it for bathing." Maddie pursed her lips and yanked on Noah's arm, tugging him to the edge of the lake.

"Get in the safe house!"

They darted from the lake, not bothering to get dressed as they grabbed their belongings. Maddie threw open the hatch and they scurried inside, an earthy scent hitting her senses. She then pulled down the door and locked it, a sigh escaping her. They should've just come in here to begin with. The noises from outside weren't as loud ... for now.

Silvery stone stairs glistened and led straight to a large space filled with crates stacked in the corner, holding packets of dried blood, same as in the other safe houses. Besides that, the room was bare except for a mattress—with a few folded blankets resting on it—against a wall.

Maddie set her things on the stone floor and tossed Noah one of the fur blankets before wrapping herself in another. She plopped down on the mattress and scooted back to the wall.

"Thank you again," Noah said, taking a seat beside her. "For coming with me, even though you are, apparently, a fugitive here. If I had known you were in more danger than what we're heading toward, I would've thought twice about asking you to come."

Lovely immortal... But he still would've had to ask because he wouldn't have been able to do it on his own. Maddie waved him off, her teeth chattering. "It's fine."

"You're shivering," Noah whispered, his face concerned. "Share with me instead—body heat will help." He shifted forward and opened his blanket for her.

As her shivering continued, she couldn't deny him or herself the chance to get warmer. She dropped her own fur and let her body mold to his flesh as she tucked herself into his side, absorbing his heat. He drew her close, then leaned them both back against the wall while holding her tight.

Maddie's arm draped around his stomach, and his muscles stiffened—she knew he was getting aroused.

"What made you want to create hats?" Noah asked, fracturing the silence, as if trying to distract himself for the moment.

"Ah, a subject I could talk about all day, immortal." Maddie smiled. "It's the one thing I'm good at, and lucky for me, it's something I love. I like creating pieces that are unusual but beautiful." She bit her lip and stared up at his bright green irises. "What do you like doing?"

Noah tilted his head up and peered at the stone ceiling. "Before coming here, I made coffee, but I didn't love it. I really don't know what I want to do, if I'm being honest. I'll be finishing college soon. My parents want me to take over their business one day. It's not something I'm interested in, though. I used to want to make movies when I was younger or write books, but my parents said it was a waste of time, that it wasn't a sure way of making money."

"I would read your book." Maddie grinned. A book was an extraordinary way of getting into one's mind, even more so than talking to them.

"Maybe when this is over, I'll help you sell your hats." Noah chuckled. "We could be hat dealers or some shit."

"A lovely plan." Except he wouldn't be staying in Wonderland, and she wouldn't be living in the mortal world. The thought made her hand slip, unintentionally brushing between his legs. She brought it back up to his abdomen, an unstoppable heat spreading through her.

"So," Noah drawled. "About last night… I haven't done anything like that in a while with anyone who wasn't my girlfriend."

Maddie's heart stilled, her stomach sinking as she thought of all the times she had. "I've never had a boyfriend. I've always just been needed when needed, I suppose."

He turned her face so their gazes met, his holding hers steady. "You deserve better than that."

Something about that one small sentence, the sincere look on his face, sent a rush of emotions barreling through her, causing her heart to flutter. Then she did the one thing she hadn't planned on doing. Her mouth collided with his. And he didn't hesitate to kiss her back. His lips tasted like vanilla, his tongue akin to sweet honey. She could drink his flavor for eternity and never grow tired of it. Not then, not ever.

Maddie hesitantly pulled back and rested her forehead against his shoulder. "Thank you for those words."

"I meant them," he whispered.

A new emotion coursed through her veins, spreading to each nerve, each fiber. An untamable desire. "Do you want to help each other again tonight?" Her voice came out husky.

"Very much."

In answer, she maneuvered herself so she was in his lap, her legs cradling his strong thighs. Her breath hitched as his hard length nestled perfectly between her slickened folds.

Maddie's heart accelerated when she pressed her lips to Noah's, his hands hugging her waist, his fingers digging deliciously into her flesh. As her tongue entwined with his, she rolled her hips forward, and her eyelids fluttered at the delectable pleasure. She continued to slide up and down his cock, releasing moan after moan. Their kisses deepened, tasting everything they could from one another. Noah groaned when her pace picked up, the friction growing stronger. One of his hands skimmed up her spine and entangled with her wet curls. He wasn't inside her, but it felt just as good—she was already too close to ecstasy and didn't want to stop.

And then a feeling rose, a sense of something she wanted to catch and hold onto. The sensation spread and built within her until everything shattered, everything becoming liquid, including her heart, at the heightened euphoria. In that moment, she yearned to have Noah feel better than good, so she took her mouth from his and trailed kisses down his throat, his chest, his abdomen, until she was at his hardened length. Maddie wanted him to come the way she just had.

"Fuck," he rasped when she took him into her mouth. His groaning turned into animalistic growls as her tongue circled the head of his cock and then let him go deeper. Slow. Fast. Faster. She sucked and licked and pumped, stroking him to his base. His hips lifted slightly while she worked him, relishing in the intimacy, until his body tightened, quaked, and he murmured her name over and over. Noah's cum tasted just as good as his mouth—every part of him did. Her fangs itched to lower, to take in the flavor of his immortal blood.

Noah drew her up, his fingers lifting her chin as he kissed her lips softly once more. "That was the best I've ever had."

No one had ever told her that before either… Not about anything besides her hats.

"Do you want me to get your clothing?" she asked, peeling herself from his body and sitting beside him.

"No," he whispered, drawing her close.

"Me neither." She folded herself around him, both of them nestled against the wall, their breaths heavy. Neither sleeping nor talking, but as she pressed her hand over his chest and felt his heart beating, it seemed to say *everything*.

CHAPTER SIXTEEN

NOAH

Growls and booming footsteps had shaken the walls of the safe house after Noah and Maddie had taken care of each other the night before. The sounds kept him up despite Maddie's assurance that they wouldn't be found, yet the noises hadn't prepared him for the paw prints in the mud outside the boulder. He froze. Dozens of them dotted the shore of the lake, each as big as his hand. With deep claws.

"What caused these?" he asked, already knowing the answer as he studied the prints.

"Werewolves," Maddie answered matter-of-factly. "Their territory isn't far now and they like to swim in the lake."

And she'd suggested he bathe in it? Well, dip into the water. He'd barely gotten wet before the howling began. "So…" He sprinted over the prints to follow Maddie. "How large are these beasts exactly?"

Maddie let out a chuckle and shrugged. "Big enough."

Noah had seen plenty of movies about the creatures but they were very inconsistent with the lore. He wasn't sure how he imagined the ones in Wonderland. Now though? He imagined them as fucking petrifying.

"Come along," Maddie said as he subconsciously fell behind. "It's only another two miles or so. Just over that ridge."

Noah squinted into the distance where the ground rose into a slight silver crest. Without stopping, he slid his backpack down and removed the gun Maddie had given him. There was no bloody way he was chancing a werewolf encounter without it. After a quick check to make sure the safety was still on, he stuffed it into the waistband of his trousers.

As he slung the bag back over his shoulders, he caught Maddie staring at him. More specifically, at his stomach where the bottom of his shirt caught on the handle of the gun, showing a sliver of skin. "What?"

"Nothing," she said, arching a brow.

A knowing grin curled his lips as he fixed the fabric to hide the weapon. She liked the way his body looked—that much he knew—but it seemed as though she was remembering their time together last night. The way she slid her wet folds over his length nearly drove him wild with the desire for more. If the way she had moved was any indication of how she would ride him with his cock buried deep inside her, it would be otherworldly. And then she'd taken him into her mouth... It wasn't only that he enjoyed what she did with her body either. He was getting more attached. Every day she grew on him a little more, and knowing himself, it was only a matter of time before he would want more than sex. Once he and Alice were cured, he would be leaving though ... he needed to remember that. Remember the way her tongue flicked over the tip of his cock, her hand pumping him, and—*enough.* He swallowed hard at the memory and forced his mind in another direction.

Monsters. Soon they would face them in order to get the

cure and he had no interest in doing so with a stiff dick.

"How long do you think it will take to get the cure once we reach the swamp?" he whispered in case any enemies still lurked near the lake. They likely had heightened senses just like Noah. He was willing to bet their sense of smell was even better than a vampire's.

Maddie chewed her bottom lip before answering, "Depends."

"On...?" he prompted when she didn't elaborate.

"How long it takes to find where it is, how much interference we receive, and many other things, I suppose." She scowled. "No one has ever mentioned how far apart the landmarks are. First, we have to find the giant fang. Then we go left until we reach the floating baskets, and finally swim toward the east until we see the glowing fish. A landmass with a lake is there—the cure will be at the bottom."

Well, that didn't seem very encouraging. The last thing he wanted to find in a swamp full of beasts was a fang. "Why would the werewolves keep it hidden if they hate vampires so much? Why not let you cure yourselves?"

Maddie opened her mouth and paused, shooting him a perplexed expression. "That's a good question."

"Don't sound so surprised." He nudged her shoulder playfully as a low rumble sounded in the distance.

"We should be quiet from here on," she whispered and retrieved her own gun from her bag.

Every step closer they took toward the ridge—and the wolves living beyond that—the faster Noah's heart pounded. Random trees sprouted along the rocky landscape. Someone had arranged boulders and smaller stones into spiraling circles or, for all Noah knew, maybe they were just naturally arranged that way. It was admirable either way, and if the circumstances weren't so shitty, he would've ventured closer to check them out.

The walk didn't take nearly as long as he'd hoped, but as

Maddie led him to the crest of the ridge, relief washed over him. He was so close to saving Alice.
Remember why you're doing this.
Easier thought than done.
He glared down at the pristine swampland, silver, twisting trees sprouting from crystal-clear water. Clumps of what appeared to be white algae floated in patches, and a stagnant scent tainted with a hint of wet dog permeated the air. Noah rubbed at his nose, the odor overpowering him.
Maddie tapped his arm and motioned for him to follow her. She took quick, light steps down the incline, and he followed, the weight of foreboding growing every minute. They were in the open, wearing dark colors against the bright white landscape, without an ounce of coverage to hide in. But he needed to trust Maddie. She wouldn't risk their mission or their lives, especially if it would affect saving her sister.
When they finally hit level ground again, she leapt through the tacky mud until they reached a large, light gray boulder. They darted behind it and peeked over the top. Noah sucked in a harsh breath at the sight of werewolf homes. Or what he assumed were their homes. Twisted, woven branches formed dozens of floating domes at least eight feet tall that resembled wolf dens. In one of the nearest, a gray tail flopped out of the round opening.
A rumbling growl—of annoyance more so than warning—prompted Noah to remove the gun from his waistband. He hoped the damn beast was having a nightmare. But that was probably just wishful thinking.
Maddie nudged him again and pointed to a moss-covered path on their right that led through the swamp. She held a finger to her lips and crept out from their hiding place. Noah tiptoed behind her, his gaze sweeping side to side. From another one of the floating dens, a large brown snout, slightly open, poked out, revealing teeth as long and wide as his fingers.

Oh, we're fucked...

The beast also seemed to be asleep, heavy breaths coming out in lazy huffs, but not all of the dens appeared occupied, which meant the residents had to be lurking around somewhere. Under their feet, silver bugs buzzed where they crawled, appearing like tiny pebbles, and claw marks scarred the trees. Some were fresh, others more violent. One trunk was nearly clawed in half, the top leaning on a neighboring branch for support.

The deeper they traveled into enemy territory, the more frequently they witnessed the signs of werewolves. Bones jutted from the pathways, snapped and crushed, and a severed human leg floated in the water. A gym shoe still lingered on the foot and frayed denim clung to the rest of the limb. Slivers of flesh peeked out near the top, black by decay.

Maddie grabbed Noah's wrist and pointed excitedly to a tall tree stump, covered in old scratches. At some point, long ago, judging by how weathered the exposed innards were, the tree had been sliced in half at an angle to resemble a …

A fang.

It did look like one, even if a little lopsided. They turned left and the path narrowed. Noah fell in line behind Maddie, his heart pounding harder as he wiped the sweat from his forehead. She had mentioned the next landmark would be floating baskets, so he turned his gaze to the water. A low growl filled the air, followed by a yelp, and he clutched the gun tighter. The sound hadn't come from the immediate area, but that didn't mean the predators weren't lurking nearby.

A few minutes later, Maddie screeched to a halt without warning, and Noah slammed into her back. He swung around, searching for danger, but instead of a werewolf crouched to attack, his eyes landed on metal cages. Massive cages. Big enough for him and Maddie to fit inside together and still have room to move about. Thank fuck they were empty, though it didn't make him feel any better. If they were caught, would they end up in a cage as a snack for later? He unconsciously grabbed Maddie's hand.

She squeezed it and shifted closer to him. He caught a hint of her sweet cherry scent, and it instantly took the edge off his nerves. Next, they were meant to swim. If he hadn't seen so many fucked-up things in Wonderland already, he would've questioned the idea of these glowing fish they had to find.

As Noah lowered his gaze to the ivory, blood-stained swamp, he second-guessed doing so. If the floating body parts weren't enough of a deterrent, the potential creatures living in the water were. He regretted not asking Maddie about that when she'd mentioned it earlier. But he would brave it regardless, for Alice, so he supposed it didn't matter.

Maddie tugged on his arm, and he froze at the worried expression on her face. "What?" he whispered.

She put a finger to her lips, then nodded at something in front of them. When he looked up, following her line of sight, he found two trees growing on a large oval patch of land. And between them, another cage. This one on the ground with only the corner peeking out from between the trunks. He tilted his head in confusion. What did it matter if there was another cage? They needed to keep moving because their luck had been *far* too good today.

An arm flopped out from between the bars and Noah jerked in surprise. *Shit.* There was someone in there.

"Hello?" a youthful voice called.

Noah shifted closer to Maddie and shook his head. It was too risky—they had no idea who was in that cage or why.

"We see you," said a second, equally youthful voice. "Please help us."

They'll call attention to us if they keep yelling, she mouthed silently to Noah.

It wouldn't matter if he and Maddie got the hell away from the cage. They had to get into the water anyway and that would mask their scent. *Maybe they're werewolves in human form,* he mouthed back.

Maddie shook her head. "The full moon was last week and that's the only time they turn human."

"Hurry!" they shouted in unison, but they didn't seem frantic. It sounded like a trap.

"Maddie, no," he whispered almost silently.

"Trust me." She pulled away from him to tiptoe toward the cage. Noah quickly glanced around and rushed after her. *The cure.* They didn't have time to be damn heroes.

When they reached the cage, they found two young boys, no older than twelve, in striped T-shirts with shaggy, matted red hair. They hadn't bathed in months, if the way they smelled were an indication. Like onions and wet dog—though the latter could be because *everything* smelled like wet dog here. Bits of gnawed bones littered the bottom of the cage as the boys—obviously twins—peered out at them.

"Shh," Maddie warned them. "What are you doing in there?"

Noah was sure that whatever put them in there was lurking in the vicinity, but he wasn't sure how far away they were. He didn't hear any rustling close or farther away.

"I'm Dee, and this is Dom," the toothless one on the left said. "We got stuck in our human form after the last moon."

Noah scowled. "So they put you in a cage?"

Maddie inched closer. "We're looking for the cure to vampirism. Do you know which way the glowing fish are?"

"Let us out and we'll show you." Dom perked up, his eyes glistening. "Please, let us out. They'll *eat* us."

Eat their own kind? Even if they were stuck as humans, someone here had to be their family. And they were young. Sure, werewolves were monsters, but this was next-level brutality. A short howl carried through the swamp followed by a slight grumble.

"Someone will catch your scent soon," Dee said.

Noah lifted his gun a little higher and glanced over his

shoulder. Nothing was coming for them yet, but he didn't doubt that would change soon. "Maddie," he whispered under his breath. "We can't linger around here."

"We don't know which way to swim," Maddie told him. She then turned her attention to the twins and hesitated. "We'll let you out if you show us, then you can be on your way."

The brothers nodded, and Maddie took a pin from her hat. As she picked the lock with it, the boys exchanged a devious grin, and Noah stiffened. *Fuck.* He needed to remind himself that these were werewolf kids, not human ones. "Wait—" he started, but the door to the cage slid open.

The boys shoved each other in an attempt to escape their prison first. Maddie stepped aside and quietly closed the cage behind them. "Hurry then," she urged the twins.

"Maddie, I don't think this is a good idea." Noah grabbed her wrist and leaned closer to whisper in her ear. "I don't have a good feeling about them."

"Neither do I," she admitted. "But what choice do we have? If we left them there, they would probably have alerted someone to our presence as revenge. Be on your toes."

Noah side-eyed the twins. They could easily lead him and Maddie straight into a trap. Were they even telling the truth about being werewolves? He was pretty sure the odor would even cling to him after they left. But what if the children were bait for unsuspecting travelers? He clicked the safety off of his gun. The blast would wake every sleeping werewolf in the swamp, but if he needed to defend himself, he would.

"It's this way," Dee said. "It's time to swim."

At least they were telling the truth about that. Noah swallowed hard and waited for Maddie to go first so he could watch her back. As he eased from the path and into the water, goosebumps rose all over his body from the freezing liquid. Three steps away from land and the water drifted up to his abdomen. Maddie and the little bastards were already treading water. He followed suit, sinking into the liquid to swim while keeping the gun above the surface, then gasped when it lapped over his shoulders.

Maddie cut him a worried look at the sound, and he offered a stiff smile. Nothing about this felt right, but his sister was dying. There wasn't time to swim through the entire swamp, searching for glowing fish. He would kill whoever he had to in order to return to Scarlet in one piece with Maddie at his side.

CHAPTER SEVENTEEN

MADDIE

Maddie swam through the freezing water, her lungs aching with each shallow pull of breath. The twins, Dee and Dom, glided through the water, but a werewolf's body, whether they shifted into their beast form or not, produced enough heat to keep them warm.

After catching the twins' sneaky smiles, Maddie wanted to leave them in their cages. A werewolf, regardless of its age, was a deceitful thing. They weren't the darlings they pretended to be—she knew that. But as long as the little wolves led her and Noah to the cure, then there wouldn't be an issue.

A golden aura glowed within the water. The *fish*. Noah gave her a slight nod, catching sight of it too, while continuing to slice with his strong arms through the clear liquid.

Dee halted and treaded water before raising a hand, pointing to a landmass covered in cerulean trees with brown leaves and bright iridescent flowers. He mouthed at her, *This way.*

Maddie nodded, heart pounding, as she followed the fish's flickering glow to the chunk of land. A scaly body brushed her ankle just before sharp teeth bit into her flesh. *Bloody hell.* She clenched her jaw to avoid making a sound and kicked at it, when another bite sliced into her wrist.

Noah growled but stopped—the demon fish must've attacked him too. She picked up her pace, shuttling past the golden carnivores.

Maddie neared the shore and peered up, her gaze connecting with Dee and Dom, standing at the edge of the shore. Pushing herself out of the water, she knelt forward to clasp Noah's hand. She dragged him to safety as a swarm of fish sailed to where they'd just been. They circled the empty water before scattering and fleeing when nothing lingered for them to attack.

Her chest heaved and water dripped down her body as she observed the area. A large glistening lake, the color and texture of milk, sat before them. No matter how hard she strained her eyes, Maddie couldn't see what rested below its surface. Curving landmasses, covered in blackened dirt, surrounded the mound she resided on, trailing to other areas in werewolf territory. Beneath her feet, brown grass shimmered like glass.

"Now what?" Noah asked, running a hand through his wet hair as he stared out at the lake. It wasn't as large as she'd expected, perhaps the size of several of her cottages stitched together.

"Go in and get your cure." Dom shrugged, propping his back against a tree and crossing his arms. His twin copied his movements, resting his head on a tree beside his brother.

"We can't see shit," Noah answered, frowning. "We don't know how deep it is."

"Go in and find out." Dee grinned, shrugging his gangly shoulders as his twin had.

Maddie narrowed her eyes at them. "We aren't both going

in at the same time." She squinted, studying the area. If they both went into the lake, then no one would be out here standing watch.

"The lake's safe and you'll feel the mushrooms at the bottom." Dee tilted his head to the side. "I would go in and retrieve the cure for you, but we did enough by leading you here already. We don't want your kind to have the cure because there's no cure for our own curse."

"It seems you're cured now," Noah grumbled. "Is that why they locked you up?"

"Our human form sickens us," Dom said with a sneer.

Dee nodded, lips curled in disgust. "We would prefer to stay beasts."

Noah arched a brow at them. He turned to Maddie and sighed. "Wait here while I go in. You have more experience in Wonderland and with weapons than I do. Besides, this is for my sister, so I should be the one to risk it. Not you."

Hesitancy coursed through Maddie, but if something happened or he didn't come back up, she could go in after him. Vampires couldn't die from drowning anyway. And from the few who survived to tell their story, their lost body parts hadn't gotten ripped off from anything inside the lake.

"Fine," she finally said. "But be quick, immortal."

Noah gave her a gentle smile and nodded, then removed his backpack from his shoulders and slipped his gun inside it. He leaned forward, softly pressing his mouth to hers. Her eyes widened as he stepped back and turned toward the lake. She placed her fingertips to her lips, her stomach fluttering.

The twins watched her as she mirrored Noah's earlier movements and took off her backpack in case she needed to dive in after him.

Once Noah had the mushrooms in his hand, they could take them back to Alice, and hopefully, after eating one, his sister would live.

Noah sank beneath the surface, and Maddie studied the

twins, who exchanged smug looks. She scowled. Something wasn't right. As her suspicion grew, she peered back at the lake when a shrill whistle penetrated her ears, followed by another high-pitched noise.

Maddie whirled around, seething as she stared at the little bastards. "What are you doing?"

"Sorry, bloodsucker." Dee giggled, pushing himself from the tree. "We needed to get back into our pack's good graces, so they'll help us get unstuck from this horrendous form."

"You, motherfuckers!" Maddie hissed, lunging forward to grip the back of their shirts as they bolted toward the swamp. But they were slippery things and ducked before diving into the water. The little chicken shits swam away, not giving a second glance in her direction.

She was prepared to go after them, but Noah still hadn't resurfaced. The twins' betrayal didn't surprise her in the least—they were werewolves, after all. At least she and Noah were at the cure's location—he just needed to hurry his arse up before something arrived and found them.

What if there were no mushrooms left at the bottom of the lake? There was always the chance there weren't any cures remaining, especially if she now knew why the werewolves didn't want vampires to have it. Maybe they'd destroyed the mushrooms themselves…

Angry growls broke through Maddie's thoughts, and she froze. Not just one or two—*many*. She jerked her head up as the land shook beneath her feet. Furred beasts, the colors of midnight, crimson, and tree bark, bounded her way, tearing across the land and swinging from trees. They hopped from landmass to landmass, headed straight for her from all directions.

Their frenzied roars grew stronger, boisterous, their shadowy shapes becoming defined as they drew closer. Maddie lifted her gun and fired a silver bullet, watching it rip through a crimson werewolf's throat. A gurgling howl escaped the beast's snout as it collapsed to the earth, its body quaking and disintegrating to fiery ash. Smoke billowed into the air.

Then she shot more and more, the savage beasts slamming to the ground. One through the eye, another the heart, the head, the stomach—each werewolf breaking into pieces. Her gun clicked—*empty*.

Maddie frantically fished out several cartridges from the front pouch of her backpack and reloaded with a click. Not in time, though, as a sharp pain pierced her back. She gasped, ignoring the throbbing and whirled around, coming face to face with an obsidian beast, its eyes the color of the orange sun in the mortal world—something she hadn't seen in so long. Blood leaked from its razor-sharp teeth as though it had come from another meal. She pulled the trigger, aiming straight through its open mouth while the beast roared, her hair flying around her cheeks. Hot blood splattered her face and she spun around, just as another werewolf swung from a tree branch and crashed in front of her. A bullet escaped her gun and struck true in its chest, blood blooming to the wound's surface before the beast fell to ash. These werewolves were about the size of one and a half of Noah—no matter how strong she was, she wouldn't be able to defeat them with her bare hands.

Bang. Bang. She continued blasting the beasts, when a splash echoed behind her. Maddie knew it was Noah by the sounds of his swimming, yet she didn't look back as she killed werewolf after werewolf.

Another gun fired from her right—*Noah*. Maddie wasn't certain if he hit his marks, but she didn't have time to check while shooting and reaching for more cartridges. She loaded and hurled bullets at werewolves on the landmasses farther away before they came nearer.

But the beasts wouldn't stop coming. It was like sewing an endless circle around and around a hat.

"We need to leave!" Maddie shouted, her heart almost breaking her rib cage as it thundered. "Those little twin bastards called their pack here. Did you get the mushrooms?"

"Yes, get in the swamp and go!"

She didn't just yet—she stayed shooting as he shoved the black and white striped mushrooms into his backpack. Maddie then grabbed her pack and jumped into the swamp, the freezing water wrapping its icy fingers around her once more, the glowing fish heading in her direction.

Maddie kicked her legs forward, dodging the bastard fish. She stayed below the surface for as long as she could until her lungs screamed for air.

Bursting through the surface, she gulped for oxygen. Noah trailed only a little way behind her, but the werewolves didn't stop as they launched their bodies into the water. Their growls reverberated across the swamp, but they were distracted by the golden fish. *Foolish beasts*. At least they were making a meal out of those for the moment, though.

She ignored the screeching pain of her back where the werewolf had struck her and glided forward, never relaxing her tight grip on the gun.

The patch from which they'd come slid into view, and she hurried to push herself out of the water as Noah followed. A werewolf leapt out from a tree and she shot, missing. She *never* missed. The beast soared toward them and, before she could pull the trigger again, Noah stepped between them. He brought his arm back and swung his fist, summoning every ounce of strength and speed he had, doubling down to do the most damage. Maddie steadied her finger on the trigger, waiting to fire. Noah's knuckles slammed into the side of the werewolf's head with a *crack*. Bright blood sprayed out from the wound as the body flew across the swamp, the beast's raging roars reverberating. Maddie fired, the silver bullet piercing the air, striking the werewolf's chest, just as its body splintered two trees in half. The beast landed in a shallow spot of water, its body convulsing before turning to smoke and ash. She didn't miss that time, but it was teamwork.

"Fuck!" Noah shouted, yanking her forward. "Let's hurry to Ivory."

She didn't know how many cartridges she had left in her backpack, but it wasn't enough to take out an entire territory of werewolves.

They sprinted down the winding path, past curving and gnarled trees, then ran through a narrow passage until just ahead, the familiar werewolf village came into view. The rows of cages glinted from the fiery posts, burning with orange flames at their tops. They slowed, treading silently behind trees so as not to draw any unwanted attention.

Her gaze fell to one of the largest werewolves she'd ever seen, bright ivory fur, its arms longer than its legs. The beast gripped two young males—Dee and Dom. Maddie grinned as the werewolf shoved the twins back into their cage. Dee scowled while Dom spouted curses.

Ah, so the little weasels didn't get the help they so desired. Maddie inwardly chuckled. The werewolf slammed the door to the cage shut, then thrashed across the ground in the direction Maddie and Noah had come from.

Once the beast was out of sight, she and Noah hurried across the land and back through the waist-deep swamp. Crows cawed from above while they trekked through the thick bog, until finally, out and away from the putrid smells, silvery trees interlacing with ivory ones appeared.

"Thank fuck," Noah rasped, placing his empty hand at his chest, the other still clenching the gun.

"The territory line won't stop all of them from entering Ivory. The bad apples will cross," she said, glancing behind her, the coast clear for now.

As the adrenaline left her veins, Maddie stumbled. She peered down at her skin, paler than usual.

"Your back!" Noah's eyes widened.

"I'm fit as a fiddle," she slurred, losing too much blood from the gashes on her back. Before she could say anything else, Maddie collapsed into Noah's arms.

CHAPTER EIGHTEEN

NOAH

"Rest," Noah encouraged Maddie. After she'd collapsed into his arms, he'd carried her back to the safe house in Ivory beside the lake in case any werewolves followed. Once she was safely off her feet, he swung the soaking wet bag from his back and unzipped it. "Blood will help, right?"

Maddie let out a weary breath. "I'm fine, really."

"If that were true, you wouldn't have nearly fainted," he said as he pulled out a sealed pouch of dried blood. Ripping open the plastic, he poured some into a half empty bottle of water. If she needed more, he would have to chance stepping outside to the lake.

The smell of the mixed blood pricked at his own hunger. After all their running and fighting, he'd built up an appetite. And the mushrooms had been *deep* in that lake. Dozens had been spread out across the mossy floor, so far apart that, once he was far enough down to reach, he'd struggled to make it from one to another. He'd spotted at least two headless human-like skeletons at the bottom from where vampires must've failed. Logically, he knew he couldn't drown, but that hadn't made the burning in his lungs any easier to bear. Most likely, the dead vampires had been killed before going into the water.

"Stop exaggerating, immortal." Maddie rolled her eyes. "My legs simply gave out for a moment."

Noah wasn't entirely sure if that were true given the huge gashes on her back. But she knew herself better than he did. As vampires, they healed differently. That didn't make him feel any better about her getting hurt so badly. It was his fault she was on this journey. He put the cap back on the bottle and shook it until the powder was fully dissolved. "Will this be enough?" he asked, handing it over to her.

"For now." She wasted no time bringing the bottle to her lips and downing the liquid.

"Maddie?" He cleared his throat. "I'm sorry."

She paused her drinking just long enough to ask, "For what?"

"Asking you to come along. If it weren't for me, you wouldn't have been injured."

She rolled her eyes as she guzzled the last few drops of blood. "Let's not waste our breath on that. More importantly, we can't stay long. If they follow our scent here, they'll leave someone near the lake to keep watch. Getting ahead of them is the only way to avoid another fight."

"As soon as you're well enough," Noah agreed. He didn't want to face the werewolves again but if they left too soon, Maddie might not be strong enough to fight or escape. However, he did have to admit using his strength to defend her and himself made him feel unstoppable. With the power to send a werewolf through trees from a single punch, was there anything he *couldn't* do?

She handed him the empty bottle and shifted as if testing her wounds. "Most importantly, you got the mushrooms."

Noah nodded and lifted them out of his bag to inspect. They were large, black and white striped, with wavy gills underneath. The stem of one had snapped—though still attached—in their escape, but the second appeared fine. Why hadn't he ignored the pain and grabbed more while he was down there? As many as he could hold. If they didn't need more than one each, Maddie could've sold the others to anyone interested and used the money to set her and Mouse up somewhere safe, somewhere far away from Scarlet.

"May I see them?" Maddie asked.

Noah carefully set the fungi into her waiting hand. "Interesting," she mused. "So frail a thing can make a vampire mortal again."

"Do we eat them like this or cook them?" he asked. Maybe there was something they needed to add in order to unlock the curing properties. "Or is there more to the process?"

"I believe you simply eat them, however, it might be hard to get them down. Solid food can be difficult to stomach. Such a change can't come without some discomfort, I suppose." She handed them to him. "You can't eat it yet though."

Noah's heart lurched painfully in his chest. "What do you mean? Alice will die if—"

"Of course, Alice needs hers right away," she amended. "We are *both* going to save our sisters, but you must wait for yours. You can't help me with Mouse if you're human again," she reasoned.

"I understand that." He wouldn't stand a chance fighting vampires unless he was one too. Being an immortal felt natural, maybe even more so than when he was human—he was in no rush to give up his new abilities. "I promise not to take it until we rescue Mouse." They'd struck a deal, and he had no intention of going back on his word. More than that, he wanted to make Maddie happy. To see her reunited with the sister she loved so much.

"Let's head out." Maddie blew out a breath and stood.

Noah eased out of his crouched position. He stretched, loosening his muscles now that the adrenaline was wearing off. His fist ached a bit from punching the werewolf, but it was worth it to save their lives. To save *her* life.

"After you," he told her with a renewed energy. Their goal was accomplished and they'd both survived to tell the tale. Now he could save Alice, too.

Maddie snuck back to the entrance of the safe house and inched the door open, sticking her head out briefly. Noah took note of the already healing wounds showing through the rips in the back of her dress. They were barely more than cat scratches now.

"All clear," she whispered a moment later and exited the house.

Noah followed her and strained his ears, listening for danger. His pulse quickened as they raced from the lake, putting as much distance between them and werewolf territory as possible. Without Maddie to lead the way, he would've gotten lost in Ivory, as he'd put too much attention into glancing over his shoulder and not enough to the path before them. So, when she stopped, he didn't notice and ran straight into her.

Maddie stumbled forward a step and tilted her head in confusion. "Look."

The trees with splashes of crimson loomed ahead, far too familiar, but that wasn't what had his brows rising. One tree in particular was worrisome—the one with torn rope littering the ground at its base and no snarky, yellow-eyed arsehole in sight.

"Fuck," he hissed.

"It was never going to hold him for long," Maddie said wistfully. "His Royal Bastard has a tendency to lurk around though."

Noah immediately peered up as if Chess would be there. He wasn't, of course, but that didn't mean he wasn't close, maybe waiting to spring a trap on them. *Let him try.* Noah just helped fight off an entire pack of werewolves—he could handle one cocky vampire. "Let's get out of here."

Maddie adjusted her backpack. "It's not too far to the safe house, so we'll stop there for a bit."

Now that they had the cure, he didn't want to wait another night to give it to Alice, but she *was* still far. After escaping the werewolves, the adrenaline wore off and his entire body ached. "Okay," he said. "But only for a few hours."

Maddie led the way back to the safe house in the tree, passing different species of Wonderland creatures, some with sharp teeth and others with curving beaks. The crows studied them as they passed but remained in the trees.

Once they reached their destination, Maddie fished the key from the front of her pack to open the door. They descended the steps, the familiar pine scent hitting his nose.

She flopped onto the ground at the bottom of the stairs with a low groan. "I could sleep for days."

"Hours," Noah insisted.

"I know, I know," she said. "And I have a hat to make."

Noah eased down beside her and yawned, closing his eyes. The urge to wrap an arm around Maddie and tug her against him rose. *Fuck.* He was never into cuddling before… His feelings for her were changing, already becoming deeper. But soon he would be leaving, right? Taking Alice and returning home as a mortal. The thought settled uncomfortably inside him as his mind drew closer to sleep.

Just when he nearly drifted off, the weight of Maddie's head pressed on his shoulder. His lips curled into a smile as he turned his head to rest on hers. It didn't matter what he did tomorrow or a week from now… Tonight, he was alive thanks to this vampire and she was beside him—apparently, with the same urge to be closer together. Noah wrapped his arm around her shoulders, letting her settle into him even more.

"Hey," Maddie whispered. "Wake up."

Noah cracked his eyes open to find her hovering over him. His pulse quickened at the sight of her, and he wanted to brush the hair from her face. Unconsciously, his hand lifted, doing just that as a warmth for her filled his chest. He wanted to pull her closer, wrap his arm around her and—reality blasted through him. "Shit." He leapt up and grabbed his bag from the floor. "How long were we asleep?"

"Three hours," Maddie said with a shrug. "Give or take."

That wasn't bad... But it had only felt like five minutes. "Is something wrong?"

"Why would something be wrong?" She cocked her head, brows lowered in confusion.

"Because werewolves are probably hunting us down and the queen's hell-spawn escaped the tree that *we tied him to*."

Maddie laughed. "The werewolves won't follow us into Scarlet. Well, not *those* werewolves. Just the regular old renegades that sneak into the city."

Noah wasn't sure why that was any better, but they'd been fine in Scarlet so far, if he discounted his attempted murder and being turned into a vampire. He hadn't seen a single werewolf before they'd waltzed into their territory, but that didn't change anything regarding Chess. He probably had already told his mother about the encounter. They could be walking straight into the queen's guards on the way back.

"Come on." She patted his shoulder, their eyes meeting. A tiny spark lit, igniting something in him. He wanted to capture her lips with his, feel every inch of her against him. But the spell broke when she spoke again. "We need to get back before Ferris thinks we were eaten."

This time, after Maddie re-locked the safe house, Noah urged her to keep a faster pace. Hours passed before the familiar red-glowing lanterns appeared on the horizon, and he was eager to give Alice the cure.

Vampires roamed the streets in large groups, all of them wearing a variety of black lace, velvet, and dark makeup. They laughed and spoke in loud, boisterous voices, and if they weren't in Wonderland, Noah would've thought they were normal friends heading to the club. Maybe they *were* going to a club in the mortal world like Rav had when he'd found Alice.

"This way," Maddie whispered, tugging him down darker alleys and away from the crowds. "Almost th—"

"Look who it is," a familiar voice drawled. Noah whirled around to find Chess striding up behind them. "The little schemer and her new pet."

"Ah, fuck," Noah hissed, and Maddie squeezed his arm.

The prince was a few feet away, then in the next instant, right in their faces with his fangs bared. "You tied me to a tree."

"You tied us to each other," Maddie countered.

"And I'll do it again," he sneered.

Maddie cocked her head and grinned. "How about with chiffon this time?"

"Chess!" A female gave a high-pitched squeal and he winced. "I would recognize that arse anywhere."

The prince spun on his heel. "Ari. I'm a bit busy right now."

Using the distraction to their advantage, Maddie ripped Noah out of the alley, and they ran as fast as their superspeed could take them. Weaving in and out of side streets, dodging around vampires who got in their way. They sprinted past a female vampire who had her fangs buried in the forearm of an elderly man, his head thrown back in pleasure. The scent of blood tinged the air and Noah's body tightened. His hunger surged. *Almost there*, he told himself as they made it the final block to the safe house.

Maddie banged a rhythm on the door so hard that Noah knew someone would notice. Sweat poured down the back of his neck as he scanned the streets, waiting for Chess to appear out of nowhere again. If he did, he'd punch the fucker in the face.

The door swung open and Maddie fell forward, straight into Ferris's chest. She quickly drew him to the side so Noah could leap in and slam the door shut.

"What the fuck?" Ferris asked. "You both look like hell."

"It's a long story," Maddie said with a carefree wave of her hand. "Is Alice still alive?"

Noah was already at her bedroom door when Ferris answered, "Yes." He pushed inside and found Alice curled under a heavy blanket. Her hair was plastered to her head with sweat, her teeth chattered, and her eyes appeared sunken and bruised. It had only been a handful of days, but she looked so much worse than before.

"Alice?" he whispered, kneeling beside the mattress, and set the back of his hand against her forehead. Her skin burned his palm as though she were on fire. "Alice, I'm back. We got the cure."

Maddie unzipped the bag that was still on his back and, a moment later, held out one of the mushrooms. "Here," she said softly.

"Thank you." Noah took it from her and gently shook Alice awake. She blinked her bright blue eyes open but they were dull, lifeless. She was almost gone... He could see it, *smell* it. The sweet scent of death clung to her like a second skin. "Alice, you need to eat this."

"I'm not hungry," she croaked, her glazed eyes fixed on the ceiling.

"It doesn't matter," he said, bringing the mushroom to her lips. "Just eat this for me. Please. You'll become human again."

Alice opened her mouth just wide enough to get the edge of the mushroom between her teeth. She chewed and swallowed with slow, laborious movements.

"More," Noah urged. He continued to feed her one tiny bite at a time until the mushroom was gone. An eternity passed before Alice managed to finish the cure while Maddie watched from the doorway with Ferris. Now that it was done ... why was nothing happening? "Alice?"

She rolled onto her back and arched her spine with a pained groan.

Noah leapt to his feet. "What's going on?"

"I told you it's hard to keep solid food down," Maddie said. "She has to digest it."

"Can one of you get her a cool, wet rag for her head?" He wouldn't ask for a bucket, though he worried Alice might need one. If she threw up, then she wouldn't get the full effect of the cure, and he refused to accept that. His sister was not dying. She had too much life left—too many years of living without their parents' interference. Their mother's expression when Alice showed up for Christmas completely decked out in her new style would be priceless as it always was. His sister needed to survive so she could truly live.

Ferris passed Noah a damp cloth, and he hurried to press it against Alice's forehead as she writhed. "You'll be okay," he told her even though he had no fucking clue if it was a lie. "Everything will be all right."

"Digestion could take a few hours," Maddie said in a solemn voice. "Ferris and I will be in the other room if you need us."

Noah nodded and flipped the rag over, swiping strands of Alice's stray hair away from her face. A few hours felt like a lifetime, but he wouldn't leave her side until he knew if the cure worked. "When this is all over, we should get you that parrot you've always wanted." They'd never been allowed pets—not even a goldfish—but he wanted to give her something to look forward to. "We can teach it how to swear in as many languages as you want. Then we should host a family dinner."

The briefest flicker of a smile ghosted Alice's lips before twisting into a grimace again. Noah wiped the sweat from her face and neck with the cloth. "I saw that smirk," he joked.

CHAPTER NINETEEN

MADDIE

The transition from a vampire to a human would be a teensy bit more difficult than the original swap from mortal to immortal. Maddie had heard the rumors, but hadn't seen a transition first-hand. Apparently, she wouldn't now either since there was another task to complete. In only a few days' time, Maddie would deliver the headpiece to Her Royal Heart-Stealing Highness. Maddie needed to start on the delightful hat-making chore *now*, and she would finish it tonight to get it out of the way.

"I don't know about this, Maddie," Ferris said, rubbing the back of his neck as he studied her beneath thick lashes.

"Just draw me the Ruby Heart Palace's floor map leading to Mouse's cell." She patted his shoulder with a smile. "That's all I need."

With a sigh, he retrieved a notebook and pen from his room. He ripped out a sheet and sat on the sofa, then sketched a rather quick yet intricate drawing. His strokes were detailed, and she spotted the sitting room of the palace right away.

Maddie arched a brow and sat beside him. "It looks like you're good at more than drums. You never told me you could draw."

"Mouse knows. I snuck her drawings while in the palace." He shrugged before handing her the map. "Don't get your arse killed."

Maddie glanced at the closed door where Noah lingered with his sister. He seemed to be comforting Alice as she groaned in pain. Maddie had risked her life to help him save his sister. Now she would be risking his to help get Mouse. To distract Imogen, she only needed the hat, and she should've come up with a plan like this a long time ago. If something did go wrong with Noah there, she didn't want him trapped in the palace like her sister, not after getting to know him.

She pulled the second mushroom from her skirt pocket, her heart speeding up, demanding this of her. When she'd collected the one for Alice from Noah's backpack, she'd taken the second one, knowing what she had to do, what Mouse would want her to do, what Maddie *chose* to do. Pushing herself up from the settee, she inspected its stripes for a moment.

"No," Ferris said. "Not after you just risked your life for that wanker."

Maddie smirked and tossed Ferris the mushroom. He easily caught it as she said, "Give him this when he comes out and keep him safe until I return. Besides, I owe him. I did try and take Alice to Imogen." Her stomach sank at the thought of what may have happened to Alice, the torture that would've been inflicted upon her before her death. But Maddie had been desperate.

Ferris rolled his eyes and drew Maddie into a hug. "You don't owe him shite."

In case this was the last time she would see Ferris, she

squeezed him tighter, more so than usual. "Remember, if I don't come back, then you'll have to find another way to help Mouse."

"I'll never stop trying," he murmured.

Maddie released Ferris and collected her things before heading out into the heavy fog. She couldn't tell Noah goodbye—it was better for him to focus on his sister. As she trekked home, the metal odor in the air was more potent than usual, and she made sure to keep her eyes peeled for Chess or Rav. Thankfully, she didn't come across either bastard, only trails of vampire blood and a couple of fingers resting in the grass, most likely more fighting. She missed the serenity of Ivory—the city needed Ever back.

The red lanterns guided her, the fog growing heavier when she reached her cottage. She unlocked her front door and slipped inside her cozy home. It felt as if she'd been gone forever. Kicking off her boots and tearing away her filthy clothing, she made her way to the bathroom and took a quick rinse.

"Much better," Maddie sang to herself as she put on a fresh dress with a poufy silk skirt, then padded into the sitting room.

Blowing out a breath, she collapsed on the chair in front of her desk. She drank a blood bag, wishing she had something warmer, but it made do for now.

Maddie collected her needle and thread, along with the supplies for Imogen's hat. Lace. Tulle. Felt. Wool. Paint. All ivory to remind Imogen of Ever, besides for the splash of crimson paint to show that the White Queen's heart bled with a revenge that would soon come. Even without Noah, the plan would still work. Once Imogen was distracted, Maddie would bind the queen's hands behind her back, tape her mouth shut, and toss her in one of the closets while she retrieved Mouse. The thought of Imogen's face as her gaze settled on the headpiece sent a rush of giddiness through Maddie.

Her fingers itched to begin when a knock sounded at the

door. She sighed, just knowing it would be one of the royal bastards.

Pulling open the speakeasy, her gaze met Chess's sparkling yellow irises. "I'm not letting you in," Maddie said.

He took a step closer, his voice coming out light. "Then I'll break down the fucking door."

"Try." If he did, it would give her an advantage to easily have a weapon ready when he crashed through it.

"If I wanted you dead, I would've killed you in the forest." He grinned. "We weren't finished talking earlier, so play nice and open the door before I get my mother involved."

Bloody hell. Maddie could handle this bastard for a few more days, so she let him in.

"Well, go on then. What do you want?" Maddie closed the door behind him as he stepped inside.

Chess smirked and stopped near the settee, his gaze sweeping across the room. "Where's your lover?"

"Finding us dessert in the mortal world." At least this time, Noah wasn't here to put a damper in her plan and get himself in a predicament.

"Ah." Chess tapped her nose, then whispered, "I know a secret, little plum."

Maddie narrowed her eyes, unsure what Chess was getting at. He always danced around the subject, so this was nothing new. But there was an emotion in his expression, as though he *did* know something. "I don't care about your secrets."

"Mm." He sank onto her settee, spreading his legs wide. Swiping his tongue across his lower lip, he patted his knee for her. "Come play for a bit."

If he wanted to chat, then he could do so as she worked, but she would never *play* with him. "I'm about to make your mother's hat, so if you don't have something you want to talk about then you might as well leave."

"Oh, I have something to chat about." He lazily unfastened each button of his vest, until he peeled it open—all of his taut abs on display.

Maddie wrinkled her nose, not knowing what he was doing. He'd been crude with her in the past, but she'd believed it was all talk. Did he really think she would fuck him after their ordeal in the woods and him admitting over and over that he wanted to murder Ever? He never said precisely what he would do with the White Queen, but she knew he would kill her in some sort of horrible fashion.

As Maddie opened her mouth to tell him to mosey on out of her cottage, he dipped his hand into the pocket inside his vest and fished something out. Maddie held back her gasp as she studied the familiar photograph in his hand. The same one Rav had shown her when he was there last.

Maddie stayed composed. "Rav and your mother already showed me this. I hadn't seen the girl then and still haven't."

"Funny thing," Chess purred, his grin growing wide. "This pubescent looks a lot like your fuck toy, doesn't he? Remove the glasses, the braces, the shitty haircut. Add muscles..."

Heart accelerating, Maddie squinted, pretending to study the photograph, and shook her head. "No."

"Liar," he cooed. "You're playing a little game to try and steal your sister away from my mother. I'm no imbecile." Chess truly was sly...

Maddie whirled around and snatched the scissors beside a stack of felt. But before she could spin around to stab him in his heart, Chess yanked them from her hand and caged her in at the desk from behind. Her chest tightened as she thought about her sister, how Mouse had been unable to escape the mortal man who'd taken everything from her. The one Maddie had slaughtered. And now, perhaps her sister would never escape her second imprisonment if Chess tipped off Imogen.

"Don't do anything foolish, or I will end your life right here," he said, taking a step back from her so she could turn and face him. "I have no qualms with your lover, and his sister isn't my top priority at the moment. Ever is. Tell me the White

Queen's location and I won't tell my mother you're trying to break Mouse out or that you have Alice's brother as a pet."

A trade. Maddie would have to give him what he wanted—it was the only way. "There's a safe house in the Red Queen's territory. She's there. But I don't have the key since each safe house only has one." She then gave him the details on how to cross through the Broken Forest of Shattered Blood and to the hidden door beside the old well.

"This was your one chance, Maddie." Chess cocked his head, sliding the scissors back on her desk. "If you're lying to me, I will come after you and your fuck toy, then drag your sister back to my mother to do with as she pleases."

Maddie took a deep swallow, not wanting to think about the things Imogen would do to Mouse that she hadn't already. "What are you going to do to Ever?"

"That's a secret for another time." With those words, Chess backed away from her, buttoning up his vest before turning around.

Once Chess sauntered out the door, she slammed it shut, knowing she didn't have much time until he would return without Ever. As always, if she'd known where the White Queen was, she still wouldn't have told him. She'd sent him to the farthest safe house she knew, but perhaps she should've sent him farther out toward the Jabberwocky. Yet this would give her enough time to complete her tasks while having him off her back.

Adrenaline coursing through her, Maddie dropped onto her chair and lifted the felt to start Imogen's hat. She stitched, tore, ripped some more, all while pretending it was Imogen and Rav she split in half. Time slipped by, and her eyelids grew heavy as she worked. Her fingers turned red and raw, but she couldn't stop. The hat needed to be just right. It needed to be *perfect*.

And then the time had finally come to drizzle crimson paint onto the veins of the alabaster anatomical heart, giving it the bloody look she so desired.

Maddie reclined in her chair, taking one final look at her beautiful white and red creation and grinned. She yearned to take the hat to Imogen at that moment, but the queen allowed Maddie a specific time only. Not early. Not late.

If Maddie succeeded in rescuing Mouse, things wouldn't get easier, but harder.

A bang at the door caused Maddie to leap out of her chair. A sharp pain ran up the length of her stiff back.

As she took a step forward, she froze. Had Chess already made it back? Impossible… Maddie grabbed the scissors from her desk and yanked open the speakeasy. She gasped when her gaze met bright green eyes

"What the fuck is this?" Noah said through gritted teeth, holding up the mushroom.

Her heart thudded in her chest at the sight of him. *What is he doing here?* Setting the scissors on a wall shelf, she unlocked the door and pulled it open. "Isn't that what you wanted? Return to your mortal life?"

He brushed past her—his face drawn into a scowl. "I promised I wouldn't take it until after we got your sister back. And then you just came home by yourself with that fucking prince waltzing around."

"About him…" Maddie hurried and closed the door as though Chess were slinking around, listening. "He knows who you are, but I was able to send him away for a bit. Let me take you back to the safe house."

"No." Noah folded his arms.

She folded hers in return. "Yes. I'll take you there, then

you can take the cure. The mushroom practically says *eat me*."

"No."

Stubborn immortal! A warm feeling washed over her at a thought. This male maybe cared about her if he was still willing to help her. Perhaps she was more than someone who was only used for fucks and not love. Either way, he couldn't go.

Maddie backed him into the wall, and he peered down at her with a hard stare. "I'm going on my own and not risking anyone else. Once everything has blown over, either Ferris or I will take you and Alice back to the mortal world." There was a chance she would die, but at least Rav should be in the mortal world as usual, and now, Chess wouldn't make an appearance.

"You can't tell me what to do." Noah whirled her around so she was backed into the wall this time, his hot breath mingling with hers. It sent a pleasureful feeling straight to her core—none of the fear that she'd held when Chess had caged her in was there. "You made me this way, and I'm choosing what to do with my immortality. We'll get your sister out, then we'll be even."

"That's what this is?" Maddie frowned, realizing she'd been wrong about his motivation. "Owing each other? Like when we got each other off?" Maddie ducked down and escaped his barrier, waving her hand in the air as she padded away.

Noah drew her back by the arm, his nose touching hers. "We don't have to owe each other anything. If you want me to get you off the whole night without me coming, then fine by me. So tell me, what do you want?"

As she peered up at him, his determined expression, an emotion washed over her, taking out any fight she had in her. Maddie relented, her shoulders dropping. All she wanted in that moment was his skin pressed to hers. "For you to stay the night."

"And to go with you to the palace," he added

Maddie didn't want him to go, but she would leave whatever happened at the Ruby Heart Palace to fate. Perhaps he was meant to go with her on this final task. He could've abandoned her and eaten the mushroom, but he hadn't.

She couldn't hold back, not any longer. Her lips captured Noah's, and he kissed her in return with equal hunger. His strong arms hoisted her up, her legs cradling his waist, and he walked her to the settee before laying her against its velvet. Noah's warm fingers slid beneath the edge of her skirt, but paused just short of the place that yearned for him the most.

"Don't stop," she said softly. "If you do, I'll grab my hatpin."

With a playful smile, Noah hiked her dress up and peeled off her panties, already drenched with her wetness. Then his head was between her legs, his delicious tongue slowly gliding up her center in one easy motion. Maddie's eyes fluttered as he circled her clit, stroking, nipping. She gripped his hair as he continued working her, tasting her, devouring her. Her entire being shattered, like breaking glass as he worshipped every piece of her bundle of nerves. She grasped his hair tighter and shouted his name, listening to it echo off the walls.

Noah grinned. "How many more times do you think I can make you feel good tonight? Should we count?"

"It doesn't matter," she said, her voice shaky from the orgasm. "I need you inside me—I want to feel you come."

"Fuck yes." Noah ripped his shirt over his head while Maddie chuckled. He loosened the ties at the front of her dress and she shoved it down her body. There was nothing cute or sweet about it as they tore away the rest of their garments. He then took her into his lap, his warm flesh against hers—she could feel every inch of him hard and ready.

Maddie lifted her body and sank onto him, animalistic growls of pleasure escaping both of them as his large cock filled her, making her moan in delight. She rolled her hips forward, and her fangs lowered on instinct. Only one thing could please her more.

"I want to taste your blood," Maddie panted, her body heating with need, *desire*. She expected him to wince, shy away, but he didn't.

Gripping her waist, Noah licked his lips. "Do it."

While grinding against him, she pressed her lips to his throat, sliding her tongue across his throbbing vein. His cedarwood scent surrounded her, his blood calling to her. She clenched his hair with both hands, tugged his head back, and pierced her fangs into his flesh, his blood spilling onto her tongue. Ecstasy washed over her as she drank and ground herself harder against him. He tasted like honey, the nectar she desperately needed.

Noah rubbed her clit, circling, until she ripped her fangs from him and gasped. He leaned down to her breast, taking a peaked nipple between his teeth. She arched into his touch, riding him harder, allowing the pleasure to draw nearer.

"Can I taste you now?" Noah whispered, peering up at her.

Maddie stilled, her gaze meeting his. "I-I...."

"Fuck. Sorry, I don't have to, Maddie," he said quickly, holding her steady, and pulled out of her.

Maddie knew he meant it, yet she *did* want him to sink his fangs into her. She lifted his face and cradled his cheeks, his green gaze meeting hers. A feeling was coming closer to the surface, one she'd wanted to avoid. Yet she couldn't in this moment... "You can, but no one's done it since Rav. Just don't break my heart." Tears pricked her eyes. She was ruining this moment that should've been about pleasing one another, but instead, she had to open her foolish mouth. "Forget I said that, immortal."

His fingers wiped at her tears, and he gave her a soft smile. "If anyone's a heartbreaker, I think it's you. You did leave me behind, you know."

Perhaps she had, but she would do it over and over because it had led to this. In answer, Maddie claimed his mouth with hers, letting him fill her with his hard length once more. She rolled her hips as Noah trailed kisses to her jaw and down her neck to her pulse. His teeth grazed her flesh, making her moan before puncturing the skin. Noah's fangs slowly pushed into her, and she growled in pleasure, his fingers digging into her hips as he sucked and tasted. Her pace quickened as she fucked him, harder and harder. She wasn't certain what was happening anymore as crimson stars sparkled across the room.

Too soon, he took his mouth from her throat and lifted her from the settee. "You deserve the bed." She wrapped her legs around his narrow waist as he walked down the hall. "Never mind," he rasped, pressing her to the wall. "This is as far as I can go."

Maddie laughed, her lips molding to his, their kisses growing frantic, wild, as he unleashed himself. She gripped his shoulders, her nails digging in, her breasts bouncing.

Noah slid his length back so only the tip was in her, then he drove into her, hitting the base of his cock. She threw her head back in pleasure as he thrust again and again and *again*, until they both shouted in unison, their bodies drenched in sweat.

Chests heaving, they stared at one another. Maddie had never seen such a beautiful male as she did in that moment.

Noah grinned. "That's number two." He nibbled the tender spot beneath her ear, sending a wonderful shiver down her body.

Finally, he walked them into her bedroom. Pulling out of her, he gently lay Maddie on the bed as though she were a porcelain doll. He lowered himself on top of her, settling in between her legs. His lips met hers in a soft, tender kiss. Heart still beating fast, she ran her palms up the length of his chest, his back. They kissed and kissed for what felt like hours, until he grew hard once more when her mouth came to his cock, her tongue running up its length.

"Again?" he asked, his smile mirroring hers.

"Let's keep counting."

This time when Noah buried himself in her, it wasn't raw or animalistic. His movements were rhythmical, musical, as he took his time with her. She learned his body, discovered what made his toes curl with featherlight touches from her fingers, her lips, her tongue.

As though Wonderland was lit up in sunlight, bliss poured over Maddie as he spilled himself into her once more. Noah rolled to his back, bringing her to his chest and folding his arms around her.

Neither moved from their positions, their hearts pounding rapidly against one another.

Maddie had made things worse. Because now she yearned for him to stay in Wonderland, at her side, as an immortal.

CHAPTER TWENTY

NOAH

A soft sound woke Noah, and he tugged the large pillow closer to his chest. *No.* Not a pillow. It was too warm for that. He looked down to find Maddie's purple hair on the pillow beside him and his heart leapt at the sight of her nestled there. He tightened his arm around her waist. Her bare back was pressed against his chest, her perfect arse against his semi-hard cock. The events of the night before flooded through him. How they moved together, how she tasted. He smiled to himself as his length swelled even more. But more than the amazing sex, he liked waking up beside her. *Well, maybe not* more. It was equally as enjoyable though. Seeing her features so relaxed and knowing she trusted him made his chest warm.

Maddie released a soft sound and turned her head to look at him over her shoulder.

"Morning," he whispered.

"Morning," she sang and rolled to face him. Grinning

mischievously, she lifted the blanket and peeked down at his growing erection. "And good morning to you."

He chuckled and traced her cheek with his thumb. "I'm tempted to suggest we make it a *great* morning."

"We have time," she said, peering up at him from beneath her lashes.

"Do we?" he asked, and quickly rolled on top of her, eliciting a surprised squeal from her. "You're not too sore from last night? I wasn't exactly gentle." The first time, anyway—the following rounds hadn't been as rough, but still…

"I liked it," she admitted and ran a hand down his chest. "And no, I'm not sore. We heal too quickly to worry about that."

"Well, in that case…" He lowered his mouth to hers and tangled their tongues in a slow, lazy kiss. His hand ran down her side, past her hip, to grip her thigh. Breaking away from the kiss, he leaned back enough to hook her leg over his shoulder and slid inside her warmth.

Bathed and dressed in a clean shirt, jacket, and trousers that belonged to Ferris, Noah held the front door open for Maddie. She spun, hair still wet as she gathered the white and red hatbox into her arms. The hat itself had been packed away before he got a good look at it. Her movements were slow and reluctant as she walked toward him, her gaze lingering on random items.

"You'll be back one day," he assured her.

"I should hope not," she said as she stepped outside, carrying a large bag with clothes for Mouse and extra supplies over her shoulder. "It wasn't ever a real home to begin with. It was just a place to create my hats which I can do anywhere. Ivory is my home."

Noah knew Maddie was right, but he felt her sorrow like a tangible thing. She loved her hats that still hung on the walls inside, but it wouldn't be safe for her to return while Imogen and Rav ruled Scarlet. They would know who broke Mouse out of the dungeons. The sisters would need to hide in safe houses for years, if not longer. So would he and Alice—but they would be hiding in their own world. He hated thinking of them alone, even if Ferris planned on joining them, and forced into hiding. While he was a new vampire, slightly impulsive, and undoubtedly a risk to them, the idea of leaving Maddie made him want to stay and protect her all the more.

"Coming?" she asked from a few paces away.

Noah shut her front door and strode to her side. They walked together in silence for a handful of streets. He took the time to notice things he hadn't before, like the goods displayed in shops. Various clothes in styles from different eras, cages with skeletal birds, and scrolling table lamps that cast elaborate shadows on the wall. Another held mirror shards pieced together along the back wall of the display, showing their selection of sex toys from every angle. Noah was torn between stopping to take a longer look and hurrying past that particular shop to avoid the distraction. If they survived long enough, he was definitely circling back if Maddie was up for it.

"This way," she said softly, noticing his distraction before they turned again.

It was early morning and few others were on the street, but Maddie was known for her hats. Carrying a box tied with a giant ribbon wouldn't be strange from the best hat maker in Scarlet, so no one spared them a second glance. Hopefully they got the same amount of attention when they went to the palace.

"I was thinking…" he started, but stopped himself. Before

he could say anything about maybe staying a bit longer to help Maddie hide Mouse, he needed to see how Alice was doing. With their parents being in Leeds he might *need* to go home with her if she wasn't recovered enough to take care of herself. And that was even assuming they could return to their London flat. They might need to move to avoid Rav or Chess dragging them back to Imogen.

"Noah?" Maddie prodded.

He sucked in a breath. "Sorry, I should probably think a bit more before I open my mouth."

Maddie arched a brow and nodded. "Speak when you're ready then."

Did she even *want* him to stay? She said not to break her heart, but that didn't necessarily mean he would be welcome to practically move in with her. There were plans in place for three: Maddie, Mouse, and Ferris. His tagging along could cause problems. But he was getting ahead of himself. Alice had still been in pain when he ran after Maddie and there was no telling what state she was in now. His sister had barely overcome her agony before he left her, sleeping, to speak with Maddie.

Only she hadn't been in the safe house—she'd left the cure with Ferris. The male had wasted no time handing over the mushroom and telling him that Maddie went home. Ferris had watched him carefully after breaking the news, as if he was genuinely curious what Noah would do. He could've sworn the vampire had smiled when he left without another word. Noah winced. And then he'd spent the entire night fucking Maddie when his sister was going through an extreme transformation.

He shook the guilt and worry away. One step at a time. First, he and Maddie needed to get to the safe house. They had three days until they had to go to the palace to talk and figure out their plan to free Mouse which gave him a little time to sort through what he truly wanted.

After a quick look around to make sure they weren't being followed, Maddie led the way, slipping around the corner, graceful as a cat, to the front of the safe house. She shifted the box and rapped the secret code on the door. Ferris swung it open a moment later and ushered them inside.

"Noah!" Alice called in a weak voice.

He spun to find his sister sitting on the sofa with a plaid blanket wrapped around her shoulders. Her damp hair framed her face, and a bit of color stained her cheeks. The vividness of her blue eyes had faded, making her look almost human again. She smelled human too, but her blood held an acrid, bitter note now. "Sis." He smiled. "You look much better."

"I wouldn't go that far." She lifted a strand of hair and dropped it back down. "But an improvement, surely."

Noah sat beside her and tugged at the blanket so it covered more of her thigh. He paused. What was she wearing? A large black T-shirt and... "Where are your trousers?"

She shrugged. "Maddie's clothes are too small and Ferris is tall so his shirt fits like a dress."

"Seems like I'm dressing everyone these days," Ferris mumbled as Maddie set her box onto the small table just inside the door.

"It's not like you were using them." Maddie grinned, tapping Ferris's nose. "You didn't even know I'd gotten them from your flat after you entered the palace."

Ferris crossed his arms and stared at the box. "Is that the hat for Imogen?"

"Yes." Maddie made a small squeak of excitement and pulled off the top, lifting the cocktail hat from inside. "It's a masterpiece, if I say so myself. Far too perfect to sit on that shrew's head."

Noah turned from them as Maddie started explaining how she crafted each piece of the hat. Something tugged in his chest as he watched how her face lit up over her craft. She was ... she was *adorable*. But then his gaze shifted to Alice and his stomach sank. His sister needed his attention more at that moment. "Are you feeling better?" he asked.

"Much. Everything's been hazy after I … after I attacked you." Her face turned bright red, and she hung her head, hiding behind her hair. "I know I already said this, but I'm so sorry, Noah."

"Don't be." He reached over and took her hand in his. "It wasn't really you. I'm just glad Maddie and I got the cure for you."

Alice chewed her bottom lip. "Ferris told me what you had to do to find it. You really shouldn't have—not that I'm ungrateful, but you could've *died*."

Thinking back on it, Noah was honestly surprised they hadn't died in the swamp. "I could have. You *were* going to die though, so how could I not risk it?"

With a heavy sigh, Alice settled into the back of the settee. "We should be able to go back home when the cure has finished setting us both right."

They couldn't go *home*—home wasn't safe anymore, but that was just another thing they needed to discuss. Noah shifted uncomfortably. "I haven't taken it yet," he said in a quiet voice. He hadn't wanted to talk about this the moment he walked in the door, and he would've preferred it be a private conversation. Though, if he were being realistic, no matter where they spoke inside the small safe house, Maddie and Ferris would've been able to hear.

"*What?*" She sat up straight and twisted to face him. "Why? Ferris gave it to you before you left."

"I promised Maddie I would help rescue her sister. What good would I be as a mortal?" The other reason—the part about not hating being a vampire—could come a little later. He pulled the semi-wilted mushroom from his jacket pocket. "See? I still have it."

"Eat it," she urged. "We don't owe them anything."

Noah's mouth parted in surprise. "I'm fairly certain we

owe them a fuck-ton. They snuck you out of the palace, hid you from Rav and the queen, and helped me save you from certain death." Maddie *had* tried to turn Alice in for her own benefit, but that didn't negate the good things she'd also done.

"You're right." Alice winced. "I know you are. I'm sorry, it's just ... I want to go home and forget this ever happened. And I need you there with me. If you stay here, you'll end up dead, and it will be my fault for dragging you into this mess."

"I'm not going to die." Noah ran a hand through his hair, hoping that was true. "It's going to be a quick rescue mission. Maddie will distract Imogen while I sneak inside with Ferris's map. By the time she finishes delivering that hat, I'll be back here with her sister, safe and sound. Okay?"

"You don't *know* that. Besides..." She paused and chewed on her bottom lip. "What will I tell Mum and Dad? That you've run off on holiday?"

"I can come back and visit sometimes." Around Christmas and birthdays, as long as it was at night...

"Come visit?" she nearly shrieked. "I meant if you were *dead*. Are you seriously considering staying here?"

Noah felt Maddie and Ferris staring at him, but he was too cowardly to look over at them. *Fuck*. He had wanted to think this through. "I'm not sure what I want," he told her honestly. Staying in Wonderland meant leaving his entire life behind. He was torn between what he *should* want and what he *did* want. "I'm going to think about it for a couple days."

Alice grabbed his forearm with both hands. "You can't stay in Wonderland. Please, Noah, you have to come home with me where it's safe."

Safe? She was clearly in denial. But, regardless, what did he have there that was really worth returning to? A job he tolerated, another year at university to then get some new job he wasn't thrilled about? A lying bitch of an ex-girlfriend who wouldn't leave him alone? Their parents rarely made an appearance so, if he did visit once or twice a year, he would be seeing them just as much. He would have Alice, of course, but he couldn't live his life for her. He needed to live it for himself. What he needed to decide was how *long* he would live—another sixty years or forever?

"Bloody hell," he growled, not meaning to sound so angry. "I'm sorry. I need to think, okay?"

"Think about what? This is *insane!*" Alice said with wide, panicked eyes.

"I'm glad you're feeling better." Noah stood and avoided meeting Maddie's heavy stare. "If you need me, I'll be in the other room." His flat tone implied *don't need me* unless it was a true emergency. He hoped they picked up on his need to be alone for a bit. To sort through everything without outside pressure, life-or-death stakes, or a sexy hat-wearing female muddling his head.

As soon as the bedroom door shut behind him, he heard Ferris whisper, "What the fuck was that about?"

"Nothing," Maddie replied, her voice uncertain. "He's probably just tired."

He *wasn't* tired though. He should've been after all that had happened. It had been almost two weeks of jumping through mental loops and days of running through danger for the cure. His body had changed completely. But that was the thing—he *liked* what he'd become. Not the idea of drinking blood so much, but even that wasn't so bad. As a vampire, he was stronger, faster, and he felt more *right* than he ever had as a human.

Plus, there was Maddie. He hadn't known her that long, but he'd known his ex-girlfriend for years. Look how *that* had turned out. Sometimes it wasn't about the length of time two people knew each other.

Fuck. He already knew what he wanted to do. All that was left was to come to terms with abandoning one life for another.

CHAPTER TWENTY-ONE

MADDIE

Three days had passed. Maddie and Noah shared a mattress in the safe house, but he'd been quiet. So quiet. Yet she knew his thoughts weren't. It was a peaceful few days, even though she wished Noah hadn't been brooding. Before they would fall asleep in the mornings, he kissed her thoroughly as if he were trying to find an answer. But that was all they'd done. Kiss, tender and slow, as though she was stitching the finest of hats.

Maddie fiddled with her arm sleeve and glanced up at Ferris. He sat on the floor, leaning against the wall, sketching in a notepad. Noah was in the bathtub, washing himself before they headed to the Ruby Heart Palace.

A door creaked open, and Maddie turned to find Alice standing there. The vein at the girl's neck thrummed and Maddie could scent the mortal blood flowing through her. Alice hadn't spoken to Maddie since discovering Noah may possibly stay in Wonderland. But that wasn't only a surprise to Alice—it was to Maddie too. However, regardless of immortality, a shadow of their human side would always linger within the heart of a vampire. And even if Noah did stay, he may decide down the line that he wanted to go back home after all.

"Can I talk to you?" Alice asked, not moving away from her door.

Maddie lifted her chin, her interest piqued. She waved a hand in the air and patted the spot beside her on the settee. "Come on then."

Alice's gaze flicked to Ferris as her fingers dug into her oversized shirt. "Alone?"

Maddie arched a brow, curious as to what was so secretive. She stood from the settee and padded toward Alice's room. Ferris didn't stop drawing, but she knew he was listening to every word.

"Why couldn't you talk to me out there?" Maddie asked while Alice shut the door behind them.

"I can't." Alice winced. "I tried to kiss Ferris last night."

Maddie inhaled sharply. "You like Ferris?"

"No. I don't know." She nervously shifted from one foot to the other. "I mean, he saved my life."

Because of Mouse… That was why he saved Alice's life. She didn't say it out loud though—she didn't want to hurt Alice anymore. Maddie also didn't know much about his past life with mortal women, but he'd never had a girlfriend for as long as she'd known him. Only that he'd fucked Imogen to get turned into a vampire so he could become a servant in the Ruby Heart Palace for Mouse. Alice was pretty but Ferris had said he would never choose mortality again. "I'm sorry. Unrequited love is—"

"Whoa!" Alice held up her hand. "I don't love him. I just wanted to thank him and have a little fun while I was at it. At home, I still haven't really found myself."

Maddie understood that better than anyone. She'd been

reckless at times, just to escape herself, her past. "You eventually will."

"Thanks." Alice bit her lip, seeming to think for a few seconds. "Please make Noah eat the mushroom."

Maddie took a deep swallow. "I'm sorry, I can't. Just as we wouldn't want to be made to do something. Even if you two both return to the mortal world, Imogen and Rav will still be alive, hunting you, regardless if you're human or not."

Alice scowled. "You just met my brother. It isn't as though he could fall in…" Her words trailed off as she stared up at Maddie, her eyes growing wide. "Do you *like* my brother?"

Maddie's heart kicked at her rib cage, screaming yes, that she liked Alice's brother very much. "He's a pain in the arse and asks too many questions."

"It's my fault for following Rav." Alice furrowed her brow. "I never should've left the club with him. I mean, how pathetic is that? All over trying to get my teeth filed into fangs."

It was a strange concept, as though she would've been dressed up for Halloween forever.

"You aren't the only one who followed Rav. And even then, you were under his influence to go down his rabbit hole or you wouldn't have gone."

Alice blew out a breath. "I never want to see a fake vampire movie, book, or club ever again."

"The clubs do sound rather terrible." Maddie chuckled, then turned serious. "Whatever you choose to do out in the world, you'll do fine, Alice. You'll discover yourself, just as I once did. As for your brother, let him decide. It's what I would do for my sister. When she wanted to turn, I didn't stop her. It was her choice in the end." But secretly, she'd been glad Mouse had chosen the path to immortality because Maddie wouldn't have to see her sister die. Yet if Noah stayed a vampire, he would have to watch Alice wither…

Alice stared at her bare toes before looking back up. "If he does stay, watch over him. He trusts with his heart too easily."

"I will." Maddie grasped Alice's shoulders, a rush of tedious guilt washing over her. "I truly am sorry for what I did. I shouldn't have tried to take you to Imogen."

"For Noah, I would've risked someone's life to save him too." Alice's eyelids flickered and she yawned. "I think I'll lie down for a little while." Hopefully soon, she wouldn't feel as drained once she regained her strength.

Maddie helped Alice to the mattress and covered her with the blanket. Alice's breaths came out even as she turned on her side. Keeping her feet light, Maddie closed the door behind her and found Ferris still on the floor sketching.

"You heard everything?" she asked.

Without looking up, he shrugged.

Unable to keep the smile from her face, Maddie knelt beside him. "So… Alice tried to kiss you?"

Ferris kept his head down, his pencil digging harder into the paper as he drew. "She's sweet but not my type."

Maddie leaned closer, catching a glimpse of his drawing. It was all done in pencil with perfect shading of a female's hand holding a caterpillar. "What made you decide to draw that?"

His body jerked and he shut the book. "Just something from when I was at the palace."

Maddie frowned and opened her mouth to speak when footsteps sounded behind her. She spun to find Noah entering, his hair wet, and him adjusting his hooded shirt.

It was time! "Ready?" Maddie asked, scooping up the hat box from the floor. "Alice just fell asleep."

Noah nodded. "I already said goodbye earlier and told her to stay safe."

Maddie grabbed the weapons that she'd gathered earlier, tucking them into different parts along her body. Scarves, to bind wrists together, went into the waist band of her skirt, a gun in a strap on her thigh, and daggers inside her boots. If she brought a backpack into the palace, Imogen would have Maddie's heart ripped out in a split second. Noah slipped a few knives into his boot and a gun, duct tape, and scarf into the waistband of his trousers.

Ferris stood with his back against the wall when Maddie spun to face him. "If I don't return—"

"Don't worry," he said. "I may have to break the world apart to get to her, but I'll do it."

Maddie grinned and patted his cheek. "That's the way to do it."

She then led Noah out into the night, the breeze blowing cold air against her flesh. Troops of bats flew above them, circling and creating their own kind of dance before darting north. A few werewolf howls tore through the darkness as they trekked farther from the outskirts of Scarlet and into the city.

"Don't worry, it's just the rogues out on the prowl tonight. You have your gun just in case." Maddie produced the floor plan that Ferris drew for the Ruby Heart Palace and shoved it into the back pocket of Noah's trousers. "When it's time, follow the path to my sister and look for pink hair and violet eyes." Once Mouse turned immortal, her chestnut strands had turned magenta, her brown eyes to violet, making her appear even more ethereal.

As she turned a corner, Noah grabbed Maddie by the elbow and hauled her to the back of a tall black building with scarlet windows. "Look"—he raked a hand through his blond locks—"I want to stay."

She figured he would want to remain by his sister's side, which was why she'd originally made an alternative to go to the palace by herself. "If you want to go back to Alice, then you should go."

"That's not what I mean." He sighed, pressing closer, his intoxicating scent enveloping her. "I want to stay in Wonderland after making sure Alice is safe."

Noah still needed time to think about it, but perhaps he'd

had enough time to do so in the safe house. "We'll talk about it once we get out." She grasped his hands and intertwined their fingers. "*If* we live, that is."

Noah drew her to his chest, brushing his lips against hers. "I should've kissed every inch of your body last night."

"Whose fault is that?" She laughed and tapped his nose as she pulled back.

He rolled his eyes.

"Come on. I'll keep that pretty heart of yours protected as best I can." Perspiration gathered in Maddie's arm sleeves as she held onto the hatbox. She kept her eyes peeled for Chess. The prince would be due back sometime today … once he figured out Ever wasn't where Maddie had said she would be. There'd been no sign of Rav slinking around either, and she prayed he was in the mortal world, per usual, at this time.

The palace loomed high in front of them as they approached its crimson glossy outer walls, its obsidian towers. Red roses filled the entire garden along with several gray gazebos stained in blood. Imogen would stick the hearts of those she felt deserved death on pikes inside the marble structures.

Maddie took the scarlet glass steps to the entrance and tapped the wooden door's anatomical heart iron knocker. A few moments later, Rine answered. She was one of the servants who Imogen had kept around for years. Most likely because she was ruthless like the queen.

"Ah," Rine said, her pale pink irises settling on Noah, "who is this?"

"My guest, Rine," Maddie sang. "We come bearing Imogen's gift."

The vampire clucked her tongue. "You were almost late. Go sit and wait." She spun on her heel and sauntered up the curving checkered staircase, her dark hair swishing behind her back.

Maddie motioned Noah to the plush black settee in the

middle of the room. She followed his gaze around the cozy area as they took a seat. Red and black checkered tile rested beneath their feet. Anatomical hearts were painted across the walls, and in between hung ornate roses. Always red roses or hearts. Maddie should've brought a bouquet of ivory roses to shove in Imogen's face.

Heels clicked against the marble steps and Maddie peered up as Imogen descended the stairs. Rine never followed, always stayed behind to do whatever it was she did. The queen's fiery curls flowed down to her waist, the hem of her black and blood-red silky gown trailing behind her. She was dressed fancier than when Maddie had seen her last. The queen always wore trousers when out in the city, but inside her home, she dressed extravagant, *dramatic*.

"What is this?" Imogen cooed when she crept closer to them. Her gaze locking on Noah, a wide smile playing across her ruby lips. "How do you like being immortal? Osanna told me the glorious details." She turned to Maddie. "Pity she has to find a replacement for Robin, though."

Anger coursed through Maddie, but she held it back as she went to stand.

"Stay seated," Imogen snapped, fishing out her deck of cards from inside her dress. Lazily, she ran her fingers across the deck, shuffling them. "Pick a color, Hatter. If you're wrong, I'll keep your lover here with your sister."

Maddie bit the inside of her cheek, knowing she needed to play along. *Don't get anxious, Maddie.* Fifty percent chance she would be right since there were only two colors in her deck. "Black," she sang.

Imogen drew out a card, moistening her lower lip with her tongue as she flashed a black five of spades. "It seems to be your lucky day." She stuffed the cards back into her dress and straightened. "But we'll see if your luck is still here next month. Now, first thing's first before we move on to other matters—show me my hat."

Maddie's heart pounded, *slammed*, against her rib cage as she handed Imogen the box. The queen's lithe fingers slowly unraveled the silky bow, peeling it away. And then she lifted the lid…

"What the fuck is this?" Bright crimson crept up Imogen's throat, her face, pure fury as she took out the hat.

Maddie tensed up, preparing to strike just as Noah was grabbing the tape out from his waist. She then jolted from the settee, barreling Imogen to the floor. Noah rushed beside her and slammed a piece of duct tape to the queen's mouth just as she was about to scream. Imogen bucked and wriggled but Maddie flipped the queen to her stomach. Maddie held Imogen's wrists behind her and pressed down on the queen's body. Noah took out the silk scarf from his waist and wrapped it around Imogen's wrists before tying it into tight knots.

"Go!" Maddie hissed once the queen's wrists were bound. "I'll take care of the rest." They didn't have any time to fiddle around. It would be better if they could both go and retrieve Mouse, but they couldn't drag Imogen down the hall with the guards and they couldn't leave her here alone. Besides that, even if she tossed her into a closet, Maddie would be recognizable without a disguise, and they would know she wasn't supposed to be there. However, Noah would blend in with the queen's newly-turned vampires. Maddie was also stronger and better equipped to fight Imogen.

Noah's throat bobbed as he stared at her, as though he wanted to say something, but then he nodded and took off down the hall.

Maddie drew out the silk cloth from her waist and tied Imogen's ankles together as she continued to buck and make strangled sounds. She didn't know how long the silk would hold, but she wouldn't have been able to sneak in chains or rope.

Gripping Imogen's upper arms, she tossed the queen into the chair across from the settee before taking a seat in front of her. With a satisfied grin, Maddie leaned back against the plush material of the settee and crossed her legs. She waved a hand in the air. "How about we discuss the different kinds of teas? Let's begin with Earl Grey, shall we?"

CHAPTER TWENTY-TWO

NOAH

Bloody fucking hell!

By some miracle, Noah and Maddie had just tied up the queen without getting their hearts ripped out. It felt as if the organ was going to pound out of his chest now though. He forced himself to walk slowly through the hallway to avoid drawing attention. Leaving Maddie alone with Imogen made him more than uncomfortable. Even tied up, the female was a threat due to her paranormal strength and the decades she'd had to hone it, but there was no other choice. He swallowed hard and flexed his sweaty hands. How had he gone from making coffee to breaking someone out of a dungeon?

The mission. He needed to focus on his whereabouts.

Ferris's map was detailed enough that, after going over it days earlier, Noah was able to easily recognize the turns he needed to take without bringing the folded paper out to check. He knew if anyone saw him standing around, examining a map, it would draw suspicion. The anatomical heart décor seemed to flow throughout every hallway with only slight differences. The material of the hearts hanging on the walls switched from metal wire to a variety of cog wheels to thread and nails. One smaller heart he found appeared to be made from real flesh, but he wasn't going to stop and examine it to be sure. S*ick bastards.*

His vision narrowed on a suit of armor with a black spade painted on its chest. There were two on the map, one with a spade and one with a diamond. Was it the spade where he was meant to turn left? He envisioned the map in his head, seeing the path Ferris had drawn, and he became sure it *was*, before rounding the corner. A dazed human with puncture wounds on her neck exited a room ahead and stumbled past him without looking up. His breath caught at the scent of fresh blood, but it smelled diluted, as if she barely had any left.

Shaking the thought away, he looked for the painting of dodo birds. It was large enough that the frame nearly touched the ceiling and floor. The artist had used heavy brush strokes to depict six of the feathered beasts seemingly dancing around a small fire. *Wait.* Noah sniffed. That wasn't paint … it was *blood*. He scowled and turned again. A few yards later, he went right at the stained-glass window of bloody red roses, down the stairs across from a velvet chaise tucked into an alcove, and through a hidden door behind a tapestry of a mortal woman on horseback.

The farther he went, the more his fear increased. Someone had surely noticed the queen was in danger, Maddie was in trouble, and soon they would be coming after him. But he had to save Mouse. That was what Maddie wanted and he owed her for helping save Alice—he couldn't slip up and get himself caught beforehand. He'd already passed by a few servants. Thankfully none had given him a second glance.

He slowed his steps, listening intently for guards. Ferris had told him one or two always lurked in the dungeons, but

Mouse was kept away from the other prisoners. Her constant ramblings apparently made the guards stay far from her door. They would pass by once in the morning and again in the evening with blood bags. He and Maddie had timed the escape to avoid both. It didn't mean he wouldn't run into anyone on the way.

Creeping from the dark tunnel, he lifted the edge of a tapestry showing the image of a moonlit lake and entered the path behind it. Noah hurried to the left to find a hallway full of metal doors. Each had a metal slat near the top with iron mesh covering it and a locked slat halfway down which, he assumed, was how they passed blood to the captives. His heart hammered in his chest as he looked inside the first door. *Completely empty.*

Noah shook his head, ignoring the urge to open the door to make sure no one was there. Curiosity would get him killed. It didn't matter who was inside these cells—only the one Ferris specified on the map. He kept his steps light and moved as quickly down the hallways as he dared. The scent of piss, stale blood, and death permeated the air, so he kept his breaths shallow—not an easy thing to do when his adrenaline was soaring through his entire body.

"Did you see the new servant Rav brought in yesterday?" a distant male asked.

"Which?" replied a feminine voice.

The male laughed, the soft pad of their boots coming closer. *Damn.* Noah needed to get the hell out of sight, but the only place to take shelter here was an unlocked cell. *Fuck...* Without any other choice, he slipped into the nearest one, shutting the door with barely a *click.*

"He'll present her to the queen later today if you want to take a look. Luke is keeping an eye on her in the south wing," the male said.

Noah held his breath and plastered himself to the wall as the duo's footfalls brought them near his door. They continued speaking but he couldn't make out the words over the fear humming through him. Once they continued past the cell he was hiding in, he waited until their voices were too far to be heard before slipping back into the hall.

His hands shook slightly as he took the map from his back pocket and doubled checked his route. This was too important a mission to fail—Mouse's life was in his hands. With a steadying breath, he continued through the dungeon. A right, a left, straight, then another right. This hallway was different than the others. The walls were seamless black stone for at least three meters with a single door straight ahead. Soft, gentle singing carried through it.

Mouse. It had to be, judging by the door the sound came from.

He rushed forward and wasted no time pressing his face to the mesh, his gaze landing on a female with a long, pink plait. Mouse sat crossed-legged in the center of a thin mattress, the worn skirt of her black dress stretched tight over her knees. On the taut fabric, a bright blue and yellow caterpillar swayed side-to-side with her song.

"Hello," she said, ending the song abruptly, her violet gaze flicking up to meet his. The resemblance to Maddie was uncanny. "You're new."

Noah smiled. *He'd found her.* "Your sister sent me." He moved back and examined the door for the handle. Three large bolts slid through metal bars and into another set attached to the walls on either side. All he had to do was slide them the opposite way.

"Maddie sent you?" she asked, her chin tilted up as she glared at him. "Where is Ferris?"

There would be time for questions later. He quickly shoved each bolt free, leaving him with only a lock to pick. He pulled out the paperclip Ferris had given him while they'd planned this and got to work.

"He's waiting for us," Noah answered. The lock clicked

and he released a breath. He stood and wrenched the door open just as Mouse screamed, "Wait!"

But it was too late—it was wide open.

"Oh, bollocks," Mouse said with a wince. Then, to the caterpillar sitting in her palm. "He's really done it now, hasn't he, Des?"

Noah's brows rose. "Done what?"

"Triggered the silent alarm," she said as if it were obvious. She raced to the flat mattress on the floor and yanked out a stack of papers tied together with twine. Noah easily recognized the artwork as Ferris's after staring at the map for days. "They installed them only last week after Ferris helped a girl escape."

"Fuck!" He leaned into the room and grabbed Mouse's hand.

She ripped herself free. "How do I know I can trust you?"

Maybe because he was breaking her out of prison? He pulled the map out and unfolded it for her to see. "Ferris really sent me. Now, we have to *run*."

Mouse offered no resistance after that as he took her hand and they bolted back the way he'd come, taking the same staircase up two flights. The secret escape Ferris had told them about was nearby—only one turn away after they emerged from the tapestry depicting the mortal woman. He'd been hoping they wouldn't need it—the ten-meter drop into a garden of thorny rose bushes didn't sound like a pleasant experience. He'd take it over death though.

"Come on," he urged, practically dragging Mouse around the corner when she stumbled.

Mouse glared at him suspiciously and repeated, "Where's Ferris?"

Before he could answer, shouts and racing footsteps echoed behind them. The guards would catch up in no time at this rate, but Mouse was gasping for breath. He spun and scooped her up, her body nearly weightless in his arms, before doubling his speed. The steel, industrial refrigerators looked exactly like the ones Ferris drew with double doors and padlocks. Behind the third one rested the tunnel they needed.

Quickly setting Mouse down, he yanked the refrigerator away from the wall, but it was stuck on something. "Shit," he hissed, giving it a hard yank. It didn't budge. He scanned the machine and an idea formed. "Climb over," he told Mouse, cupping his hands in front of him, knowing she was too short to reach without a boost. "There's a tunnel on the other side."

"How are they running these without electricity?" she mused. "The guards mentioned generators—is that true? It seems like a lot of energy to run these."

"Seriously? *Now?*" He couldn't give two fucks about how the refrigerators worked in this place. The boots were close enough that the guards were probably at Mouse's cell now. His heart pounded painfully against his sternum.

Mouse set her foot in his hands and leapt up, then slid behind the steel machine. Noah followed, but the space wasn't wide enough for him, trapping him between the coils of the refrigerator and the wall. *No!* Mouse's hands wrapped around his ankle and pulled hard.

He felt his ribs crack from the pressure, but there wasn't time to completely register the pain before gravity took hold. He slid down a tunnel at an alarming speed.

Mouse squealed in fear as the faint moonlight glowed at the end. Stomach in his throat, Noah closed his eyes and hoped he wouldn't land on top of Mouse, crushing her. He could only tell they'd exited the tunnel from the distinct lack of stone digging into his back. Wind whistled in his ears as he dropped.

And dropped.

And dropped.

A *thunk* sounded—what he assumed was Mouse hitting the ground—only seconds before his hip smacked into something solid. It sent him careening sideways and his eyes flew open to find a blur of red roses. "Fuck!" He brought his arm up just in time to shield his face from the thorns as he slammed into the bushes.

He sucked in one breath. Two.

"Hey," Mouse whispered, hugging the stack of artwork to her chest. "Are you conscious?"

"Unfortunately," he grumbled as blood trailed down his arm from a deep cut.

His entire body hummed with shock, and he felt dull pain that he was positive wouldn't remain that way once he calmed the fuck down. He shoved himself up, ignoring the bleeding scratches and throbbing in his hip. Glancing over his shoulder, he took in the palace. Red light flickered over the glossy stone walls as figures inside moved past windows. Maddie was still in there…

"We can't stay," Mouse said, clutching the caterpillar gently in her hand. "Take me to Maddie and Ferris."

She was right—they couldn't stay. Every second they wasted made their capture more likely, but … *Maddie.* He shook his head. They had to leave her. That was always the plan—to escape and she would catch up to them. He had to trust in Maddie's own strength and do his part.

He tightened his jaw and nodded. Telling her Maddie was in the castle might make her run back in, and he couldn't risk it. "Come on then."

CHAPTER TWENTY-THREE

MADDIE

Ginger? Mint? Hibiscus? Maddie mulled the different teas over in her head before settling on chamomile. "Back in London, this was my favorite tea. Even now, I'll put a hint of it in the blood I'm drinking while creating a hat. It enhances the flavor. Silkier. Sweeter." She paused and smiled, staring into Imogen's raging yellow eyes. "You should try it sometime."

The queen jerked out of her chair and lunged for Maddie. She easily grasped Imogen by the shoulders, then pushed her back down into her seat.

"Tut, tut," Maddie sang in a hushed voice. "Do that again, and I may have to take you outside."

A hard kick came to Maddie's stomach and she gasped. Her gaze fell to the queen's freed ankles, the bindings torn and resting on the checkered floor. Imogen rammed her leg forward again, but Maddie stepped around the chair, holding the queen's shoulders firmly against the velvet back.

"A pity," Maddie said, observing the shredded cloth on the floor. "But alas, make another move, and I'll rip your head off after stabbing you in the throat and heart. Understand?" She released Imogen and drew out two switchblade knives from her boot, then shifted back in front of the queen.

Imogen narrowed her eyes but didn't lift from her seat again. Even though Maddie's heart pounded ferociously, she held her casual expression as she set her switchblades on the settee beside her. There wasn't much time left until she needed to go back to the safe house. She'd told Noah she would give him fifteen minutes to retrieve Mouse, then she would meet him there. And if he wasn't there, then she would return to the palace. But she wouldn't make it far, not with Imogen still alive, knowing what Maddie had done to her. If Maddie killed her though, it would only make matters worse. She would be hunted harder, and if Mouse was free, her sister and Noah would be as well.

Maddie was about to move on to discuss the dainty flavor of lavender tea when loud stomping stormed down the stairs. She glanced up, stilling as she saw Rine's hair swishing around her face, the female's lips curled into a snarl.

"The alarm, my queen," Rine shouted to the back of Imogen's chair. "Mouse has escaped."

Noah did it. Maddie couldn't contain a grin. He'd gotten her sister out. Relief didn't wash over her yet though—she was unsure if they were out of the palace and safe.

Maddie grabbed a switchblade from beside her and stood, preparing herself.

"What is this?" Rine's eyes widened as she stepped farther into the room. Her gaze focused on Imogen, her duct-taped lips, her bound hands. Vicious sounds emanated from the queen's throat, her words trapped inside her mouth.

Before Rine could attack or free the queen, Maddie hurled herself at the female and thrust the switchblade into her chest, a squishing sound emanating. Maddie grasped the female's head and twisted hard to the left, tearing it from her body, the crack of her spine filling the room. Rine's body thumped to the floor, bright crimson pouring out from the gaping hole and pooling near Maddie's feet. She took a step back, making sure to not get blood on the bottom of her boots—she didn't want to leave a trail behind. As she dropped the head beside the body, more blood splattered the floor.

"If only this could've been done without getting messy." Maddie shrugged and spun to face Imogen with a grin. "Now, I must apologize about Rine, even though she always was a nasty little thing, but I do have to go. Our time is up. Ta-ta."

As Maddie's eyes shifted to the settee to collect her other knife, she froze. It was *gone*.

The tear of fabric came and in a split second, Imogen was standing, her hands free, the tape off her mouth. *Idiot, Maddie.* If Rine hadn't distracted her…

"You shouldn't have done that, you crazy bitch," Imogen seethed. "I'm taking you to the dungeons where you will wait and watch as I kill Mouse, then I will bite the flesh from your bones, piece by piece. You'll suffer for a long, *long* time before I rip your heart out, Hatter."

Well, that didn't sound pleasant in the least.

"Not today," Maddie said, waving her hand in the air. She lunged for the first object she could find, grasping a metal vase from a shelf on the wall, just as Imogen came forward. The queen growled, her fangs sliding out, and knocked the vase from Maddie's hand.

With a grunt, Maddie whirled to the side and caught the object just as it was about to crash to the floor. She didn't need the loud sound reverberating. As Imogen swiped again, Maddie struck the queen's hand with the heavy metal.

"Now now, we were having a much more relaxing time discussing teas." Maddie darted around the chair and tossed the vase in its seat. All she needed to do was get to the front door, but Imogen blocked it. She patted her dress for a weapon—the gun would be quick but too loud.

"Hatter, I've played enough games over the years and I always win." Imogen hurled the switchblade forward and a sharp pain pierced Maddie's shoulder.

Maddie held back a scream as she yanked the blade out. She ground her teeth together against the pain while hot blood oozed from the wound. But it would heal quickly, and she didn't have time to waste. Imogen shot toward her and Maddie dove for the other side of the room. Spinning around, Maddie hurled her knife forward and it lodged in Imogen's chest, but the queen didn't falter.

"Bloody hell," Maddie hissed, her fangs dropping. She'd missed the heart.

Imogen ripped the blade out and tossed it back, this time striking Maddie's other shoulder. She clenched her teeth at the deep ache.

"Thank you for giving it back." Maddie grinned, staring at the door. If she played this game a little longer, she could eventually draw closer to the exit.

"I've had enough! Guards!" Imogen yelled.

Oh no. This will not do.

"Just wait until you watch what I do with your sister," Imogen purred, her lips pulling into a cruel smile.

Anger coursed through Maddie, and she launched the knife forward, driving it into the queen's heart. Imogen's eyes rolled back, and she lurched to the side. Maddie felt fulfilled as she watched the evil shrew try in vain to suck in a breath. This was for Mouse. The queen swayed and crumpled to the floor.

Maddie stared at the door—this was her chance, her escape. Only Rine had seen Maddie thus far. A thought spun in her head, something dark, yet a necessity that would make this a bit easier for everyone. She didn't know if she could be quick enough before the guards got there, but she had to try. Maddie jolted forward to Imogen's still body and thrust her hand into the queen's chest, shattering her rib cage. She clenched Imogen's bastard heart and yanked it out, crimson splattering the floor.

Maddie's hand shook as she held the bloody organ, squeezing it. She liked the feel of the wet heart, one that had brought so much torment to her and her sister, in her hand.

The distant clomp of boots reminded her of where she was, what she'd just *done*. Now that she'd killed the queen, she knew she'd truly made a mess of things. A servant dead was one thing, but Rav and Chess were still alive. Rav might not know Maddie was responsible for her death, but Chess would.

Imogen being dead wouldn't make things easier—it would make them *worse*.

Footsteps drew closer, and she looked at the door, which was directly across from the hallway. *Hide.* Her gaze fell to the large statue of the queen from a chess board in the corner. She collected both her switchblades from the two bodies, along with the hat and box she'd brought, then rushed to the statue with light steps and ducked behind it.

"What are you yelling about now, Mother?" Chess said, his tone bored. He lazily strolled in with his vest unbuttoned while rolling his eyes at the ceiling. His gaze dropped to his mother's body, and he came to an abrupt stop. Maddie's heart slammed so much she feared it would burst, and her hands trembled as the prince studied Imogen's torn-open chest, her empty gaze. Chess's arms dropped to his sides, tears streaming down his face, as he stared at Imogen for what seemed an eternity, as if he was waiting for her to stir.

"Mother!" he finally shouted and fell to her side, scooping her dead body in his arms. Blood smeared his bare chest as he held Imogen close.

Maddie covered her mouth with her shaking, bloody hands. Did he love her? Imogen was his mother, but she didn't think Chess was capable of love. Then again, Imogen had loved Rav and possibly Chess as well.

Glancing toward the door, Maddie didn't know if she would get the chance to escape. Just as Chess lifted his mother's bloody heart with his free hand, boots pounded down the hallway.

"Imogen, Mouse escaped!" Rav screamed. He stopped in his tracks as he rounded the corner of the hallway in front of the stairs. *Damn it, they're both here.* His breathing hitched as he studied Chess holding Imogen. "What the fuck have you done?"

Chess's face paled and he opened his mouth, but no words escaped.

"You killed her!" Rav roared.

Maddie sucked in a sharp breath.

"No, I didn't," Chess stuttered. She'd never heard him sound so weak, so small. But she couldn't feel sorry for him, not after he'd tried to kill Ever. Not when he'd threatened to hurt Mouse. Yet still…

Three guards rushed in from the hallway and halted.

"Seize him," Rav growled. "He killed the queen."

The guards glanced at each other for a moment, then two came forward and grabbed Chess by his arms while the other gently returned Imogen's body to the floor.

Chess didn't fight back, only whispered, "I didn't do it."

"Then, who did?" Rav took a step forward, his fangs down, eyes wild.

Chess licked his lips, his eyes narrowing as he seemed to piece something together. "I don't know. But you have no purpose here now. Go back to Ivory, and I'll handle my mother's death."

"The murder of the queen does not make you king, regardless if you're the heir. You're now a traitor. I will come to you in the dungeon soon enough."

Chess didn't say another word as the guards hauled him out of the room and down the hall.

Why was Chess protecting Maddie? Then she realized he

wasn't protecting her. He was making sure he was the only one who knew she was a traitor. If Chess ever found her, he would kill her.

Rav peered down at his dead wife, then fell to his knees beside her with a sob. "I know he's your son, and I know you wouldn't want me to kill him. But for this, he has to die." He ran his hand over her hair and pressed his lips to Imogen's.

He then stood and grabbed a heart vase from a shelf on the wall and threw it against the floor, shattering it to pieces. Maddie clenched her jaw, remembering everything he'd done, not just to her but so many innocents, turning them without their consent.

She remembered what he and Imogen had both done.

Rav's cheeks reddened as he ripped paintings from the wall, snapping them in half and throwing them across the room. He drew closer and closer to Maddie. She quietly fished out her gun, knowing she wouldn't miss his heart, even though the entire castle would hear the fateful shot.

As he stepped in front of the chess piece statue, one of the guards from earlier crashed into the room. "My king, the prince has escaped."

Rav whirled around. Maddie couldn't see his face, but she could hear every vicious word in his voice. "What kind of guards are you if everyone keeps escaping? First, the girl and Knave, then Mouse. Now you allowed Chess to murder Imogen before fleeing himself!" Rav shot forward and buried his teeth in the guard's throat, shredding it until the spinal cord split in half.

Dropping the guard, Rav straightened and wiped the blood from his lips and chin as he looked at his queen. "I suppose everyone will have to die since we can trust no one."

Maddie swallowed deeply while Rav stormed down the hall, seeming to prepare himself for a killing spree. Screams echoed, loud and shrill, and faded. This was it. Her opportunity. She dashed for the door and peered down the hallway where Rav had left. Bloodied bodies littered the area—crimson stained the walls. Slowly opening the door, she slipped out into the cool breeze and ran out into the night.

Maddie hoped Noah had made it home with Mouse because if Chess escaped the palace already, she didn't know what he would do next. But as she ran through the rose gardens, passing the marble gazebos, and entered the outskirts of the city, she didn't see a sign of Chess anywhere.

Still, she had a sinking feeling that the prince was somewhere out there lurking, watching her.

CHAPTER TWENTY-FOUR

NOAH

In all his life, Noah never thought he would slide out of a palace tunnel and land in a damn rose bush. All that lingered of his wounds now were dried blood and a dull ache in his hip. His heart hadn't stopped racing since he and Mouse had run from the queen's gardens. He was sure guards would catch up to them at any moment, yet no one chased them through the streets of Scarlet. Someone had to have seen them running from the garden...

Noah rapped on the door using the rhythm Maddie had taught him. It immediately swung open as if Ferris had been standing there with his hand on the knob. *Thank fuck.*

Shoving Mouse over the threshold, straight into Ferris's chest, he slipped inside behind her and slammed the door shut. They were either safe or they had led the enemy to their doorstep. He slunk along the wall, tuning into his vampire hearing to see if he could pick up on anything suspicious outside. The only thing audible was muffled chatter and laughter.

"Ferris!" Mouse shouted. Noah turned around just in time to watch her leap into his arms.

For the first time since he met the vampire, Ferris's face softened into a smile as he caught her. "Good to see you again, luv."

"You did it," Alice said, rushing from her room, straight for Noah. He stepped forward and pulled her to him. "I was so worried."

"I told you I'd be fine." And he'd never been more relieved to be right. When he'd told her that lie, he wasn't sure of anything at all. Neither he nor Maddie had voiced it, but he knew she felt the same. He stepped away from Alice and looked around the safe house. The most important person was missing. "Maddie…?"

"She's not back yet," Ferris answered in a low voice.

Her part had been easier than his. Keep an eye on the queen—that was all she'd had to do after they tied her up. Unless the alarm he'd set off while rescuing Mouse had blared through the entire palace, sending guards to warn Imogen. He swallowed hard. Maddie wasn't back yet. She wasn't fucking *back*. He couldn't wait another minute. Mouse and Alice were safe. He had to go back, had to—

Someone pounded on the door, making him jerk Alice behind him for protection. It took a moment to recognize the secret knock. Ferris must've realized it sooner than Noah did, because he cracked the door enough to let a body slip through. *Maddie*. A weight lifted from his chest to see her alive and in one piece, despite her rumpled clothes and mussed hair. Then he noticed something that made his breath catch when she dropped the hat box on the floor. *Blood*. Slick crimson covered the tips of her fingers all the way up to her elbows, saturating the arm warmers. More splotches were on her face. "What—"

"Maddie!" Mouse cried and brushed past Noah to get to

her sister. Maddie flung her arms out wide to welcome Mouse into her embrace.

Noah dragged in a harsh breath. He didn't want to ruin their long-awaited reunion, but he needed to ask. "What happened? Are you hurt?"

Maddie looked up at him from over Mouse's shoulder. Her expression was tight as she shook her head. "It's not mine."

"It smells like the queen," Mouse whispered.

"What did you do?" Ferris asked in a serious voice that made Noah's heart beat even faster. Why would the thought of Imogen bleeding put Ferris so on edge?

"She's dead." Maddie eased away from Mouse and took her hand, leading her sister to sit on the settee. "I don't know what happened precisely. I planned on leaving her knocked out but then something came over me."

Ferris ran a hand down his face. "What did you do with the body?"

"Oh, they know she's dead," Maddie clarified. "They just don't know I did it."

Noah's brows rose. He and Maddie were the last two to be alone with Imogen. It didn't take a genius to put the pieces together. "Who do they think murdered her then?"

"Don't worry, Noah, I killed Rine first, so you're in the clear." Maddie held her stained hands up in surrender. "Chess *may* know it was me, but Rav and everyone else think that the prince is the culprit." She bit her lip. "Chess escaped but I'm confident he didn't follow me."

"We're all safe at the moment," Mouse piped up. She shuffled closer to Maddie on the sofa. "That's the most important thing right now. That we're safe and together."

Alice slipped her hand into Noah's and squeezed. "She's right."

Mouse took a long inhale of the air, her eyes fluttering, her canines lowering. Her gaze landed on Alice and the tip of her tongue darted from between her lips, licking as if she were hungry. "She's mortal again?"

"Yes," Noah replied, shifting to partially hide Alice behind him. "She's my sister."

"I'll get us all something to drink," Ferris announced, his worried stare still trained on Mouse.

Noah protectively inched backward into his sister, remembering all too clearly how Alice had lost control of herself and attacked him in this very room. Given how long Mouse had been in captivity and knowing what he did of Imogen, she was likely starving for fresh blood instead of bagged. He turned to Alice and ushered her toward the bedroom. "Why don't we let them have some time alone? They haven't seen each other in two years."

Alice appeared to take the hint and went straight into the other room. "We should probably talk about going home now," she said the moment the door was shut.

"She won't bite you," Noah assured her. "No one will let her."

Alice scowled. "I trust you, but I can't stay here. I just … I really want to go home."

Noah flopped onto the mattress and sighed. He knew she wanted to go home and that it needed to happen as soon as possible, but not tonight. Now that the adrenaline was beginning to wear off, the ache in his hip throbbed. It was probably shattered, or at the very least, cracked. He was sure it would heal like everything else, but until it did, he just wanted to lay down. The exhaustion hit him like a truck.

"Tomorrow," he promised her. "I need a little rest now."

Alice mumbled something to herself and plopped down beside him. "Don't fall asleep until you drink some blood, okay? It will make you feel better."

"I feel fine," he lied. Alice smelled *mortal* and his gums tingled, fangs threatening to descend. But he would *not* bite her—even if his instinct for blood told him to. So he would drink whatever Ferris brought to ensure Alice's safety, then he would sleep with one eye trained on the door.

"You were limping." She lightly smacked his arm. "Don't argue with me."

Noah smirked. "I wouldn't dream of it."

When Noah opened the bedroom door the next evening, he found Maddie nervously weaving a needle and thread into some sort of cloth. Mouse's head was in her lap as she slept, but it looked as if Maddie hadn't gotten an ounce of rest. He'd meant to have a chat with her after finishing the blood Ferris had brought him, but he'd fallen asleep as Alice listed out options for returning to London. Or *outside* of London, since they couldn't risk Rav finding her again.

"Give me a minute?" he asked over his shoulder to Alice.

"Sure," she whispered, shutting the door at his back.

Maddie silently slipped out from beneath Mouse's head and nodded toward the other side of the room. Ferris had taken the second bedroom, and they couldn't ask Alice to wait near Mouse, so it was as private as they could get. Noah followed her into the corner and cast a glance back at Mouse to make sure she was still asleep before turning fully to Maddie.

"Are you okay?" he asked, brushing the stray hairs from her face. Flecks of blood had dried in a few places.

She wrapped her arms around his waist, burying her face in his chest. "Thank you."

Noah hugged her back, soaking in the feel of her against him, and placed a kiss on top of her head. Warmth stirred inside him at her sweet scent, and he tightened his arms slightly. "For what?"

"You got Mouse out." She pulled back and looked up at

him with a bright smile. "She's safe now because of you."

"Not because of me. Because of *us*. You, me, and Ferris." Noah may have physically broken Mouse out, but he never could've done it alone.

"It feels a bit like a dream to be with her again after all this time."

He could only imagine. But, he supposed, he wouldn't have to wonder for long. Once Alice was back in the mortal world, there wouldn't be a day that went by where Noah wouldn't wonder if Rav had found his sister. Still, Alice was smart and he liked to believe that she would make sure to cover her tracks.

Maddie's smile faltered as she peered at him, seeming to notice something in his expression. "Are you taking Alice home now?"

"We thought it best to get it over with." Before anyone figured out it was Maddie who killed Imogen and came looking for her on the streets. One of the guards could recognize Noah from when he had wandered the halls looking for Mouse. Or worse—Chess.

Maddie's gaze fell as she stepped back, nodding. "You're probably right."

Noah tilted his head, studying the way she bit her lip as if she were fighting with herself not to speak. "I'm coming back," he told her. "I know we haven't gotten the chance to hash everything out, but I want to be here."

"Why? It could potentially mean a life in hiding."

It would also mean a life with *her*. He tilted her chin up with the tips of his fingers so she met his eyes. "I think it would be nice to stick around and get to know you a bit more. Besides, we won't have to hide forever."

She scowled. "We could literally be doing just that … *forever*."

"No," he said with conviction. "At some point, we would have to fight back, but I want to do that with you too."

"Fine, immortal, fine." Maddie grinned and stretched up to kiss him, her lips pressing against his. Noah tugged her closer so their bodies melded, her heat warming him. A primal part of him didn't want to give her up, even though he hadn't known her long. But did it fucking matter? She was different. The world here felt more like home, the immortal body he was in now felt more like his than it ever had before. He wanted to learn everything about this place. And to see Maddie's smile and determination when she created the hats she loved so much, to know what new things they could do with their mouths, their bodies. They fit together too perfectly and he wanted *more*. He slipped his tongue between her lips, reveling in her sweet taste.

Someone cleared their throat and Noah groaned as he pulled away. Mouse sat on the settee, rubbing her eye. "Maddie, I think you left a few things out last night," she said with a sleepy grin. "You said he was a friend."

"He *is* a friend. And maybe a few more things," she admitted as Ferris joined them. "Noah's taking Alice back tonight."

Ferris nodded. "We should get out of Scarlet too."

"Hang on." Noah wasn't sure what the vampire thought of him exactly, but Ferris needed to hear he wasn't planning on abandoning Maddie from his own lips. "I'm coming back. Don't leave until I do. I'll only be gone a few hours."

Ferris looked between Maddie and Mouse and gave a shrug. "That'll give us time to pack all of our essentials, but we can't wait longer than that."

"We'll wait for you," Maddie told him, casting Ferris a hard stare. "You'll be less noticeable if I stay here, and I don't want to leave Mouse alone just yet."

"Stay. It will be faster this way, anyway." He took a deep, fortifying breath and glanced at his sister. "Alice, it's time to go."

The door opened and his sister poked her head out, her

gaze landing immediately on Mouse. When the pink-haired vampire didn't move to attack, Alice stepped into the room. Ferris held his hand out to her and they exchanged their final goodbyes.

"Is there anything you need me to bring back?" Noah asked Maddie.

"Just yourself." She leaned forward and pressed her warm lips to his once more, then flicked her hand in the air and gave Alice a curtsy. Noah arched a brow as Maddie sang, "Stay safe." It was a very Maddie goodbye, but one that made him want to come back even more.

"You too," Alice said. She studied Noah and nodded toward the door in a silent plea to leave.

"All right then." He took his sister's hand and headed for the door. On one hand, he was eager to get Alice back to the mortal world where she was safer, but on the other, he hated to leave her. "We won't be long."

Their flat in London had been ransacked. Tables were toppled and sofas torn to shreds. The stuffing littered the floor along with glass from shattered photos. Noah took note of the broken frame that once sat on the mantle, displaying the family photo Chess had somehow taken from Rav. The entire contents of the kitchen cupboards were scattered about and the mattresses in the bedrooms had been flipped.

"What a mess," Alice muttered, nose wrinkled as she stepped over a piece of her broken bedframe.

Noah grunted in agreement. There wasn't anything he truly cared about that had been destroyed—it was just … stuff to him. Things his parents had bought because of how the objects looked, not because there was any attachment or because it was comfortable. In fact, the sofa was like sitting on stone, but it was more the audacity Imogen and Rav had to destroy everything because his sister escaped them. And that they so easily found where his sister lived since Rav had taken Alice's purse. *Arseholes.*

Alice would have to break the news about the flat to their parents—perhaps it could be part of why she needed to leave London. Someone broke in and scared the living shit out of her, she fled before getting hurt, and ... something. Alice would be the one to maintain the lie, so he would leave the details up to her. As for his absence, he was granted a last-minute opportunity to study abroad. Sure, his parents would be pissed he didn't inform them and that he left Alice alone, resulting in her being endangered by the robbery, but what could they do? Ground him? Cut off his allowance? He was twenty-two years old for fuck's sake.

"Only grab what you need," Noah said. Their parents would make sure she had a new wardrobe and whatever else, so she wouldn't truly need anything. But that didn't make up for the things she loved that were ruined.

The hair on the back of Noah's neck suddenly stood on end. He tensed, sensing someone behind him. Tuning into all his heightened senses, he took in their nearly weightless footfalls and the lingering hint of metallic in the air. Not a concerned neighbor checking on them then. He moved to the console table in the hallway and made a show of pretending to look for something while he curled his fingers around the silver letter opener.

A floorboard creaked just behind him, and Noah whirled around, grabbing the vampire by the front of his black hoodie. The male was young—at least he had been when he'd been turned—with a gap between his teeth. But the only thing that mattered were the fangs. Noah shoved the letter opener into the side of his neck and ripped it out before the male could make a sound. Hot blood splattered across his face and the wall.

Noah carefully dragged the vampire into one of the spare rooms and laid him down so as not to alert Alice with a loud thump. *Fuck.* Rav must've had the place under surveillance. He grabbed the vampire's head and set a foot on his chest, holding him in place, then easily ripped the head the rest of the way from his body. They didn't need him recovering and telling Rav that Alice had come back. He'd simply have to return and deal with the body after sending her off.

He quickly left the space, shutting the door to hide the vampire, and climbed through his disaster of a bedroom. After sparing a moment to switch out of Ferris's bloody outfit, he yanked some of his favorite shirts off their hangers, stuffing them into a bookbag, along with other necessities.

"I'll need to buy a new phone," Alice said from his doorway. Noah flicked a quick glance in the mirror to make sure he didn't have any blood left on his face. It was clean. "Mine was in my purse so Rav probably still has it."

Noah nodded. He wasn't keen on the idea of her traveling alone, especially at night, and definitely not without a phone. His old one was somewhere at Maddie's cottage. "Grab one as soon as you can, yeah? We'll get you settled in a hotel tonight, and you can head out in the morning."

She hoisted an oversized bag over her shoulder and sighed. "All my credit cards and money were in my purse too."

"No worries." He tossed her a pair of his folded socks.

"What's this?"

"My emergency fund." He'd been saving up for his own flat so he could live independently from his parents' money, but he wouldn't need it now. Not in Wonderland.

Alice unrolled the socks to find a neatly rolled stack of bills. "Bloody hell, Noah."

"I figured I might need to bail you out one day. Thought it would be from jail, but hey…" He laughed. "Come on then.

There's a place a few blocks over."

Alice shoved the socks into her bag and followed Noah from the flat. "Will I see you again?" she asked when they hit the sidewalk.

Noah put his arm around her shoulders. "Of course you will. There are plenty of portals and it's not as if I'd miss the holidays. I'll just be there a bit later to avoid, you know, burning to death."

"But you'll be fugitives."

"True." Noah sobered. That part would definitely be shitty, but it wouldn't be forever. They would make their stand against Rav eventually, and Chess too when he resurfaced. "I might miss a few holidays, but don't worry, sis. After all I did to save you, I'm not about to vanish from your life."

Alice thought for a moment, a line forming between her brows, before she relaxed under his arm. "That's true, I suppose. But Noah, I'm really sorry about ... everything."

"Sorry?" He smiled. "Don't be sorry. I wouldn't have met Maddie if it wasn't for you, and I actually *like* being a vampire."

Alice uncomfortably shifted on her feet. Noah could tell she still felt both guilty and grateful by the way she studied him, but he didn't want that. He wanted her to heal and live her life, knowing he was living his.

"Just don't come looking for me," he warned, his tone joking, though he was serious.

Alice chuckled, the sound thick with unshed tears. "I don't think you need to worry about *that*."

Noah laughed with her to distract himself from the mounting pressure behind his own eyes, but then he winced at the thought of anyone else searching for him. "Don't let Mum and Dad worry about me. Maybe buy a second phone since I lost mine and text them as me once in a while."

"I can do that," she whispered.

Noah caught the scent of the blood flowing in her veins

again. He held his breath for a moment, pushing down his urge to feed. "Good. Then you'll need to remember a few important things to make it look real. What was I going to uni for?" he quizzed.

Alice jabbed him playfully in the side with her elbow before answering correctly. Noah asked her several more important questions, sprinkling in a few smaller things to keep up appearances.

"When in doubt, be vague or ignore them. It's what I would do," he suggested as they reached the front of the hotel. "I'll walk you in."

"No." Alice sighed. "I'm not the best at goodbyes, so let's say them now."

Noah swallowed hard. "Are you sure you'll be okay?"

"Positive." She gave him a strained smile, her eyes filling with tears. "Thank you for saving me."

Noah sighed, wrapping her in a fierce hug. "What are big brothers for?"

"I mean it," she said into his shirt. "Thank you."

"You're welcome." The words came out tight around a lump in his throat. He didn't want her to see him cry, but *damn* if it wasn't hard to hold back. Even if he would see her again, he didn't know how long it would be or if she would be safe until then. "I love you, sis."

"I love you, too." Alice pulled back and adjusted the bag on her shoulder. "Go on then. Keep yourself safe."

"I will." He nodded at the hotel. "But I'm not leaving until you get inside."

Alice rolled her eyes, tears slipping from the corners, and turned away from him. "See you soon."

"See you," he called as she entered the brightly-lit lobby, hoping *soon* would be the truth. But, for the time being, he had to figure out how to clean blood out of carpet and dump a body in the Thames without being seen.

CHAPTER TWENTY-FIVE

MADDIE

"We can't wait forever," Ferris said as he zipped up his bag.

Maddie shot him a glare. "It's been less than twenty-four hours."

"It's been precisely twelve hours," Mouse pointed out, her pink plait falling across her clean lacy black dress. The gown she'd arrived in hadn't even been fit for a rat. The gothic frock she now wore fell between her knees and ankles—it was her usual dark and brooding style.

Her sister had been quiet most of the time since she'd been back, except for when she would hum to herself. She'd never sang before being captured, but she must've had to entertain herself somehow.

"He's taking his sweet time." Ferris walked out of the room and Maddie rolled her eyes at his back. He wasn't usually this impatient, but she knew he wanted to get Mouse farther away from Scarlet as much as Maddie did.

Mouse hummed while fishing something out of her front pocket. Something that wiggled, curled. Maddie squinted at the blue and yellow thing in her sister's palm. A caterpillar. What in all of Wonderland? It slowly crawled along the center of Mouse's hand.

"Why do you have that?" Maddie arched a brow, watching as the caterpillar stood on its hind legs, seeming to sway to Mouse's song.

Mouse let out a breath but didn't take her gaze from the small creature. "She's my friend and kept me company while at the palace. Her name is Desdemona, but I call her Des."

Maddie's lips tilted at the edges. Her sister always did love a good Shakespeare piece. There wasn't a single one she could recall that her sister hated. "Othello is still your favorite play, I take it?"

"It is." Mouse watched the caterpillar, her expression unreadable. Maddie waited for a smile to cross her sister's face like it always had, but there was nothing. Only a solemn look that Maddie wanted to wipe away and see her laugh instead. As she studied Mouse's hand, the caterpillar—something inside her mind clicked.

It wasn't a random hand or caterpillar that Ferris had drawn … it had been her sister's and Des. A memory from his time spent at the Ruby Heart Palace...

"Do you want to release Des outside?" Maddie asked softly. "Since you're both free now?"

Mouse jerked her head up, a horrified expression crossing her face. "No."

"What happened to you in there, Margo?" She hadn't used her sister's real name in so long. It was reserved for dire situations. After facing Imogen in the palace, Maddie should've been stronger. She should've attempted to rip out Rav's heart when he'd been alone.

Mouse's gaze grew haunted, her lower lip wobbling.

"Nothing. I was treated fine." She straightened and shrugged, her eyes becoming distant once more. "I've been through worse."

She was lying. Mouse may have survived a horrendous act when she was human, but Maddie believed something worse occurred in that palace. Her sister had never looked like this before. Since she'd been back, Mouse hadn't really spoken much after their hug when her sister had arrived.

Maddie circled her arms around her sister and held her close, breathing in her gardenia scent. "Just talk to me when you're ready."

"I'm tired," Mouse mumbled into her shoulder.

Taking a deep swallow, Maddie rubbed her sister's arm. "When we get to the next safe house, you can sleep for as long as you want."

A familiar knock at the door sounded and Maddie's breath hitched.

He'd come back.

Maddie took her arms from Mouse and went to answer the door. Her heart sped up as she cracked it, peering out into the street, worried it was Chess or someone from the palace, but it wasn't.

Noah stood there, his blond locks falling at his brow. He no longer wore Ferris's oversized clothing, but a tight solid black T-shirt and jeans that showed off his muscular arms and legs.

"Maddie," he murmured, his green eyes brightening as his gaze fastened on hers.

"Noah." She grinned.

"You're back," Ferris grunted from behind them. "Good, because we need to leave."

They really did. Maddie knew that no inch of Scarlet would be left unsearched as Rav hunted down Chess for supposedly killing his queen. She was pretty sure Chess hadn't followed her because she would've already been dead if he had. Once Rav found Chess, she didn't know how long it would take before the prince voiced his suspicions that Maddie murdered his mother.

Earlier, she had taken a quick rinse to wash away any traces of Imogen's blood so no one would scent it on their travels. As Maddie scooped up her pack, she decided not to worry about Chess now. She needed to focus on the others and get them to a safer house.

The group headed outside into the cool breeze of the bare streets. Not a single bat flew in the air as Mouse and Ferris walked ahead. He took Mouse's bag from her, then hoisted it over his shoulder. Neither one of them talked but Mouse shifted closer to Ferris, her humming stopping as though he was her cure.

Maddie realized then that her sister had grown even closer to Ferris in the past two years. Her stomach sank—she knew she'd missed two years of her sister's life, but she hadn't realized that Mouse wouldn't want to confide in her. Perhaps she could with Ferris though.

"Are you all right?" Noah asked, his deep voice relaxing her a fraction.

"I'm perfectly peachy." Besides having to leave all her hats behind at the cottage, but she couldn't risk going there. She was almost certain Chess would be sitting on her settee, with his legs spread open and his vest unbuttoned, lazily waiting for her to arrive so he could remove her heart like she had his mother's.

"You don't look it."

"How was Alice?" Maddie asked, changing the subject.

"She's safe. Our flat was in shambles and one of Rav's goons showed up. I had to dump him in the Thames and ruined my favorite jeans. Yet I'd have to say I'm perfectly peachy too."

Maddie sucked in a sharp breath. She should've known Imogen and Rav wouldn't have left his flat unwatched. "I should've come."

"You can't save me every time." He grinned. "I'm an immortal in training."

"Ah, that you—"

Mouse stopped, sniffed the air, her eyes growing wild as she gazed around the tall stone buildings. It was almost as if she was a new vampire... "I need to eat."

Ferris grasped her shoulders. "Hold Des and I'll get you a packet."

With a nod, Mouse held the caterpillar. She took the powdered blood and water from Ferris.

Something wasn't right here. Ferris's gaze met Maddie's and he shook his head, telling her not to question it.

As they kept to the shadows, Mouse seemed to perk up a bit yet still focused on Des, who was crawling up her arm.

"What's with the caterpillar?" Noah asked. "She was singing to it back in her cell."

Maddie shrugged, but her chest tightened for her sister. "It's her friend from the dungeon."

She kept her eyes peeled as they ventured away from the city. They walked for hours until they reached the same white and silver trees that she'd traveled past only days before with Noah. All remained quiet as they drifted deeper through the outskirts of Ivory, staying clear of the city. The abandoned lands of the Red Queen would've been the ideal place to go, but Chess knew the location of its safe house. She feared he would try to return there at some point to look for them.

As they entered the opposite side of Ivory, Maddie scanned the trees, searching for the trunk with a mark across its belly. Some thin and wide, others gnarled or drooped. Her gaze fixed on a curving line in the middle of a mossy trunk. *Aha*! This was it.

Maddie drew out the key from her skirt and shoved it into the thick trunk. A soft click echoed and she opened the door, allowing everyone entry. When she stepped inside, the smell of flowers and fresh rain snared her senses.

Closing the door behind her, she ascended the white marble flight of stairs. All around her, the room was entirely white, its surface giving off a glittery sheen. Down below, an ornate dinner table surrounded with high-backed alabaster chairs took up the open space. When she hopped down the last step, she peered up at a chandelier, covered in pearl beads, hanging above her. In the center of the table rested a chess game that looked as if it ached to be played. Six doors surrounded the room, and Ferris opened each one. Five bedrooms and a bathing area. It was almost like a miniature palace underground compared to the other safe houses she'd spent nights in.

"I think I'm going to lay down for a bit." Mouse yawned and padded into one of the rooms, leaving the door wide open. Maddie's stomach sank at the thought that her sister didn't shut it because she feared being caged in again.

Ferris's brow furrowed as he studied the room where Mouse had entered.

"Was she like this when you were there?" Maddie whispered to him.

"Sometimes." He ran a hand across his strong jaw.

"Watch over her tonight. I think she'll confide in you more than me."

"Of course." He set his and Mouse's bags on the floor and walked into the room.

Tomorrow would be a new day. Each day her sister was gone from the palace would get better for Mouse—it would have to.

A warm body slid up beside her, reminding her she wasn't alone in the room. This male, who'd become immortal not too long ago, had decided to stay in Wonderland, to remain a vampire.

To be with her.

She turned to face Noah, her chest swelling as she studied

each of his chiseled features, his bright eyes. But she wished she could pull back each of his layers and see everything that rested inside him too, including his tender heart. It could be considered morbid, but she just wanted to see everything that ticked within him, what made him caring, determined, loyal.

For the first time in her life, she wasn't sure what to say, what their next step would be, or how long they would stay there hiding. Yet the most important thing had happened—both their sisters were safe for now. Ever was still gone, but Maddie knew she would meet up with her again one day.

Her gaze flicked to the chess game on the table, studying each of the black and white pieces once more. Her fingers twitched, wanting a challenge.

"So," Maddie said, adjusting her hat and taking elegant steps toward the table. She then picked up the white queen piece and whirled around. "How about a game? Winner gets to choose what we do next."

Noah smirked, sauntering up to her until his broad chest pressed against her breasts, his arms caging her in at the table. "You want to play chess?" His deep voice was like silk caressing her ears.

"Of course," Maddie sang, ducking down and out from his cage. She then ran the tip of her finger along his jaw and traced his soft lips. "Unless you're afraid I'll beat you, immortal."

Noah pulled out a chair and took a seat, stroking the black king as he studied her. "I highly doubt it. I was the best player at my school when I was twelve."

She wanted to pat his head and congratulate him on that rather cute remark. "Ah. You forget I have many more years than you playing the game."

"You want to play by the rules and go first?" Noah continued to brush the king, and she couldn't help thinking about his long, lovely fingers or how good they felt pressing into her flesh.

"White always goes first, but I suppose I'll allow you to."

She drew out the chair opposite him and sank down, resting her elbows on the table. This was just the distraction she needed from Imogen, Rav, Chess, Mouse, Ever...

"I'm glad I met you, Maddie," Noah murmured. Her heart drank in that comment and before she could reply, he straightened in his seat, growing serious. "Now, let's focus."

Maddie grinned wide. "Let's do this."

Noah went first, both of them staying quiet while they played, as though they were at a tournament. The game came naturally to her because of Ever's past lessons. Maddie moved. Noah slid. She jumped. He swiped. She took. He claimed. But in the end, she still won. However, he was incredibly close to conquering her.

Maddie set the pieces back into their proper places and stood from the chair, rounding the table until she was beside him. "We can play again tomorrow. Should I go easy on you next time and let you win?" Maddie teased.

"I already won." Noah pushed the chair back from the table and pulled her into his lap as she gasped.

Taking a deep swallow, she studied his hooded eyes, his dilated pupils. Butterflies swarmed in her chest and neither uttered a word. Instead of trying to discover what words were, she brought her fingers to his face, like before, and cradled his warm cheek.

Noah leaned into her touch and whispered, "I know I'm being needy, but damn, I can't control myself around you." His mouth captured hers and she wanted every inch of him.

If she was a needle, then he was her thread, and together, they would figure out the next step, and the next, and the next after that. But, for now, she wanted more of his lips on hers.

CHAPTER TWENTY-SIX

NOAH

Noah lifted Maddie, her legs encircling his hips. Their lips remained sealed as he carried her into the nearest bedroom and kicked the door shut behind him.

"Ah, aren't you the eager one, immortal?" Maddie grinned against his mouth without pulling away. "It was me winning the chess game that turned you on, wasn't it?"

"Exactly that." He nipped her bottom lip and set her gently on the plush fur blankets covering the bed. A gilded mirror hung above the headboard, matching the simple yet elegant room. With the floors and walls both glimmering white, the two small dark tables beside the ivory bed, were a stark contrast.

Maddie twiddled her thumbs, her grin growing wider. "Well, are you going to kiss me?"

Hell yes, he was. Purple curls spread around her head like a halo on the white quilt, her hat askew. The way she looked at him made his heart pound faster than it ever had. Noah slowly crawled over Maddie until he caged her in. He leaned close, only a hair's breadth from his lips touching hers. "I want to kiss every damn inch of you." He ran the tip of his nose up her lips, inhaling her enticing cherry scent, then pressed his lips gently to hers.

Her fingers fell to the edges of his shirt, and he let her lift it over his head and toss it somewhere on the floor. They had pleasured each other several times now, but this was the first time he felt in control of his lust since turning. He wanted to take his time. Explore her thoroughly.

Noah sat up and placed his finger at the top button of her dress. Teasing them both, he slowly unfastened each button, all the way down to her navel. He then peeled the fabric back over her shoulders, exposing the perfect swells of her breasts. She bit her lip as she stared up at him, and he couldn't control himself when he took her perfectly peaked nipple into his mouth. As he circled it with his tongue, he drew down the remainder of her dress while she moaned.

He then pushed up from her, his gaze meeting hers once more. "I'm going to continue kissing you."

"Where next, immortal?" She grinned.

He smiled wide as he crawled down her body until he was off the bed and standing in front of it. His eyes raked her in, wearing only a pair of see-through purple panties that didn't hide any inch of her.

Dropping to his knees, he grasped her legs and tugged her to the edge of the bed with one swift movement. She laughed as Noah smirked mischievously and placed a kiss on the side of her knee. He hooked his fingers beneath the sheer fabric and shifted back only long enough to slide them off, his gaze never leaving her glistening core. Then he returned his lips to her flesh, just above the knee, dragging his mouth across the soft skin of her thigh, biting at her gingerly. Maddie sighed as he traveled to her other leg and repeated the motions. Only, this time, he kissed higher and *higher*. His chest swelled with an intense emotion. The other woman he *thought* he'd loved ... how wrong he'd been. *This* was what they wrote books about—this was the beginning of their story, and he wanted to see where it would lead.

"Are you going to kiss me?" Her voice came out breathless, with a tinge of craving ... for him.

"Yes, right here," Noah whispered. He leaned in and flicked her sensitive clit with his tongue. Her gasp made his hard length throb. *Patience*, he urged himself, and lowered his mouth to her. His tongue circled and flicked until her hands found his hair, entangling, gripping, driving him wild. Hooking one of her legs over his shoulder, he plunged his tongue deeper into her before slipping a finger inside.

"Noah," Maddie begged, growling.

"Hmm?" he asked without pausing. She tasted so damn good—he could kneel in front of her like she was his queen and drink her like this forever.

"More." Her voice was low, and Noah's breath caught in his throat. How could he deny her that? Deny her anything? As he gazed up at Maddie, her eyes glazed, she was the prettiest thing to ever grace this world—*any world.* He added a second finger and her legs shook. Increasing his speed, he pumped and licked, relishing in her quiet sounds of ecstasy, until she shattered with his name on her lips. A sense of pride filled him as he took in her flushed face and lowered eyes. But he wasn't finished with her yet. Sitting back on his heels, he wiped her arousal from his face.

"Stand up," Maddie whispered, trailing a finger down her side.

Noah tilted his head and did as she instructed, his body anticipating her next touch. She slowly sat up, her fingers grasping his belt loops and tugging him to her.

"Come here," she whispered, peering up at him from beneath her lashes. That emotion was there again as they studied one another. Neither said a word, their eyes doing the talking, as she slowly unbuttoned his trousers, the sound of the zipper filling the room, and shoved them to his knees. His hard length pulsed with need as she wrapped her hand around him. A deep groan escaped him when her warm tongue ran from the base of his cock to the tip.

Noah swept the hair away from her face so he could watch as she took him between her lips. With a moan, he tilted his head back, committing the sensation to memory. *Damn.* In that moment if she were to ask him for anything, he would do it. Even if it was bringing her the fucking moon itself.

Her mouth left him a second later, her hand continuing the pace she'd set as she trailed kisses up his chest, to his neck, to right behind his ear, her fangs grazing the flesh. "That's enough of that," she sang in his ear.

Noah's eyes fluttered as she pumped him and he couldn't help smiling at her words, her adorable and sexy oddness.

"I agree." Using his newly-acquired speed, he scooped her up with the intention of setting her down gently. Instead, he forgot his trousers were still around his knees and they flopped sideways onto the mattress. Maddie covered her mouth as she laughed, and Noah quickly kicked off the denim.

"Found that funny, did you?" Noah climbed over her, settling between her legs. Biting his lip, he tucked a curl behind her ear. He never thought he would be in this position again after his disastrous breakup, but here he was. With the immortal who saved his life, faced a pack of werewolves at his side, and took down an evil queen to save her sister. The same immortal who'd stolen his heart with her peculiar hats and bright soul.

Her eyes glittered with amusement as she shrugged. "Maybe I did."

Noah's heart gave a warm, pleasant *thump* and he dove in for a kiss. Their lips collided, tongues dancing to a perfect symphony. Everything about her was perfection. And he would worship her for all eternity.

"You're beautiful," he mumbled and kissed her again. His hand cupped her breast, the pad of his thumb rubbing her nipple. Without warning, his own fangs dropped.

He slid his mouth down her neck, kissing, licking. A soft, satisfied sound left Maddie when he traced her vein with his tongue, the saltiness of her skin hitting his taste buds. It spurred him to graze the same spot with his teeth and her hips rose to meet his cock.

He lined himself up with her entrance and paused to admire the expression on her face. The look that mirrored his—needy, dazed, flushed. *Fuck.* He placed a lingering kiss on her throat—

Then he sank his teeth into her tender flesh at the same time he slid into her heat. The taste of metal flooded his mouth, coating his tongue, as her delicious folds took in his length.

"Noah!" she growled, arching in pleasure.

Her nails dug into his back, her legs quaking as she wrapped them around his waist. He drew her blood into his mouth with a gentle suck, and she moaned quietly, a hand over her lips to stop Ferris and Mouse from hearing.

Forcing his fangs from her skin, he started to move within her. Slowly at first, shifting his hips in a circular motion, learning every inch of her. Which movements made her gasp hardest, which made her back arch off the bed, and which had her shifting beneath him for a new angle. Finding one spot that made her nails dig into his back deeper, he skimmed his hand down from her breast to rub her bundle of nerves. *Shit.* He wasn't going to last long.

"Keep doing that," she murmured. "But faster."

Noah groaned and thrust harder. Faster and faster, just as she requested. His eyes fluttered while trying to fight the urge to spill into her, but he wanted one more orgasm from her first. Just. One. More. She deserved to come many, *many* times. He ground his teeth together in an attempt to hold himself back, but his rhythm turned more frantic. More desperate.

Maddie's finger traced his shoulder as she buried her face in the crook of his neck. She gave him open-mouth kisses, her tongue flicking the sensitive area. A moment of intoxicating pain flooded him when her fangs pierced his flesh and bright stars floated in his vision. His release barreled out of him without warning at the same time her walls squeezed with her own release.

"Fuck!" he growled as he rode out the pleasure.

When he finally stopped moving and the flutterings of Maddie's second orgasm abated, she drew her fangs from his neck. He rolled off her, distrusting that he had the strength not to crush her. That was the most intense pleasure he'd ever experienced. His cock was already growing stiff again, wanting *more*. And not just physically. He wanted more of Maddie's laughter, her bravery.

"Thank you," Maddie whispered.

Noah turned his head to stare at her, their noses almost touching. "You don't have to thank me for good sex," he teased.

"No, silly." She grinned. "Thank you for coming back."

A smile spread across his face. How could he have stayed away from this alluring female who constantly made his heart race? "You don't have to thank me for that either. It was the only logical choice."

"You could've taken the cure," she reasoned, a guarded look slipping into her features.

"No," Noah said firmly. He wanted to erase that look from her face forever, wanted her to know *why* he'd come back. "Becoming a vampire wasn't something I could've predicted, but I've never felt more like myself than I do now. You're here and I think... I mean, I *know* that I'm falling in love with you, Maddie."

Her lips parted as though she must've misunderstood what he said.

"Bloody hell, after all we've been through, I might as well just say it. I love you, all right?" He rolled his eyes and smiled.

She blinked rapidly for a moment, a tinge of nerves building in his chest while he waited for her to say something. *Anything*. Did she not feel the same way? It was okay if she didn't—they could work up to that if she gave him the chance.

"How could I not love you, too, immortal?" Maddie finally said, her honey-colored eyes brightening as she took his face between her hands. Warmth spread through him while she pressed her lips to his forehead, his nose, his mouth, his neck, just before whispering in his ear. "Now, how about you help me make a new hat and ask me more of your wonderful, inquisitive questions."

"Only after I make love to you one more time."

"Fine, immortal. Fine." She laughed as he hauled her into his lap, then her laughter was replaced by beautiful gasps of pleasure when he sank into her once more.

He would never get tired of her sounds. He would never get tired of *her*. She was something unexpected, but somehow he knew, she was his messy, unpredictable, wondrous, immortal match, nonetheless.

EPILOGUE

MADDIE

A hat was still like a heart.

But now Maddie's heart was full of more than her love for hats, her sister, and Ferris. It had opened up to something new, *someone* new, something wondrous. A new kind of love. With Noah.

She didn't know what was next, though. The four of them were still hidden below ground in Ivory. As for Alice, she was safe. Noah had snuck out once, only briefly, to check on her in Leeds.

Maddie glanced up from sewing and leaned into Noah, who was reading a book. Mouse sat beside Ferris on the floor, playing a game of chess with him. Her caterpillar, Des, rested at the edge of the board, silently watching them. Ferris hated the game, but he did it for Mouse. After a month away from the Ruby Heart Palace, her sister still hadn't smiled like she used to.

One day, she will again.

Maddie brought up her scissors and cut out several Queen of Night tulips that she'd drawn into the thick fabric. She was making a hat for her sister in an effort to cheer her up. For weeks, Maddie made do by using fabric from one of the beds and breaking it apart over and over again to reshape. Then while checking on Alice, Noah had retrieved materials for Maddie to make a few hats. After that tiny gesture, Maddie had given him the utmost pleasure. He'd returned the favor—her body unintentionally heated at the reminder of that night.

"Do you want me to help you with that?" Noah whispered in her ear and set down his book.

Maddie tilted her head. "You want to do it right here in the open?"

His cheeks pinkened, but his eyes still sparked with desire. "I meant with the hat."

"So boredom made you turn to hat-making then?" She grinned. "Take this." Pressing a needle in between his finger and thumb, Maddie placed the fabric in his other hand.

He lifted her and sat her in his lap, making her laugh. Together, she helped Noah weave in and out of the fabric, even though he didn't need the help—she just wanted to keep touching him.

A knock sounded at the door, echoing throughout the house. Everyone stilled. Ferris stood, grabbing the gun he kept beside him.

Maddie leapt off Noah and grasped hers from on top of her backpack while Noah retrieved his from the bedroom. Weaponless, Mouse padded toward the stairs, unafraid.

Then another knock came, familiar. A knock Maddie *knew*. The same one she and Ferris had shared at the safe house back in Scarlet.

Jolting forward, she raced past Mouse, in case it wasn't who she believed it to be.

Maddie held her gun tightly, aiming it upward, as she

swung open the door to a female with black hair and brown eyes, wearing jeans and a raggedy old Dracula T-shirt.

"Is that the way you greet a friend?" Ever arched a brow, her gaze focused on the gun pointed at her face. "Next time"—her long fingers touched the tip of Maddie's weapon and brought it to her chest—"remember to aim for the heart."

With a grin, Maddie lowered the gun and yanked the White Queen inside before sealing the door shut. Maddie then folded her arms around her friend and squeezed her tight, inhaling her lily scent.

Ever took a step back and smiled. "My attire is rather drab, isn't it?"

"You look positively human," Maddie said. She'd never seen her friend not wearing something white and lacy.

Ivory's ruler placed her hands on her hips and blew out a breath. "Do you know how many safe houses I had to visit before I found you?" She took the wig from her head, exposing her white hair pulled back in messy pinned-up curls, while descending the stairs. The queen's shoulders relaxed as she peered around the room, her gaze landing on Mouse. "She's safe." But then Ever cocked her head as she gazed at Noah. "So it seems all of you are wanted in Scarlet. But I don't know you."

"That's Noah. I'll explain it all." Maddie shrugged while Noah studied the new guest with a furrowed brow.

Ever walked to the middle of the room, removed her backpack, and took a seat on one of the chairs at the table. "I heard from my spy that Imogen is dead, but my bastard brother still isn't. I would've come back from the mortal world sooner if I'd known they'd had Mouse. After hearing of Imogen's death, I knew it was time, but it shouldn't have taken me this long to return. I was also informed that not only are you all wanted, but my dear, precious, Prince *Chess* is." Her lips curled up into a smug grin.

Even if Ever had come back sooner, she likely would've

been dead before she'd found Maddie anyway.

"Do I have the story for you," Maddie sang. "But first, what were you planning to do next?"

Ever reclined in the chair and peered up at the ceiling. "The time has come for me to reclaim what is mine and intimately acquaint my brother's heart with a stake."

Did you enjoy Maddie?

Authors always appreciate reviews, whether long or short.

Want more Vampires in Wonderland? Check out Book Two, Chess, in the Vampires in Wonderland series!

He's a villainous prince. She's a virtuous queen. Their despise for one another will ignite desire.

Chess has been the Queen of Heart's perfect, devious son all his life. With Wonderland as his playground, he revels in consuming blood and pleasuring lovers in his bed. That is, until he's blamed for his mother's death and a price is put on his head.

Ever has been in hiding for years, biding her time until she can reclaim the Ivory kingdom. Until she can drive a blade through the heart of the cruel prince who once tried to murder her.

With a mutual enemy hunting them both, Chess offers Ever a bargain, one she has no choice but to agree to.

A bargain neither can keep.

To stay updated for current book news and giveaways from Candace and Amber, sign up for their newsletters!

ALSO FROM CANDACE ROBINSON

Wicked Souls Duology
Vault of Glass
Bride of Glass

Cruel Curses Trilogy
Clouded By Envy
Veiled By Desire
Shadowed By Despair

Faeries of Oz Series
Lion (Short Story Prequel)
Tin
Crow
Ozma
Tik-Tok

Cursed Hearts Duology
Lyrics & Curses
Music & Mirrors

Letters Duology
Dearest Clementine: Dark and Romantic Monstrous Tales
Dearest Dorin: A Romantic Ghostly Tale

Campfire Fantasy Tales Series
Lullaby of Flames
A Layer Hidden
The Celebration Game

Merciless Stars
The Bone Valley
Between the Quiet
Hearts Are Like Balloons
Bacon Pie
Avocado Bliss

ALSO FROM AMBER R. DUELL

The Dark Dreamer Trilogy
Dream Keeper
Dark Consort
Night Warden

Forgotten Gods
The Last Goodbye (Short Story Prequel)
Fragile Chaos

Faeries of Oz Series
Lion (Short Story Prequel)
Tin
Crow
Ozma
Tik-Tok

Darkness Series: Temptation
Darkness Whispered

The Prince's Wing
When Stars Are Bright

Vampires in Wonderland Series
Rav (Short Story Prequel)
Maddie
Chess
Knave

Acknowledgments

Thank you so much for stepping into our retelling of Wonderland! Maddie gives you a bow while Noah waves.

This world and these characters were so much fun for us to write! And there are some very important people who helped in the process of this! Thank you to the editors, Brandy and Jess, for helping to pick out things we couldn't find and make the story better!

To Amber Hodges, who rooted for this book early on and helped so much! Jerica, for your endless support! Elle, for letting us be a part of your amazing author team! Hayley, for your wonderful British skills! Ann, Vic, Lindsay, and Tanya, who plucked out the quick fixes that needed to be done!

Our families who continue to support us through thick and thin, we love you! And now, are you ready to read Chess and Ever's enemies to lovers' story next?

About the Authors

Candace Robinson spends her days consumed by words and hoping to one day find her own DeLorean time machine. Her life consists of avoiding migraines, admiring Bonsai trees, watching classic movies, and living with her husband and daughter in Texas—where it can be forty degrees one day and eighty the next.

Amber R. Duell was born and raised in a small town in Central New York. While it will always be home, she's constantly moving with her husband and two sons as a military wife. She does her best writing in the middle of the night, surviving the daylight hours with massive amounts of caffeine. When not reading or writing, she enjoys snowboarding, embroidering, and snuggling with her cats.

Seeds of Sorrow by Elle Beaumont & Christis Christie

Wishing for more adventure in her life, Eden, a fae of the sun, accepts an invitation to a ball in another king's court. Despite her over-protective mother's ire, they travel away from home for the first time and into the middle realm.

Draven, known as the Nightmare King and ruler of the dark realm, desires only to remain in his kingdom to maintain control and order over his ravenous creatures. However, he finds himself drawn away by the mysterious summons of his brother, who desperately needs his aid.

In one evening, thrust unwittingly together, Eden and Draven find themselves beguiled, betrayed, and betrothed. Neither are prepared for what it means for them, or for the immortal realms.

As politics and death intertwine, can two entirely different fae learn to rely on one another? Or will the chaos of the dark realm bleed into the other courts, destroying every last hint of light, including Eden.

Come True by Brindi Quinn

Recent college graduate Dolly Jones has spent the last year stubbornly trying to atone for a mistake that cost her everything. She doesn't go out, she doesn't make new friends and she sure as hell doesn't treat herself to things she hasn't earned, but when her most recent thrift store purchase proves home to a hot, magical genie determined to draw out her darkest desires in exchange for a taste of her soul, Dolly's restraint, and patience, will be put to the test.

Newbie genie Velis Reilhander will do anything to beat his older half-brothers in a soul-collecting contest that will determine the next heir to their family estate, even if it means coaxing desire out of the least palatable human he's ever contracted. As a djinn from a 'polluted' bloodline, Velis knows what it's like to work twice as hard as everyone else, and he won't let anyone—not even Dolly f*cking Jones—stand in the way of his birthright. He just needs to figure out her heart's greatest desire before his asshole brothers can get to her first.

CPSIA information can be obtained
at www.ICGtesting.com
Printed in the USA
LVHW101225210422
716759LV00007B/237

9 781953 238436